KT-495-133

LIBRARIES NI
WITHDRAWN FROM STOCK

The Castle of Tangled Magic

SOPHIE ANDERSON

ILLUSTRATED BY SAARA SÖDERLUND

LIBRARIES NI
WITHDRAWN FROM STOCK

USBORNE

AIR DOME

FLOATING TOWER

WATER DOME

KOSHKA'S OAK TREE

DOORWAY TO CASTLE MILA

FORBIDDEN MAGIC

EARTH DOME

CHERNOMOR'S
FORTRESS

MAZE

FIRE DOME

GOLOV'S
HEAD

SCORCHED
LAND

CRUMBLING
CLIFFS

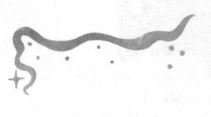

So dense the forest no light gleams
Where I, aglow with youthful dreams,
With rapturous hope and expectation,
Summon up with invocation
The spirits…

From *Ruslan & Ludmila*
by Alexander Pushkin,
translated by D.M. Thomas

PROLOGUE

Castle Mila rises from the shore of a lapping lake, as vast and bright as a sunrise. Built entirely from wood, and being five hundred years old, the castle is a little crooked with age. But the pine-log walls gleam like gold and the endless roof domes, which curve higher and higher into the sky, shimmer and sparkle like silver.

The topmost, and biggest, of the roof domes is as dazzling as the sun itself and the thin spire on top of it reaches all the way to the stars. I call this dome Sun Dome, and I've often wondered what lies inside it. Castle Mila is full of secrets. There are hidden doors, passageways behind walls and long-forgotten chambers. Though I've lived in the castle all my life, I can still get lost and, with a thrill of delight, discover untouched rooms.

One of my favourite things to do is explore the castle, looking for ways into the roof domes. Each one contains a small, round attic, but the staircases that lead to them are all concealed. So far, I've found my way into fourteen of the thirty-three domes. Most have been empty, aside from dust and spiderwebs and a warm, tingling feeling that I always get in Castle Mila's hidden spaces. But a few have contained treasures: rolled-up maps and gilt-edged books; fine art brushes and half-full pots of coloured inks; carved wooden boxes filled with hand-blown glass beads, and other trinkets that must have belonged to my once-royal ancestors.

My family aren't royal any more, but Castle Mila is still our home. I was born in the warm and cosy kitchen on the ground floor, and learned to walk along the castle's long and winding corridors. Mama has sung me to sleep in my third-floor bedroom that overlooks the lake, and Papa has shown me where I can climb onto the roof safely, to watch hawks hunting over the meadows and cranes dancing in the marshes.

Both my parents are carpenters, and they use one of the old ballrooms as a workshop. The floor and walls are covered with enormous pictures I've been drawing in there since I was old enough to hold a piece of chalk. Some of the other big rooms in the castle are used by the villagers who live nearby. My school puts on a show in the old theatre once a year. And the biggest room, the Great Hall, is used for almost every birthday, wedding and wake.

At these gatherings, I hear stories about the castle's history that are seasoned with myth and legend. There is a tale that Castle Mila was built by a lone carpenter, using one perfect axe. No nails were used, because the wooden pieces were cut to fit precisely together. And when the carpenter finished, the axe was thrown into the lake, which is why no other castle like it has ever been built. In the summer, I've spent whole days diving into the lake with my friends, looking for the axe. The search is fun, but I'm always slightly relieved when we don't find it, because there is another tale that I'd rather believe instead.

My grandmother, Babusya, says Castle Mila was built from magic, and that to understand why, I should talk to the spirits who live in and around our home. I've memorized her descriptions of house spirits, water spirits and tree spirits, and searched for them all my life. A few times I think I might have seen or felt *something*. But after thirteen years, I still have no proof these spirits exist.

I keep on exploring though. There is nothing like the excitement of finding hidden spaces and forgotten treasures. I'm determined to find my way into every inch of the castle and discover all of its secrets. Now more than ever, because I have a new baby sister.

Rosa is three weeks old and makes my heart swell with love every time I look at her. I haven't figured out how to be the best big sister for her yet, but I want to be strong and brave and good, and show her all the wonders in the world. So, if there *is* magic hiding somewhere in our home, then I'm going to find it, and share it with my sister.

CHAPTER ONE

THE MORNING CHASE

I wake at sunrise, ready for the morning chase. The honeyed light oozing through my bedroom window makes the pine walls glow warm and smell sweet. I sit up in bed and peer out into the light, until I spot the silhouette of Babusya. She's wobbling through the long yellow grass in the meadow, leaning on her two walking sticks. A large birch-bark rucksack is on her back, and she's halfway to the fruit grove by the lake already. I narrow my eyes and start to count.

One. I slide the huge woollen socks Babusya knitted me over my bare feet.

Two. I leap over the rag rug I made with Mama, swing open my bedroom door and swerve into the long, third-floor corridor.

Three, four, five. I take three running strides, then skid along the corridor, my woollen socks sliding over the smooth spruce floorboards quicker than skates over ice.

Six. I reach the first staircase, jump onto the sweeping oak bannister and zoom down it so fast that my heart races to catch up with me. Several of the portraits of my royal ancestors frown at me, but I ignore them with a whoop.

Seven, eight, nine, ten. I skid along two more corridors, past the ghostly outline of the secret door that leads to the dome I call Musician's Dome, because in it I found a viola and some ancient handwritten sheet music that crumbled apart when I touched it.

Eleven, twelve. There are two more bannisters to slide down, past more frowning ancestors and a faded and torn tapestry of the royal crest that puffs dust into the air in annoyance.

Thirteen. I land on the wobbly block flooring of the ground floor and start running, because my socks don't skid so well over the mosaicked patterns.

Fourteen. I race through my favourite part of the

castle, our kitchen, waving to my dark-haired papa, who is frying what smells like *grenki* – eggy bread – on the enormous tiled stove, and my red-haired mama, who is pouring coffee from a long-handled copper pot. The only sign of my sister is a few silk-soft dark curls peeping out from the bright green baby wrap that Mama is wearing to hold Rosa close to her heart.

Fifteen. Sixteen. I stumble to a halt by the kitchen door that leads outside, pull on my boots and the oversized cardigan Babusya knitted me, and smile because I'm making good time.

Seventeen. I burst through the door and fly into the gold-and-rust-coloured autumn world outside. I take a deep breath and squeal with happiness because everything is so beautiful.

Eighteen, nineteen. I sprint down the hill towards the lake shore. The air is cool and brimming with the earthy, maple scents of fallen leaves and ripening nuts.

"Twenty!" I shout as I reach Babusya. "Two seconds faster than yesterday."

"But you're still wearing your pyjamas," Babusya replies without looking up. "And you haven't eaten breakfast." She's focusing on where to place her walking sticks and feet on the rough, hummocky ground.

"My pyjamas are comfy and I'm not hungry yet." I hold an arm out.

A small growl of annoyance rumbles in the back of Babusya's throat, but she passes me one of her walking sticks and grips my elbow instead. "You don't need to keep chasing me out here every morning, Olia. I can walk fine with my sticks." Babusya lifts her head and her big, dark eyes shine as they reflect the rising sun.

"I know you can. I just like the morning chase. And…" I hesitate, wondering whether to tell Babusya the other reason I follow her out here every morning. "I think I'm more likely to see magic when I'm with you."

Babusya chuckles. "Magic is everywhere you believe it to be."

My brow furrows. Babusya has a way of explaining things that seems both simple and complicated at the same time, and the true meaning of her words often feels just beyond my grasp.

We reach the shade of the overgrown fruit grove, and Babusya leads me through it to the sprawling yellow-leaved trees on the far side. "So, what are we collecting today?" I ask.

"Ranet apples." Babusya stops and I help remove her rucksack and pass her walking stick back. We both peer into the trees. The fruits from the lower branches have already been picked, but the branches higher up are loaded with small, red apples.

I kick off my boots and socks and clamber up the nearest tree, my bare feet gripping the thick, rough trunk and my hands grasping each branch, until I'm surrounded by fruits. Then I swing a leg over a sturdy branch to sit, and pick three perfect apples. I try to pass them down to Babusya, but she's wandered to the next tree along. She lifts a walking stick, rattles it against a branch, and five apples drop to the ground at her feet. She leans down to pick them up.

"What are you going to cook?" I ask, letting the apples I picked fall into the grass below.

"A *sharlotka* apple cake, for the harvest moon feast tomorrow night," Babusya replies, hitting another branch with her walking stick until a few more apples fall.

I lick my lips, thinking not just of apple cake, but of all the foods that will be at the feast. Once a year, when the harvest moon rises, fat and red, Castle Mila glistens like a ripening blackberry and its Great Hall fills with people carrying the last fruits of autumn, baked into pies and boiled into jams of every colour and flavour imaginable.

There will be music and dancing all through the night, until the harvest moon sets and the sun rises again over Lake Mila. This year, the celebrations will be bigger and merrier than ever before, because this year is Castle Mila's five hundredth birthday.

I'm most excited about the patch that I've made. It's a small square of fabric, about the size of my palm, with a picture stitched onto it. Someone from our family makes one every year, and tomorrow I'll add mine to the four hundred and ninety-nine other squares that make up our patchwork family blanket.

I've always dreamed about having a brother or a sister, and since Rosa was born all I've wanted is to be the best big sister for her. The patch I've made feels like a start. It shows how much I love her, and once I've sewn it onto the blanket it will prove for ever how glad I am that she is part of our family.

I turn to look at the castle, thinking of all the adventures I want to have there with Rosa as she grows up. The huge, round roof domes reflect so much light that I have to shield my eyes to look at them.

"Every year they glow brighter." Babusya straightens her back and follows my gaze.

"Papa says the aspen shingles that cover the domes get more silvery as they age, reflecting more light." I reach up into a branch so full of apples that it's bowed under their weight.

Babusya snorts. "Your papa is a fine carpenter who knows all about the wood of Castle Mila, I'm sure. But he's never paid any attention to the castle's magic, even when he was a young boy. The castle domes are filled with magic that has been locked away from the world, and they glow brighter every year because that magic is trying to escape."

I look up at the domes again. They are radiant,

shimmering like quicksilver. "Why is Sun Dome the brightest?" I ask, hoping Babusya will tell me again, but that this time I'll understand her explanation.

"Because the key to unlock the magic is hidden inside that dome." Babusya's eyes twinkle. "No one has ever found a way up there. I've spent years of my life looking, but the spirits tell me even they can't get into that dome. And if they could, the key isn't a key anyway, and the lock is hidden somewhere else."

"That doesn't make any sense." I shake my head, pick a few more apples, then lean over to drop them near Babusya. "Do you think it's even possible to unlock the magic trapped inside the domes?"

"If you believe you can do it, then you will. Belief is *everything*, Olia. You can never have enough of it."

"I want to believe." I gently sway, like the leaves rustling above me, and sigh dramatically. "But I don't see magic the way you do, Babusya."

"Nobody sees things the same way." Babusya laughs. "That's why it's important to look from different angles."

I lean even further over, until I'm dangling upside down from the branch. "You mean like this?" I smile.

Babusya rolls her eyes, but smiles back. "What would happen if I did unlock the magic?" I ask.

Babusya stares long and hard at the domes, as if she's trying to figure something out.

"Then the magic would be free," she says finally.

"Would that be a good thing or a bad thing?" I ask, unable to read Babusya's expression.

"Like everything else, it depends on how you look at it and where you're standing." Babusya frowns as a wind blows from the direction of the castle, rakes through the meadow and agitates all the trees in the grove. It smells faintly of the castle's hidden spaces – of warm pine, dust and old books – but also of something far more ancient, like sun-baked stones and dry, cracked earth.

Cold air needles through my cardigan and pyjamas. I shiver, and grip the branch I'm holding tighter. My hair whips around my face and flashes of golden light dance in front of my eyes. I stop breathing and stare at the sparks in wonder. I've never seen anything like them.

Then, as quickly as it arrived, the wind falls away and the lights are gone. I'm left feeling ruffled and breathless. It's as if – just for a moment – a veil over the world blew back, and I saw something glittering and tangled beneath.

I swing down from the tree and land next to Babusya, my pulse racing.

"You saw magic, didn't you?" Babusya leans towards me and looks right into my eyes.

"I don't know. It might have been…" I bite my lip. "How can I be sure?"

"Your heart knows the truth." Babusya leans even closer and whispers into my ear, "Time is running out, Olia. If the magic isn't unlocked soon, it will break out on its own. And that would be a bad thing, from whatever angle you look at it."

Babusya's words land heavily, sending waves through my mind. I've always looked for magic because the idea of it makes me feel curious and excited, but I've never considered that something bad might happen if I didn't find it. What if I'm meant to be looking harder or doing something more to reach it?

Another breeze whirls around me, and I nestle deeper into my cardigan. "I think it's just a cold autumn wind," I say to Babusya, trying to reassure myself rather than her. Because I feel in my heart that this is no ordinary wind, and I feel like *something* is about to happen. Excitement is fizzing up from deep inside me, but my stomach is flipping with nerves too, because I'm not sure that I'm ready for whatever this thing is.

CHAPTER TWO

BREAKFAST PICNIC

I pick the last apple off the ground as my parents walk into the grove, hand in hand. Papa is carrying a basket and has our faded blue picnic rug thrown over his shoulder. Mama is cradling Rosa, who is still tucked into her baby wrap, but she lifts a hand to wave when she sees me.

"We thought we'd bring breakfast to you, seeing as you were too busy chasing your grandmother to eat this morning." Papa smiles and the dimple in his left cheek deepens. Mama calls it the mark of Mila, because Babusya, Papa, me and many of our ancestors in the castle paintings have the same dimple. I've even seen a tiny version of it on Rosa. We all have the same eyes too – big, dark and wide set – and the same dark curly hair, although Babusya's is now white with age.

"Shall we eat in the sun?" Mama looks towards the lake shore, away from the shade in the grove. Her green eyes are as bright as the horsetails growing at the water's edge, and her long hair, tied back in a plait, is as red as the fireweed among them. Although I didn't inherit any of Mama's bright colours on the outside, Papa says that I did on the inside. He says Mama and I are the kind of people who make rainbows out of rain.

I stow Babusya's rucksack, which is now brimful with apples, beneath a tree in the grove, while Mama, Papa and Babusya lay out the breakfast picnic near the lake. There is a small mountain of the *grenki* I smelled Papa cooking earlier, along with *syrniki* – cottage cheese pancakes – plus pots of sour cream and cloudberry jam, fresh blackberries and bilberries, and tomatoes and ham for Babusya, who prefers savouries to sweets.

Mama beckons me to sit next to her and passes me a pancake topped with blackberries, which she knows are my favourite. "Did you sleep well?" she asks. I nod and take a bite out of my pancake as I peep into the baby wrap to look at Rosa. She's asleep, one of her tiny hands curled close to her lips. She spends most of her time sleeping at the moment, but I don't mind. I love watching her peaceful face, especially when Mama lets me hold her and she snuggles against me, all warm and soft.

"So what are you doing today?" Papa asks. "Are Dinara and Luka coming over?"

Dinara and Luka have been my best friends for ever. They live in the nearest village, which is a twenty-minute walk away – or a ten-minute run. We spend nearly all our time together. I stop at their house on the way to school, then we sit next to each other all day. Most weekends we're together too – either in the village or here, near the castle and the lake. Today is Saturday, but Dinara and Luka are visiting one of their aunts. I shake my head at Papa and reach for another pancake. "They're coming over tomorrow. I thought I could help you and Mama today."

"There's plenty to do," Mama says. "The tables need setting up for the feast, and the Great Hall needs decorating. Some of the villagers are coming to make straw wreaths and clay statues of the harvest spirits."

A clattering of jackdaws wheels through the sky and Mama beams up at them. She stands and breaks the slice of *grenka* she's holding into small pieces as she walks towards them, then she throws the bread up into the air. The jackdaws swoop down and grab it mid-flight, shrieking and cackling with delight. Mama laughs and I smile. Mama has the loveliest laugh, light and easy, like wind chimes in a breeze.

"I could do with some help looking for a way into Aurora Dome, if you have time," Papa says. Aurora Dome is the smallest and most easterly dome of the castle. It got its name because, when I was younger, I thought I saw ribbons of golden light streaming out from it one morning. Papa said they were most likely reflections of the sunrise. But now, after seeing those lights on the wind in the grove, I wonder if they were more. "I heard rattling up there last night," Papa explains, "so I'd like to check the roof, but I can't find a way in. You've always had a talent for spotting the secret doors."

"I'd love to help." I look from Papa to Babusya, wondering if she has a tale about Aurora Dome, but she isn't paying attention to us. Her gaze is focused on an oak tree further along the shore. A breeze whispers through its crisp copper leaves. Three of them break free and flicker in the light as they're carried towards us. Two land at my feet, but the third is swept up and away, until it disappears into the brightness of the sky.

Babusya pokes the leaves at my feet and frowns. Then she pulls a fingerful of salt from her pocket and throws it into the wind. Babusya makes salt offerings all the time, to chase away what she thinks are bad omens or to please the various spirits she believes in.

"What do you see?" Mama asks Babusya. While Papa has logical explanations for the strange things Babusya sees and hears, Mama has always been more accepting. She once told me that there is more in this world than most people ever see or understand, and that Babusya is one of the few people lucky enough to realize it.

"A journey." Babusya's frown deepens. "Because of a fierce storm."

I shift uncomfortably and draw my feet away from the leaves. I don't want there to be a storm, or a journey. I don't want anything to disrupt the feast tomorrow.

"All the farmers have been predicting a mild autumn." Papa looks up. "And there isn't a cloud in the sky."

Babusya makes a short grunting sound that manages to express her complete distrust of farmers and clouds predicting the weather, compared with whatever omen she's just seen. "I'm going to have my morning nap," she announces loudly, and picks up her walking sticks.

I jump to my feet, eager to escape the unsettling breeze. "I'll help you back to the castle," I offer and, for once, Babusya doesn't argue.

"Perhaps you could make Babusya some of her tea, then come to find us in the Great Hall," Mama suggests.

"I will. Thanks for bringing me breakfast."

I head back towards the castle with Babusya, stopping in the grove to collect the rucksack full of apples. As I lean down to pick it up, another cold wind raises goosebumps on my arms.

"Do you know what the winds of change are, Olia?" Babusya asks suddenly, making me jump. The curly mass of her white hair is like an enormous cloud around her head, and there is a flash of lightning in her eyes. "They tear things down." Babusya's eyes widen. "To make you *see*."

Confusion swirls around me like the breeze. "I love you, Babusya, but sometimes you don't make any sense."

Babusya laughs her familiar, croaking chuckle. "You don't need to understand, Olia. You just need to be willing to see. *Here*." She points at her eyes. "And *here*." She puts a hand over her heart. "And from all around." She waves her walking stick vaguely and laughs again.

"I'll try my best." I nod, though I still don't understand. Then I secure the rucksack on my back before guiding Babusya on to the castle.

When we reach the kitchen, I offer to make some of the bitter-smelling frankincense tea that she drinks for her rheumatism, but Babusya says she's too tired. So I help make her comfortable on the bed she has next to the stove, and she starts snoring happily almost as soon as her head touches the pillow, her mouth wide open.

Babusya's talk of a storm and a journey scampers through my mind, like a mouse looking for seeds in the meadow. I decide to go to one of the highest domes of the castle to take a good look at the sky. So, after making sure that Babusya is tucked up warm, I race to my bedroom, where I quickly change into my cord trousers and favourite green jumper that used to be Mama's. The wooden box on my dresser catches my eye and I open it to look at the patch I made for the family blanket.

It shows me, holding Rosa. Our parents and Babusya are beside us, and all around, in the shape of the castle, are the faces of our friends and the spirits that Babusya sees too. I used some golden thread that I found in one of the dome attics to make swirling patterns in all the empty spaces, to represent the magic that I want to find and share with my sister. I stroke the image of Rosa, before tucking the patch

into my jumper pocket.
Talk of the feast has made
me excited about sewing
the patch onto the
blanket tomorrow, and I
want to keep it
close until I do.

I continue up
to the fifth floor of the castle. At the end of one of the
long, winding corridors is a door hidden behind a
cobweb-filled bookcase. The door groans as I push it
open, and the narrow stairs behind it creak as I run up
them two at a time. I emerge through a small trapdoor
into the attic of a dome I named Astronomer's Dome,
because it contains an ancient, dilapidated telescope.
The telescope doesn't work, but when I look out of
the small, arched windows dotted around the dome, I
can see for miles anyway.

At night, millions of stars can be seen from here,
glittering over the lake, the fields and the meadows.
Sometimes Mama and I come up to gaze at them and
she tells me their stories, and how the stars are where

we all came from and where we'll all return to. But now, the sky is bright and blue. Papa was right: there isn't a cloud to be seen.

Something rattles on the east side of the castle, and I tense when I see flashes of light whizzing around the domes there. But then a wood pigeon takes off with a flutter, and I realize the bird might have knocked the roof shingles, making sunbeams bounce off their shiny surfaces.

The gentle lapping sound of the lake drifts up to me on the lightest of breezes. "It's a beautiful day," I say aloud, "not a storm in sight." I turn away from the window, ignoring the creak of Sun Dome's spire – it doesn't take much wind to make it sway.

I slide my hand into my jumper pocket to feel the patch once more, and tell myself that everything will be fine for the feast tomorrow. Then I race to the Great Hall to help with the preparations, trying to unknot the small tangle of worry in my stomach and banish Babusya's strange talk about tearing winds, by sliding down every bannister on the way.

CHAPTER THREE

THE WINDS OF CHANGE

The Great Hall is on the ground floor, in the centre of Castle Mila. It's enormous – as long and wide as the field we play games on behind my school – and it's almost the full height of the castle. The round ceiling, which is painted with green and gold swirls, is directly beneath Sun Dome. Between the ceiling and the bright dome there must be a hidden attic. Babusya's talk of a key to unlock the magic inside it and time running out makes me burn with even more curiosity than usual. I'm desperate to find a way up there soon, but right now the hall is filled with people, as busy as squirrels gathering nuts.

I help sweep the floor, assemble the tables for the feast, and load them with glowing jam jars, baskets of shining fruits, and stripy pumpkins and squashes. When some of my friends from school arrive, we stack up more pumpkins into the shape of a giant, who manages to look both benevolent and slightly angry. Then we sit and weave straw decorations beneath him.

When Mama appears holding the family blanket, my heart leaps. I drop the straw bear that I've been making and rush over to help her hang it at the far end of the hall. Unfolded, the blanket is big enough for the whole family to snuggle under in winter. It has loops sewn onto the top two corners, and we use the poles for opening the castle's windows to lift the blanket high, then dangle it from two hooks in the wall.

I step back and stare at all the patches. Every year since Castle Mila was built, someone in my family has added a patch to the blanket, showing a scene from their life, so it has become a record of the castle's and our family's history.

The first patch shows a prince and princess holding hands beneath the newly built golden domes. Then there are patches showing huge parties, babies in long white dresses, dark-haired children growing into crowned adults, ageing monarchs in fur-lined robes, and rooms filling with treasure.

After the patch with the fallen throne, which represents the revolution about one hundred years ago, there is a patch that shows my great-great-grandfather turning the ballroom into a carpentry workshop, and more patches showing my family working alongside villagers to plant seeds and harvest crops.

Babusya appears as a toddler talking to a tree spirit about seventy years ago, and Papa's birth is marked by a huge picnic attended by hundreds of people about forty years ago.

Papa sewed the patch showing my parents' wedding and, a few years later, the patch of me as a baby in their arms. My first steps, my first swim and my first day at school are all sewn onto the family blanket. There are pictures of my friends and all the villagers during feasts and celebrations too.

Last year's patch, which Babusya helped me sew, shows my parents and me rowing on the lake. I added

Babusya sitting on the shore, and she added a water spirit between us.

There is a space on the bottom right corner of the blanket, waiting for the patch in my pocket – the first patch I made all by myself. When I sew it on tomorrow night, the blanket will be a perfect rectangle, and Rosa will become part of this patchwork history too.

"Have you finished making your patch?" Mama asks, following my gaze.

"Yes." My hand hovers over my pocket. It takes all of my willpower not to pull it out now to show Mama, but I want it to be a surprise tomorrow. I lean down to look at Rosa instead, tucked into her wrap, and her eyes peep open.

"Oh, she's awake." Mama's eyes glitter as she looks from Rosa to me. "Would you like to give her a cuddle?"

"Yes, please!" I find the nearest chair, sit down and wait for Mama to lift Rosa out of her wrap. The first time I held Rosa was just moments after she was born. I held her close to keep her warm, looked into her tiny squashed-up face and said, "You're as new and sweet as a rosebud," and that's how she got her name. I can't believe how much she's grown since then – although she's still the tiniest person I've ever seen. Especially now, when she emerges from the baby wrap all bunched up.

Rosa sinks into my arms. Her limbs unfurl and she waves her hands around, as if searching for something. I offer her a finger and she wraps her own tiny fingers around it and stares up at me. Love balloons through me until I think I might burst. "I'm going to be the best big sister for you," I whisper. Rosa keeps staring at me, and I think I see a smile twitching on her lips, but then her mouth opens and she moves her head from side to side, the way she does when she's looking for milk. "I think she's hungry," I say, offering Rosa back to Mama.

"I think you're right." Mama gently lifts Rosa out of my arms and sits down to feed her. I watch for a while, until the pumpkin giant topples over on the other side of the hall, and I rush over to help my friends rebuild him.

The day whizzes past like a dragonfly. It's not until the sun sets, and Babusya wobbles into the hall to tell us she's made dinner, that I remember I was going to help Papa look for a way into Aurora Dome. But Papa says he's starving and that can wait for another day.

There are only a handful of people left in the hall now and they're packing up to leave too. We wave them goodbye then head to the kitchen, which is filled with the warmth of the stove and the rich, savoury smell of Babusya's *solyanka* soup.

After we've eaten, I get ready for bed. But thoughts of a key hidden in Sun Dome buzz in my mind. I know I won't be able to read or sleep, and it's too dark to look for a secret staircase now. So I pull my cardigan over my pyjamas, slide the patch I made into my pocket, and return to the kitchen.

I curl into my comfy chair in front of the stove like a field mouse curling into a nest for winter. Rosa is asleep, resting against Mama's chest. Babusya is propped up by pillows on her bed, trying to do some mending, but she's soon snoring. Mama lifts the torn blouse from her hands and finishes sewing it for her, while humming a lullaby she once told me her own grandmother used to play for her on a *balalaika*.

Papa reads one of the puzzle books he keeps by his chair, and I stare at the flames dancing in the stove. Usually I'd be solving riddles with Papa, but tonight I can't concentrate.

A crackle comes from inside the stove, followed by the gentle pop of a stick splitting. Then, as fast and fierce as a hawk hunting, a gust of wind slams into the kitchen window, cracking the glass. Everyone in the room jumps in shock, except Babusya, who carries on snoring.

The wind swoops and zooms up the walls outside, hissing through the pine logs and making threads of moss fly into the air from between them. I grip my chair, my muscles tight with fear, and stare at my parents with wide eyes. Mama and Papa look at each other, concerned frowns rumpling their brows as the wind reaches the roof. It squeals with glee as it whirls around the domes.

Rosa starts crying and Mama stands and sways back and forth, patting her back to soothe her. There is a creaking noise that gets louder, and for a moment I feel like the whole castle is tilting... Then there is a bang so loud that I cover my ears, followed by a clattering that sounds like a herd of moose clashing antlers.

"What was that?" I whisper nervously when the noise subsides. In my heart I know the wind must have broken some part of the castle – and judging by the loudness of the noise, it was something big.

CHAPTER FOUR

THE KERCHIEF OF SALT

"The bang came from the Great Hall." Papa rises to his feet. "I'll take a look." Another burst of wind explodes against the kitchen window, shaking the already cracked glass. Papa crosses the room and swings the interior shutters closed, then picks up his tool bag. "I won't be long." He disappears out of the door and worries crowd around me.

"Why don't you put some spiced milk on the stove?" Mama whispers as she sits down. She's managed to rock Rosa back to sleep, but is still patting her gently.

Glad of the distraction, I fill a pan with milk. I can't stop Babusya's words about a storm from thundering through my mind. And I can't forget the lightning in her eyes when she spoke of winds tearing things down.

Wind whistles down the chimney, long and loud, and my hand shakes, making a few drops of milk splash out of the pan and sizzle on the stove top. I've never heard winds like these before. And I've never felt Castle Mila shake. But right now the walls, the floor and the ceiling all seem to be trembling in fear. What if something happens to the castle? Or to Papa while he's trying to fix it?

"Your papa knows how to keep himself safe," Mama says softly, as if she's read my thoughts. "And whatever the wind has broken, we can repair or replace."

I nod, not wanting to speak in case I wake Rosa up with the fear in my voice. Then I add two of Papa's secret spice sachets to the milk. A fierce gust raises the pitch of the wind's whistle, and panic hurtles through me. If this storm is strong enough to shake the castle, then what might it be doing to the houses in the village? What if my friends and everyone I've ever known are in danger? My thoughts are broken by something scuffling behind the stove. I peer into the shadows, wondering if it's mice, scared of the winds.

"The *domovoi* wants an offering," Babusya croaks without opening her eyes. I sigh with relief, because if anything can take my mind off the storm, then it's Babusya and her talk of spirits, like the *domovoi* – the house spirit who she says lives behind our stove.

"I thought you were asleep," I say to Babusya, opening the cupboard where we keep the salt pot. There is a stack of neatly ironed white kerchiefs and a bundle of ribbons next to it. I try my best to stop my fingers from shaking as I pour salt into one of the kerchiefs, fold it up and tie it with a ribbon, the way Babusya does when she leaves an offering for the *domovoi*.

Babusya says the *domovoi* is as old as the castle, and protects it from dangers. She says that all homes have a *domovoi*, and that ours looks like a fox, although he can take the form of a foxlike old man as well. She says she's seen him hundreds of times, and that if I looked with my heart, then I would see him too.

When I was younger, I believed in the *domovoi* completely and spent hours chasing scuffling sounds along the corridors, hoping to catch a glimpse of him. Once I thought I saw the tip of a fluffy fox-tail poking out from behind the stove. At the time I was sure of what I saw, but now I don't trust the memory. It was late at night, so I could have been tired or half-dreaming.

The wind roars louder still, rattling the window shutters, and my heart rattles with them. All of a sudden I want the *domovoi* to exist more than ever before, and I want this offering of salt to help him protect our home. I walk over to the stove and place the kerchief near the back of it, just beyond what I imagine might be a *domovoi*'s reach. I started doing this when I was very young, in the hope that I'd see the *domovoi* as he leaned out to take his offering.

The shutters fly open, slamming against the log walls, and I rush over to close them again. Behind the window, the night is full of shadows. Winds beat against the castle and small branches zoom past like startled birds. A silvery roof shingle swoops down, then disappears in the direction of the lake. I peer after it, scowling at the winds, before closing the shutters once more.

"The milk is bubbling." Babusya sits up in bed. "Why don't you come and pour us some?"

I move back to the stove, feeling hot with anger at the storm, and cold with fear at the same time. "The castle is strong, isn't it?" I glance from Mama to Babusya as I pour three cupfuls of milk and stir a little honey into mine and Mama's. Usually I'd savour the scents of ginger, cinnamon and vanilla wafting into the air, but right now all I can think about is the winds and the damage they might cause. "I mean, the castle has stood for five hundred years, so it must have survived a storm or two?" I ask nervously. The thought of our home being torn apart, especially before I've had the chance to explore it with Rosa, makes my stomach tighten even more than it did the time I ate bad mushrooms.

"Castle Mila has withstood many storms." Babusya takes the cup I offer her. "But that doesn't mean it will withstand *every* storm."

Mama opens her mouth, but her words are drowned out by the wind. The whole room shakes. Something high above creaks and a sad wail flows down the chimney. I feel it deep in my bones. What if

Babusya is right and our home is in danger? How can I keep all of us safe?

"What about the *domovoi?*" I glance at the kerchief of salt by the stove. "Won't he protect the castle from the storm?"

"There is something strange about this storm." Babusya tilts an ear towards the sounds skirling in the chimney. "There's magic in these winds. The *domovoi* is a powerful spirit, but I don't know if he's strong enough to protect the castle from this."

I sink into my chair, feeling dizzy as I try not to picture the castle tumbling down.

Mama gives Babusya a concerned look, then reaches over and rests a hand on my shoulder. Babusya's eyes soften. "Of course, the offering will give the *domovoi* strength, as will asking politely for his help. A *domovoi's* magic grows when they feel needed and appreciated."

I stare into my milk, wishing I felt comforted.

"Come and rest on the bed." Babusya pats the empty space beside her. "And try not to worry. Your mama is right about your papa keeping himself safe. And we're in the strongest room in the castle."

I abandon my cup and slide onto the bed. Babusya strokes my hair, like she used to do when I was little. Mama hums her favourite lullaby again and I hum too…and I carry on humming long after Mama and Babusya have joined Rosa in sleep. Then, just as I'm finally drifting off myself, I see a tiny pawlike hand covered in fluffy orange fur reaching out from behind the stove.

Two small, bright, but somewhat melancholy eyes blink up at me from a furry face almost hidden in the shadows, and two large, triangular, black-tipped ears twitch in my direction. I don't know if this is a dream, or an imagining, but I hear myself ask, "Please, *domovoi*, will you help protect our home?"

And the *domovoi*, if that's what he is, nods. Then he snatches the kerchief filled with salt and disappears back behind the stove with a swish of his long, fluffy tail.

Chapter Five

After the Storm

When I wake, the kitchen is so peaceful I wonder if I dreamed the storm. Babusya is asleep beside me. Mama is sat humming softly to Rosa. The smell of fresh coffee and hot buttered toast wafts from the table. Papa is standing in a pale shaft of light that is falling through the window. I watch him fiddling with the glass for a moment before realizing he's replacing the pane that cracked last night.

Everything comes rushing back to me: the fierce winds, the crashing and clattering, Babusya's talk of magic, and my glimpse of the *domovoi*. I sit up and look at the space near the back of the stove where I left the offering. The kerchief of salt is gone.

A shiver of excitement rushes through me as I wonder if I really did see the *domovoi*, and if he somehow stopped the storm because I asked him to protect our home. I slide out of bed and give Mama and Rosa a morning kiss, pick up a slice of toast, then walk over to Papa. I kiss him and look out of the window, wondering if the winds have completely stopped.

The sight of all the glorious autumn colours gone, blown away by the storm, makes my heart sink. The grass in the meadow has been flattened and there are no leaves or fruits left on the trees in the grove, making them look frail and vulnerable. The sky is overcast, the sun hidden behind a cold, steely haze, but there are no obvious storm clouds and the lake is fairly calm, with just a few waves rising and falling, like the water is sighing with relief.

"The storm ended as abruptly as it started." Papa follows my gaze. "When the sun rose about an hour ago, the winds stopped."

"Is the castle all right? What was the huge bang last night?" I ask.

"Part of Sun Dome collapsed into the Great Hall." Papa runs his hand through his curly hair, ruffling it up. "It's all a bit of a mess in there."

"Sun Dome…" I whisper, my eyes widening at the thought that the hidden attic might have been revealed – the one Babusya says holds the key to unlock magic. But then I remember all the work everyone did in the Great Hall yesterday. "The preparations for the feast…" My voice falters as I think of the family blanket. I hope it's not torn or damaged in any way.

"I'm afraid the feast is going to have to be cancelled. I'm sorry, Olia," Papa says gently. "Your mama and I are going to the village shortly to tell everyone, and to ask for help with the clearing up."

"We can't cancel the feast! Everyone has been looking forward to it all year." I think about the patch in my pocket and how much I want to sew it onto the family blanket, the same way a patch has been added for the last four hundred and ninety-nine years. I pull my shoulders back and give Papa my most confident look. "There must be a way for the feast to go ahead. We've got all day to clear up the hall."

"It's not just the mess." Papa shakes his head sadly. "There are some big repairs needed to Sun Dome too, and I'm not even sure how to get up there."

"I'll help you find a way." I try to think, for the millionth time, where the secret staircase might be.

"We've looked for a way into that dome so many times that I'm starting to doubt there is one." Papa scratches his head. "I might be able to persuade some of the wild-honey collectors to bring their climbing equipment over here so we can get in through the hole in the ceiling. But getting up to that dome and repairing it before tonight is going to be tricky."

"But not impossible." I finish my toast and push back my sleeves so I'm ready for action. "I'll start clearing the hall while you and Mama go to the village. Maybe I'll even find a way up to the dome."

"Please don't go into the hall by yourself." Papa packs his tools away. "It's not safe – there's broken glass and splintered wood all over the floor."

"Why don't you come with us to the village?" Mama rises to her feet, swaddling Rosa into her wrap.

"I'll stay with Babusya," I say, wondering if she might take me into the hall when she wakes.

"All right." Mama gives me a hug and opens the wrap a little so I can kiss the top of Rosa's head. "We'll be back by lunchtime, hopefully with lots of people to help."

"Your grandmother and I had a talk early this morning so she knows what a mess the hall is in." Papa tucks Babusya's blanket carefully around her. "Please don't let her go in there either."

"But we could go together and start clearing up. We'd be careful…" I give Papa my best pleading look, eyebrows raised and a wide smile to make my dimple deepen, but he shakes his head firmly.

"Please stay safely in here until we return." Mama puts Papa's coat on. She's been wearing it lately because it's big enough to fit around her and Rosa together.

I nod reluctantly and wave goodbye to my parents. Then I sit by the window and watch them disappear into the spruce grove by the lake. There is a path through it that leads to the village.

Restlessness courses through me like a blustery wind. I'm desperate to see the damage to Sun Dome for myself, and I want to get the family blanket and make sure it's all right. I stare out of the window, frustrated that Papa told me not to go into the hall. But my heart lifts when I notice two figures down where the spruce grove meets the shore.

I slide my bare feet into my boots and rush out of the door. I forgot Dinara and Luka were coming over today. We were thinking about going fishing, so we arranged to meet by the rowing boat I built with my parents two summers ago. An idea swells in my mind as I race down the hill. Papa said not to go into the Great Hall *by myself*, and not to let Babusya go in there. But if I went in with my friends, maybe that would be okay. We could rescue the blanket and while we're in there take a quick look at the damage.

The wind whispers Babusya's words into my ears...*the key to unlock the magic is hidden inside that dome... No one has ever found a way up there... Time is running out.*

A thrill gusts through me and I pick up speed because today, there is a chance that I'll discover the mysterious secrets that have remained hidden inside Sun Dome for five hundred years.

CHAPTER SIX

DINARA AND LUKA

Dinara and Luka are twins, but they don't look alike. Dinara is tall and slim, with a wide smile and short brown hair that she teases into spikes. She always looks like she's about to take off into a run or climb up a tree. Right now, she's bouncing on her toes at the water's edge, skimming stones across the lake.

Luka is sat on the upturned rowing boat, drawing inky monsters into his notebook. He's shorter and broader than Dinara, and has lighter hair that flops over his face. He does everything slowly and carefully, always carries a fat black notebook under his arm, and at every opportunity draws pictures in it with a fine black pen.

I'm in between Dinara and Luka, both in height and build, and the way we go about things too. I'm not as speedy or impulsive as Dinara, but I'm not as wary as Luka either. I like to think that I balance them out; that I'm the midpoint of their see-saw.

"Hello, Your Highness." Luka looks up from under his hair and grins as I sprint up to them. Sometimes Dinara and Luka and the others at school tease me about living in a castle and being descended from royalty. But I don't think they mean any harm by it.

For hundreds of years, my ancestors were rich in a land of poor people. They gathered treasures while the villagers often went hungry. The thought makes me feel hot with shame and guilt, and I have to fan it away by reminding myself that was all a long time ago and things are different now. After the revolution that promised to make everyone equal, Castle Mila was stripped of its treasures. Now we live the same as everyone else, only in a bigger home.

"Can you believe the storm last night?" I lean over to catch my breath. "Are the houses in the village all right?"

"What storm?" Both Dinara and Luka stare at me in confusion.

"You can't have slept through it?" I ask, incredulous. "I've never heard a storm like it. It shook the castle walls and made part of Sun Dome collapse."

"Are you joking?" Dinara peers between the spruce trees, trying to glimpse the castle.

"No. Come and see." I beckon Dinara and Luka out of the grove and point up at my home. In my rush to reach my friends, I hadn't looked back at Castle Mila myself until now, so the sight of Sun Dome is a shock. It looks like the wind blew itself into a fist and punched the dome, full force.

A hole has been torn in one side and the thin spire that reached all the way to the stars has snapped. I stare at the damage in dismay. Sun Dome should be shining in the sky, not tumbling towards the ground. But as my gaze is drawn into the darkness through the hole, my only thoughts become what might lie inside. I wish I could see into the hidden attic, but it's too shadowed and far away.

"That looks bad." Luka's eyebrows draw together.

"But it doesn't make any sense. We didn't hear a storm last night. Nothing in the village is damaged, and nobody said anything this morning."

"Maybe the dome just collapsed?" Dinara suggests. "Your castle is pretty old, Olia."

I shake my head. "There really was a scary storm – I saw it. The winds were howling around the castle and screaming down the chimney. You must have heard something! And the worst thing is the Great Hall is a mess. My parents have gone to the village to get help, but there's a good chance the feast tonight will be cancelled."

"That's a shame." Luka's face falls. "I was looking forward to playing music with the band. I've been practising."

"Is there anything we can do to help?" Dinara asks.

"Yes…" What I'm about to suggest is making my conscience buzz around me like a hoverfly, but I quickly silence it. "Will you come and help me get the patchwork blanket that was hanging in the Great Hall? I want to check it's all right."

"Of course. We know how important it is to you and your family." Dinara starts running towards the castle.

"Is it safe in there?" Luka takes a slow breath in, like he always does when he gets anxious. Then he tucks his notebook under his arm and together we run after Dinara.

"Papa says there's broken glass and splintered wood on the floor, but we're all wearing boots."

"What about the dome?" Luka stares up at it. "What if it collapses further?"

"It won't." I shake my head firmly enough to squash the seed of worry that just sprouted. "It was the storm that made the dome collapse, and that's over now."

A ray of light breaks through the overcast sky and falls through the hole into Sun Dome, making something inside glow dazzlingly bright. I shade my eyes and squint up at it.

"What can you see?" Luka asks.

"There's something shining inside the dome." My words fizz on my tongue.

"Like treasure?" Dinara turns around, but carries on running backwards. Dinara always hopes to find real treasure – gold, silver or jewels – when we explore.

"Maybe something even better." My mind whirrs with thoughts of a key that is not a key; *something* with the power to unlock magic. I don't understand what Babusya thinks is hidden inside Sun Dome, but I'm desperate to find out. "Come on!" I shout to Luka and race after Dinara. I overtake her and lead the way to the west entrance of the castle, because I don't want to go through the kitchen and disturb Babusya.

The west entrance is a huge set of wooden doors that rise at least three times taller than me. If the doors opened, they would lead straight into the Great Hall, but they swelled shut long ago and now we leave them closed. There are, however, two loose panels in the bottom corner of the left door that I always sneak through. I pull them aside so Dinara and Luka can enter the hall, then I follow them in. I hold my breath and brace myself for the mess I expect to find, but it's still a shock.

I stare at the devastation, wide-eyed. I can't even see the wooden floor I helped sweep yesterday, because it's buried beneath a mound of debris. Broken planks and green-and-gold painted panels of wood from the fallen ceiling are jumbled amongst smashed jam jars, squashed pumpkins, scattered leaves and flowers, and baskets spilling fruits and berries. A cracked clay statue of one of the harvest spirits reaches out from the chaos like she wants to be saved. My hands cover my mouth in shock. I know Papa said it was a bit of a mess, but I wasn't prepared for this.

"This is terrible," Dinara groans. "I think you're right about the feast not going ahead."

"If my parents come back with enough helpers, we might be able to clear it up in time." I try to sound confident as my gaze is drawn up to the ceiling, high above us. There is a huge hole on one side but I'm at the wrong angle to see through it so I start walking across the hall, wincing as my boots crunch over debris. "Let's just find the blanket to start with. It must be over there somewhere." I scan the far end of the hall, looking for the blanket. It isn't hanging on the wall any more and my chest tightens as I think of it torn and crumpled in amongst the mess on the floor.

As we draw close to the wall, I notice it looks different. A few of the logs that make up the wall have slumped down, revealing a dark, empty space behind them. A soft breeze flows from the space and whispers in my ear, about secrets and magic and locks and keys. I feel myself being pulled towards the tumbled logs, and I pick up speed.

"Be careful, Olia," Luka says. "That wall doesn't look safe."

"There's something behind it." I stare into the dark and my heartbeat quickens. "It's a hidden staircase!"

Dinara runs to catch up with me, her feet crashing through the mess.

"It must lead up into Sun Dome!" Excitement bursts through me. "Oh, I've looked for this all my life and lots of my ancestors have looked for it too. No one has ever found a way; Babusya says even the spirits can't get up there and she says…" I pause, unsure how to explain Babusya's talk of a key that unlocks magic. "She says incredible things are hidden up there."

"Treasure?" Dinara beams.

"The most amazing treasure ever." I look from Dinara to Luka, a huge smile growing on my face. "And we're going to find it."

CHAPTER SEVEN

SUN DOME

"No wonder this staircase has never been found." I step closer to the tumbled wall. "There is no secret door. Someone built the wall right across the entrance to conceal it completely."

"They must have done that for a reason." Luka frowns. "What if the stairs aren't safe?"

I lean into the hidden space and prod one of the dusty wooden steps. "They're solid." I move back a little and gaze upwards, imagining the path the stairs must take behind the wall, all the way up into the dome. Through the hole in the ceiling I can now see tantalizing glimpses of a curved attic space.

As I stare, something glows inside the dome again. Whispers swirl in my ears, like the sound of the ocean in a shell, and I feel myself being pulled upwards. "Do you see that?" I ask.

"Something is shining up there!" Dinara bounces with excitement, cracking some debris beneath her feet.

"I see it too." Luka pushes his hair away from his eyes.

"I have to find out what it is." I try to climb into the hidden space over the lower logs of the broken wall.

"Wait! I'll come too." Dinara crunches over to me.

Luka shakes his head. "You're not careful enough to go up there, Dinara. Besides, the stairs and the attic might not be strong enough for two."

"I can be careful." Dinara scowls at Luka.

"You're never careful." Luka scowls back at her.

"Please don't argue. Shall I go up first and make sure it's safe?"

"All right. But you have to share any treasure with us peasants, *Princess* Olia," Dinara jokes with a grin. She puts her hands together to make a step to help boost me up through the hole in the wall.

"Of course I will." I give Dinara a regal wave and

step onto her hands, then scramble into the secret space. It's narrower and darker than any of the other hidden staircases I've been in, and a warm tingling skirrs over my skin. I know in my heart these stairs lead to something magical and, right now, I absolutely, truly believe that I'm going to find it.

It takes a moment for my eyes to adjust to the darkness. Everything leans slightly to the left, but I tread carefully. I peer back into the hall, give Dinara and Luka a thumbs up followed by another regal wave, then begin my ascent.

The steps give slightly beneath my feet and I find myself springing higher and faster up them, eager to reach the dome. As the staircase curves I'm plunged into even deeper darkness, but I carry on, feeling my way with my hands along the walls. Then, all of a sudden, there is a bright circle of shimmering light ahead. I stop and stare at it in wonder. My breathing quickens. The air feels thin and smells of ancient things, like sun-baked stones and dry, cracked earth… *like the wind in the grove!*

Something like heatwaves shift in the light and

slowly a round attic comes into focus. It's a little wonky and part of its domed roof has been torn open so I can see the grey sky beyond. Dark clouds are massing out there, and for a moment I wonder if another storm is coming, but then I'm distracted by the faded paintings on the walls.

One is of a boy who resembles a tree and a girl who appears to be made of water. They could be a tree spirit and a water spirit, like the ones that Babusya talks about. Then there are winged horses flying through a pale blue sky, and an ocean with a huge golden fish splashing in it. Silver eyes stare out from a picture of a red fortress, sending a chill down the back of my neck. Babusya has never told me anything about a fortress.

I edge into the attic and feel a stretching sensation in the air, followed by a brief pop and the tingle of something raining down, as if I've walked through a giant soap bubble. My face squinches up at the strange feeling. Then I spot the glowing *something* on the floor and almost squeal with excitement.

It's a small, old and dusty wooden chest, but it's wrapped in golden chains that glow as brightly as summer sunlight. I creep towards it and feel the floorboards bending beneath me. A thought buzzes through my mind that the floor might not be safe, but I blow it away and, treading as lightly as possible, draw closer to the chest. My fingers reach towards it and the air fills with sparks of warm light, while whispers of magic swish in my ears...

My fingertips graze the golden chain wrapped around the chest and electricity sizzles through me. Then there is a terrifying crack and everything drops away beneath me. For the briefest moment, I'm falling through the air, surrounded by broken planks and ceiling panels.

Above me, I think I see a small, foxlike old man, reaching for me with panicked eyes. Somehow the walls of the Great Hall wave and warp towards me, bending impossibly to cradle my body like a hammock. Then I land, hard, in Dinara's arms. She collapses to the floor with a groan. And the walls are straight again.

Something heavy crashes down beside us, making my racing heartbeat leap. Dust and splinters are thrown into the air, along with flashes of golden light. All I hear is my too-fast breathing, then the worried voice of Luka asking if we're okay, before Dinara laughs hysterically.

I sway to my feet, every muscle in my body shaking, and stare up at the dome I fell from. It's so high above us, it doesn't make any sense that I could have fallen so far and still be alive. I look down at myself to check I really am okay, then lower my gaze to the wooden chest, which has split open within its chains, on the floor beside us. The darkness inside the chest looks like a swirling storm cloud, but deep within it there is something else, glowing and pulling me towards it.

Chapter Eight

The Treasure Chest

The glowing chest holds my gaze like a weasel hypnotizing a rabbit. It takes all my effort to look away from it, to check that Dinara and Luka are okay. Luka is pale, his eyes wide, and Dinara is cradling her wrist. "Are you hurt?" I ask her.

"Just a bruise, I think." Dinara tries to move her hand and cringes. "You're heavier than you look, Olia." Her face relaxes into a smile. "But I'm glad I caught you."

I glance up at the dome again, feeling foolish for walking on floorboards when I felt them bending. "I think you saved my life." I throw my arms around Dinara in a huge hug and she laughs.

"I thought you were both going to…" Luka takes a slow breath in. "It was terrifying."

"But thankfully we're fine." Dinara nudges Luka, looks down at the chest and grins. "Shall we see what's inside?"

We all kneel next to the smashed chest and pull pieces of its wood away from the golden chains. Except the chains don't look golden any more. They look old and rusty, and crumble as we move the wood. But I'm sure there are still sparks of gold dancing amongst the splinters.

Dinara slides the last piece of broken wood away and lets out a long, disappointed sigh. There is only a small mound of dust on the bottom of the chest. "I can't believe it's empty," she groans.

"It can't be." I shake my head in disbelief. "I saw something glowing inside."

Luka pokes the dust mound with his pen and lifts up something floppy and grey.

"What *is* that?" Dinara screws up her face as she peers at it in confusion.

I lift the thing off Luka's pen. It's fabric – soft, dusty, old fabric. I rise to my feet and brush it off away from the others, so the dust doesn't get in their eyes. "It's a hat!" I exclaim, turning around to show it to them. "A green, velvet hat."

Dinara leans in to take a closer look. "There aren't any jewels on it. Why was it locked into a chest?"

"I don't know." I turn the hat over in my hands. It feels strangely warm. "It's very odd." I frown, wishing I understood all of this: the stretching and popping sensation in the attic, the way the chains around the chest glowed, the glimpse of the small, foxlike old man trying to help me, and the walls bending. I lift a hand to my head, wondering if I bumped it.

Luka takes the hat from me and examines it closely. "It's a nice hat," he says. "Old and worn, but carefully made. The stitching is neat and it has a silk lining too. Try it on."

My fingers tingle as I take the hat back, and my nerves jitter. The hat feels powerful somehow, and I don't feel ready for what might happen if I put it on. "Umm...maybe later." I slide the hat into my cardigan pocket, and as I do so, my hand brushes the patch I made, reminding me why we came into the hall in the first place. "The blanket!" I crunch back over to the wall. "We never found the family blanket."

Dinara and Luka follow me, picking their way over the mess, which is even worse now that I've brought more of the ceiling down. Dinara is still cradling her wrist and looks thoroughly disappointed, as she always does when we don't find treasure. Guilt gathers over me like a mound of wet leaves. Because of me Dinara is hurt and the dome is even more damaged than before.

The interior door to the hall creaks open and Babusya steps in, leaning on her walking sticks. "I heard a bang." She looks up to the top of the hall, then scans the ruins around us. Her eyebrows lift and I flush with shame. "My eyes see you clearly," Babusya chuckles, "but my heart not so much. You wouldn't come in here when your papa told you not to, would you?"

"He said not to come in here by myself." I recoil from my own words, knowing full well that my parents didn't want me to come in here at all. More heat rises into my cheeks. "I wanted to check the family blanket was all right, but then I found stairs to the dome attic." I point to the hidden staircase. "I had to go and see what was up there. But some of the floorboards broke and I fell…" I stop, not sure how to explain about the bending walls and the glowing chest. "I'm so sorry, Babusya. I shouldn't have come in here."

"It's lucky you weren't hurt. But everyone makes mistakes. In fact, to live is to make mistakes." Babusya chuckles again and my brow furrows, because I don't know what she means or why she's laughing.

"I caught Olia when she fell," Dinara says proudly. "And we're all fine, so no harm was done."

"There's the blanket!" Luka points at the floor and my heart clenches as I spot a corner of it, prickled with splinters. I kneel down and start to move chunks of wood and broken jars off it. Luka and Dinara come over to help, although Dinara only uses her one uninjured hand.

"Be careful." Babusya looks pointedly at Dinara. "Looks like we've already had one injury this morning."

"I'm fine, Mrs Solnyshko," Dinara says as we extract the blanket. It has splotches of jam on it and a rip down one side. Tears well in my eyes as I notice which patches are torn: Babusya as a toddler, talking to a tree spirit; Papa's birthday picnic; my parents' wedding; my first day at school.

I try to bundle the blanket into my arms and a trailing thread catches on my fingernail. It pulls at the stitching, several patches separate and the whole blanket starts to fall apart. "No!" I shout in panic and move my hand, but I only make things worse.

"Just stay still!" Luka says and I stop moving. He unhooks the thread from my fingernail and he and Dinara help me fold the blanket, with the loose patches tucked safely inside.

"I can clean and mend it, Olia." Babusya beckons us over and I carry the blanket across the hall, blinking away my tears. Babusya is right. We have all day to fix the blanket, and then I can sew my patch on as planned tonight.

"I'll bandage your wrist," Babusya says to Dinara, "but then you and Luka must go home. There is another storm coming, even bigger than the last."

"Really?" Dinara raises her eyebrows quizzically as we follow Babusya to the kitchen.

"Dinara and Luka said there was no storm in the

village last night," I explain as I kick off my boots. The sight of my bare feet and pyjama trousers reminds me it's still so early in the day that I haven't even got dressed yet.

"It can't storm everywhere at the same time," Babusya mutters. She finds a roll of bandages in a cupboard and looks sternly at Dinara until she holds out her arm. "Right now, a huge storm is coming *here*, to the castle, and you two must go back to the village." Babusya glances up at my friends as she wraps the bandage around Dinara's wrist. "You need to get this checked properly, Dinara, and I don't want you two getting stuck here and your parents worrying where you are. When the storm hits, people will need to stay sheltered inside."

I look out of the kitchen window. Wind whirls around, whipping up leaves and strands of loose grass. My stomach knots at the thought of a storm even worse than last night's. "Should we stay here if another storm is coming?" I ask Babusya. "Maybe we should go to the village too, and find Mama, Papa and Rosa, and all stay together somewhere safe."

"There is something you must do here, Olia – something that will help your parents and sister and everyone else." Babusya's fingers tremble as she secures Dinara's bandage, and that sends uncertainties fluttering through me.

My friends look at each other in confusion and Dinara opens her mouth, but before she can say anything Babusya ushers her and Luka to the door. Wind gusts into the kitchen when she opens it. "Go straight home," Babusya orders.

"Will you be all right, Olia?" Dinara cranes her neck to look back at me.

"I think so." I hug the family blanket I'm holding tight, feeling baffled by Babusya and scared at the prospect of another storm. "I'm so sorry about your wrist."

"It's fine." Dinara smiles reassuringly and waves her hand gently.

"I'll make sure she gets it checked." Luka's hair blows around his face as he steps out of the door. "And we'll come to see you when the storm has passed?" He looks from me to Babusya.

"Yes, yes – now go quickly before the storm arrives," Babusya urges. She closes the door, shutting out the wind…but I still feel tension growing in the air until it chafes against my skin. It's like a hurricane is building both inside and outside the castle.

"Are you ready?" Babusya turns to me with a twinkle in her eyes.

"For what?" I whisper nervously. In my heart I have a strange inkling about what Babusya might say, but my head is tangled with doubts.

"To unlock the castle's magic of course," Babusya replies. "And stop this storm, before it destroys everything."

CHAPTER NINE

THE HAT

A gust of wind howls down the chimney, so fiercely that the fire in the stove roars back at it. Fear wraps around me, as icy as the lake in winter. "This storm could destroy everything?" I look at Babusya, hoping I misheard her. "You can't mean the whole castle…" Blood drains from my face and I hug the family blanket tighter. The blanket is more than squares of fabric, and the castle is more than a building made of logs. They are our history and our home. We can't lose them to a storm.

"Yes. The storm could destroy the castle, and even more than I can explain right now. But you found the key, didn't you? You got into Sun Dome and found the key, Olia!" Babusya pulls me into one of her bony, awkward, walking-stick filled hugs and almost jumps up and down with excitement. "I knew you would. I'm so proud of you. Now, if you are to stop this storm, you must hold onto the belief that won you the key."

"But, Babusya, there was no key. And I don't know how to stop a storm!" My voice rises in panic as the winds outside crescendo and rattle all the windows.

Babusya lifts the blanket out of my arms. "I'm getting ahead of myself. Sorry. Tell me what you found." She glances at the lump in my cardigan pocket.

"Just this." I pull out the velvet hat and offer it to her, but she doesn't take it. She only stares at it, wide-eyed.

"Do you *see* it?" Babusya whispers.

"Well…er…yes. It's a green velvet hat. With a red silk lining," I reply, silently thanking Luka for his careful observations, which seem much more sensible than my private ones about flashes of gold dancing in the dust and the strange warmth of the hat.

Babusya shakes her head as if disappointed. "Put the hat back in your pocket. Keep it close to you.

And try to *see* it." She pauses. "I want you to go to your bedroom, Olia."

"My bedroom?" I ask in confusion.

"You can see Aurora Dome from your bedroom window, can't you?" Babusya asks. I nod. "Good. That's where the lock is."

"What lock? How do you know all this? And what about the key?" I ask in exasperation, opening up the hat to look inside again. "There's nothing in here. What am I meant to do?"

Sudden inspiration strikes me. "Is the hat the key? Should I put it on?"

"Goodness, no!" Babusya exclaims. "You should never wear someone else's hat. Just look at Aurora Dome, *see* what is happening, and listen to the spirits. Then you'll know what to do." Babusya waves her walking sticks, shooing me away. "Go now, time is ticking!"

"Are you all right, Babusya?" I ask, although really I'm wondering if *I'm* all right. I feel so topsy-turvy, I'm starting to think maybe I truly did bump my head during the fall.

"I'm fine, Olia." Babusya kisses my cheeks. "Off you go. I need to do some urgent baking." She puts the family blanket down. "I'll clean and mend this later. It will be even better than new when you return." She shoos me away again, so I turn, as if in a dream, and begin the long walk to my bedroom.

The winds wail outside and beat against the castle walls. I wonder where Mama, Papa and Rosa are, and whether they're safe and warm in a house in the village, or stuck somewhere, cold and windblown, between the village and the castle. Worries flap in my chest at the thought that this storm could destroy *everything* and before my fears overwhelm me, I remind myself that Babusya said I can stop this. Fantastic as that sounds, if it's true then I must try. I pick up speed, determined to figure out how the hat, Aurora Dome and the storm are linked.

I reach my bedroom, so breathless from running up the stairs and confused from trying to make sense of it all that dark spots are clouding my vision. I pour some water from the jug on my washstand into a bowl, splash it onto my face and take a slow breath in. Then

I sit on my bed and look out of my window towards Aurora Dome, as Babusya told me to.

The sky over Lake Mila is overcast and grey, and it gets darker closer to the castle. Directly overhead are thick, bruise-coloured storm clouds, which make it feel like midnight even though it's barely mid-morning. Winds tear at the roof like claws. They scare me, but I try my best to ignore them and the damage they're causing and focus on Aurora Dome, in the hope that Babusya is right, and it will help me figure out what I need to do.

Because my bedroom is on the third floor, and because Castle Mila's domes are arranged in layers, I can see four domes from my window. Aurora Dome is the smallest and most easterly of them. It perches far out, right on the edge of the roof. I rest my chin on my hands and look hard at the dome. It's a brighter silver, and less shaken by the winds than the others.

I stare at it until my eyes blur and my heart can't ignore the escalating storm any longer. The sound of it battering against the castle walls and roof makes me tremble. I'm overwhelmed by an urge to go back to the warmth of the kitchen and see what Babusya is doing. She said she needed to do some urgent baking, which is weird, but her company along with something warm to eat might help me feel calmer. But just as I decide to leave my room, it's as if something silently explodes inside Aurora Dome.

Winds blast out from beneath its shingles. The currents of air are tinged with gold and I peer at them nervously, remembering the ribbons of light I saw streaming from this very dome when I was younger. The winds zoom, split and accelerate, faster and faster, until they're screaming along the flat parts of the roof and spinning around the domes.

Something cracks and crashes beyond my sight and I tighten with fear, for my family and for the castle. All of a sudden, the world feels like a strange and dangerous place. My bedroom walls shudder. The glass in my window shakes.

Then, as suddenly as they came, the winds subside. Only a whisper of a draught remains, prying through the gaps in my window frame. The draught is bone-chilling, unsettling, like the wind that creeps through a graveyard at night.

My pulse races as I scan the floor of my bedroom, desperately searching for my socks, because I want to skid and slide as fast as possible all the way down to Babusya. I don't feel brave enough to face this storm alone, and I certainly don't feel able to stop it.

But before I can find my socks there is a knock on my bedroom door. I turn around, hoping maybe Mama or Papa will enter, having come home early from the village. But no one opens the door, not even when I call out, "Come in." I keep searching for my socks and am beginning to think I imagined the knock when I hear it again.

I open the door. There is nobody there. I frown in confusion and am about to close it again when I look down and see a fox, staring up at me with bright blue eyes. Even though he looks like an ordinary fox, I know in my heart he is more.

"*Domovoi?*" I whisper, my whole body fizzing and popping with excitement.

The fox gives me a curt nod, then rises onto his

hind legs. As he does, the air shimmers around him and he changes into the small, foxlike man I saw when I fell earlier. A long, green coat appears on his body and black boots appear on his paw-feet. His bushy fox-tail remains, curving up from beneath his coat, and his fluffy, triangular fox ears stay pricked up attentively on the top of his head. But his snout flattens slightly, making him look more human, and although his face remains covered in neat, orange-brown fur, some of it grows into a flowing moustache and beard that hides his mouth and reaches halfway down his chest.

"Olia," the *domovoi* replies. His voice is rough like a growl and yet soft like downy fur, and his blue eyes gleam with a look that is strangely familiar but entirely new. "You asked for my help. To protect Castle Mila."

I'm too stunned too speak, but I also feel relieved – that the *domovoi* Babusya has talked about and I have searched for all my life really does exist, and that he's here now. A moment ago I felt powerless against this storm. But if I have the help of a magical spirit, maybe I can do something to protect my family and my home after all.

CHAPTER TEN

FELIKS

"My name is Feliks, and we have very little time, so I suggest we don't waste it standing here. May I come in?"

"Sorry." I open the door wider and watch, incredulous, as Feliks the *domovoi* walks into my bedroom. His paw-hands are buried deep in his coat's curved pockets and his back is very straight. There is something of a march in his short, quick steps and his boots make a scuffling sound on the floor.

I turn around, my gaze following Feliks intently. His looks and mannerisms are familiar, but I don't understand why. My brain feels tangled and I'm not sure whether to believe what my eyes are seeing. Does this mean that all the other times I thought I saw something, I really did? A smile grows on my face. Feliks is right in front of me, proof that I *can* see magic and spirits, just like Babusya! I shake my head, feeling foolish for doubting myself before.

Feliks jumps onto the window sill in a single swift and elegant movement, and for a moment, when he's mid-flight, he is a fox leaping. Then he lands with a thud and opens the window.

Wind rushes into my bedroom, along with sounds of the roof rattling and the log walls groaning. I gasp for breath as the force of the rising storm hits me once again, along with the echo of Babusya telling me it could destroy *everything*.

"You will need to bring the hat!" Feliks shouts to be heard over the wind. I fumble with my cardigan pocket until my hand closes over the green velvet. I pull it out and Feliks's eyes gleam. He leans back into my bedroom so he doesn't have to shout so loud. "You did well to find it, Olia. I just hope there's enough magic left in it."

"Magic?" I peer into the empty hat wonderingly.

"That hat was once filled with enough magic to

fold the fabric of the world.
I'm not sure how much
remains in it now, but
hopefully it will be
enough to take us
in and out of the
land, and protect
you in times of
need." Feliks offers
me his hand. "We
should embark on
our journey
immediately if we
are to save the castle
from this storm."

"But I don't understand." I stare at Feliks's hand,
desperately trying to untangle my thoughts. "What
journey? What land?"

"It will be easier to explain once you've seen it
for yourself." Feliks extends his hand closer to mine.
His palm is plump and round, like a paw pad, and his
fingernails are tiny black claws. "You can trust me,

Olia. You've known me all your life."

I frown in confusion and for a moment Feliks looks disappointed, but then he smiles and I glimpse tiny pointed teeth behind his beard.

"I was there when you were born in the kitchen," Feliks says eagerly, as if he expects me to remember that day. "You learned to walk while chasing me along the castle's corridors," he continues hopefully. "You've left me salt offerings since before you could talk. I've mended your clothes and glued your broken cups back together more times than I can remember."

I stare at Feliks and the feeling of familiarity swells. I remember marching along the corridors, copying Feliks's short, quick steps. And a game of hide and seek, where Feliks's bushy tail swishing gave him away. Sometimes my torn clothes would be mended with stiches too small to be my parents' or Babusya's, and when I hid a cup I broke under my bed, it appeared, fixed, on my pillow the next day. I remember Feliks's smile too, and his eyes gleaming as he led me to hidden doors and staircases. "I do know you," I whisper. "But how is that possible?"

"Sometimes your mind denies what your heart sees." Feliks taps his fingers against his chest and shakes his head sadly. "And magic is easy to forget when you doubt it exists."

"You were there earlier, weren't you?" I venture. "When I fell from Sun Dome you reached for me."

"I saved your life." Feliks's tail fluffs up with pride. "I bent the castle walls, so they cushioned your fall. That's what I do – protect the castle and everyone in it. And that's why I'm here now." Feliks glances at the storm outside: the dark sky, the winds howling and the domes shaking. He turns back to me, his gaze urgent. "Unless we do something, these winds will destroy the castle. I feel it breaking already. At this rate, there will be barely anything left by moonrise."

"No!" I shake my head, not wanting to even think that's a possibility. Castle Mila is my home. My family's home. My baby sister's home, bursting with hundreds of wonderful, hidden places that I want to explore with her as she grows up.

Something creaks above us, then there is a deep crunching noise, followed by a bang that makes me jump. Part of a dome crashes down, smashes onto the roof near Feliks, then is whipped away by the wind. Feliks falls to his knees, clutching his chest.

"Are you all right?" I rush to him in concern.

"Yes. It just gave me a shock. Can we leave now?" Feliks rises to his feet and holds out his hand again, but I hesitate.

Then questions spin from my mouth, as fast as the wind. "What about Babusya? Will she be safe? Shouldn't I tell her where I'm going? And what about my parents and sister? I don't even know where they are!"

"You can help your parents and sister get home safely by stopping this storm. And your grandmother is in the strongest room in the castle and knows where we're going." Feliks reaches into his coat pocket and pulls out a neatly folded piece of paper. "I was going to give you this once we got into the land, but you can read it now, if you're quick."

I take the note and unfold it. Babusya's crooked handwriting stares up at me from the letter-writing paper she always uses, which has magnolia flowers around the edge. I was named Magnolia, after Babusya's favourite flowers, though I'm nearly always called Olia for short.

Dearest Magnolia, the letter reads, *I have heard the land you are journeying to is bursting with wonders. The spirits have told me many tales of it, and I have searched for a way into it all my life. Though I never found one, it fills me with joy to know that you did. Please, if at all possible, could you bring back a vial of the waters of life? Feliks tells me it's good for rheumatism.*

I glance up at Feliks, who is now tapping one of his boots on the window sill impatiently. He gives me a quick nod and I look back down at the letter.

I'm not sure what you will need to do to stop this storm, but I know your actions have the power to change everything. Remember to look from all angles, see with your heart and believe in yourself. Feliks will endeavour to keep you safe, although you should be vigilant and careful and consider any advice he gives you. I will see you tonight. If all goes well, perhaps the harvest moon feast will go ahead after all!

Yours, with love, Babusya x

My fingertips tremble nervously, but a bubble of hope is growing too. Even though she doesn't really explain anything, Babusya believes I can travel to another land with Feliks! And that I can stop the storm and make everything better in time for the feast tonight. Although I'm scared, I'm excited too – and I can't just stay here and watch these winds destroy my home.

"She told me to give you these too." Feliks passes me a small empty green glass vial. "This is to collect the waters of life." Then he pulls a brown paper bag from his pocket. It expands as he slides it out, until it is almost half the size of Feliks himself. My eyes widen in wonder. "Shapeshifting magic," Feliks explains proudly.

I take the paper bag and peer into it nervously. It's full of still-warm, freshly baked *bulochki* – the poppy-seed buns Babusya always makes for journeys. Their sweet smell reminds me of expeditions with my family and friends to explore the woods around the lake or row out across its shining waters. *Bulochki* are the taste of adventure.

"Are you ready to leave now?" Feliks raises his furry eyebrows and his pointed ears twitch with anticipation. He pulls something else out of his pocket which expands in his hand: a carriage clock, actually shaped like a carriage, with golden wheels that tick round and a clock face studded with jewels where a driver might sit. "It's almost eleven o'clock in the morning. The harvest moon rises at about six o'clock this evening. We must save the castle before then."

I look past Feliks to the winds surging outside and I think of Mama, Papa and Rosa out there somewhere, unable to get home. "I'm ready," I say, pulling my shoulders back. "We must stop this storm to protect my family and save our home."

Feliks shrinks the clock into his pocket and takes

a step out onto the roof. The wind parts his moustache and beard and I glimpse his smile again. "Come and see the land inside Aurora Dome, Olia." Sparks of light dance in Feliks's eyes like tiny stars glittering in a dawn. "There, we can make everything right."

A thrill explodes through me as I realize I'm going to do this. And though I'm not really sure what *this* even is, I know it involves a magical spirit who I had almost stopped believing existed, a climb to a roof dome I've always wanted to go inside, and the hope of doing *something* to untangle the magic of this castle and save everything I love. And that hope is enough to blow away any doubts faster than the shingles are being torn from the roof.

So I push the velvet hat, the letter from Babusya and the green glass vial into my cardigan pocket, next to the patch showing me holding Rosa. Then, clutching the paper bag full of *bulochki* in my hands, I follow Feliks, barefoot, out onto the roof.

CHAPTER ELEVEN

THE DOOR

I've climbed onto the roof outside my bedroom window many times before. Usually, the exhilaration of being high up on the castle, so close to the sky, is enough to overwhelm my fears. But right now, my body is so filled with dread it's hard to take even small steps.

The wind is relentless. It pushes against my arms and legs, making it difficult to balance. Every time I wobble, I remember my fall earlier and my heart rises into my throat.

Feliks is ahead of me, bounding along as a fox, but when he turns to beckon me on, he shifts into his more human-like form. "Hurry," he urges, "there is no time to waste."

The wind gusts and my cardigan, which was only fastened with its loose woollen belt, whips open and flaps around me. I struggle to tie my belt again while still holding the paper bag full of *bulochki*, shivering in my pyjama trousers and wishing I'd found my socks and put on warmer, more sensible clothes.

"Pass me that." Feliks quick-steps back to me, points at the paper bag and I give it to him. It shrinks as he slides it into his coat pocket, then he waves me onwards.

I double-knot my belt and take another step along the roof. It's flat here and wide enough for me to feel fairly safe, but after a few more steps it narrows and my head spins when I glimpse the ground far below. "I'm scared to go any further." My voice wavers as I call to Feliks over the wind. "I'm worried I'm going to fall."

Feliks stops and waves a hand over the roof, as if smoothing it out. Tiny golden sparks flash around my toes, and the section of roof we're standing on expands until it's wide enough for me to stop feeling like I'm about to slip over the edge.

"How do you do that?" I ask in amazement.

"The castle and I are made of the same magic," Feliks says proudly. His orange fur is ruffling like grass in the wind, and his long beard and moustache blow around his face and over his shoulder like a scarf.

"Thank you." I smile. Despite the storm billowing around us and shaking the castle, it feels incredible to finally know, for sure, that magic and spirits exist in my home. I feel like a cloud of doubt that has shrouded me for years has lifted and revealed my hopes weren't just fanciful dreams but something with real meaning.

I walk on until Feliks stops abruptly. The roof has ended with a sheer drop. Aurora Dome is ahead of us, but across a wide, empty space. Feliks shifts into a fox and leaps effortlessly onto the dome, then turns and beckons me to join him. I shake my head, and am about to explain I can't jump that far, when the whole of the dome leans towards me until it's just a step away. I hop onto it. The roof is warm and tingling so much that it makes my toes vibrate.

"This way." Feliks waves a paw-hand over the dome roof and two sections of it draw back like curtains, revealing a small, round attic inside. Feliks jumps down and disappears into darkness and I clamber after him as quickly as I can, eager to see what is inside.

The space is so small I can only fit by sitting cross-legged. As I lower myself to the floor, the roof sections swing shut and shadows fall over us.

Feliks nudges my elbow. "There really is no time to waste."

"But I don't know what to do," I whisper. My eyes adjust to the darkness a little, and I notice Feliks is fully a fox again, leaning forwards, his ears and whiskers twitching. I'm not sure if he's impatient or anxious.

"Look with your heart." Feliks nods to the wall in front of us. "Do you see it?"

I follow his gaze, but see only the underside of the roof. Then, out of the corner of my eye, I spot something tiny nestled halfway up the wall, glowing like a firefly. "What is that?" I raise a finger towards it, but am too nervous to touch it.

"The keyhole of the lock." Feliks's tail swishes

back and forth. "You do see it. Excellent. Now, you need to pull the key out of the hat."

I slide the hat from my pocket. "But there's nothing in here, Feliks."

Feliks makes an impatient growling sound that reminds me of Babusya. "You really do need to look and think with your heart. Put your hand into the hat," he says slowly and clearly, as if talking to a toddler, "and feel the magic. Then picture the key, and it will form. It's called folding – the act of turning magic into objects. The hat can also help you unfold objects back into the magic that made them. Everything is made of magic, Olia, and the hat helps you see and use it."

My brow furrows, but I do as Feliks says. I put my hand inside the hat and my fingers tingle. I close my eyes and imagine a key, glowing like the keyhole. Something grows in my palm. "I can feel it!" I exclaim. The sensation is both familiar and unfamiliar, in the same way that Feliks was when I first saw him, and I wonder if I've used magic before, but lost that memory too.

I pull my hand out of the hat and stare at the key I'm holding. It's bigger than my palm, glows gold, and is so warm it feels like it's been sitting on the stove in the kitchen. I beam at Feliks. "I have the key! I folded it from magic!"

"Well done, Olia." Feliks's smile widens and I swell with pride. "Now, put it in the keyhole."

I lift up the key, but for a moment it flickers, like a guttering candle, disappearing and reappearing in my hand. "Oh no! Did I do something wrong?" I ask.

Feliks shakes his head. "No. I thought this might happen. It's because there's so little magic left in the hat, the key isn't perfect. It will flicker from time to time, and it might fade too. We need to move swiftly, because if the key fades too much it won't work, and we'll need it to return home."

"How long do we have?" I ask, my nerves quivering.

"I'm not sure. But we'll be able to see if the key fades, so we'll know if we have to rush home."

Doubts close around me at the thought of becoming trapped in some strange place, away from my family, friends and home. "What's on the other side?" My voice trembles. I'm itching to know, but there's a cold trickle of fear curling down my spine too.

Feliks's ears twitch towards the keyhole. "Open it and see."

Could there really be another place somehow locked inside this dome? A place filled with magic? I lift the key towards the keyhole and my heart pounds as they both glow brighter...but a squeeze of uncertainty makes me stop still. "I'm nervous," I whisper.

"Olia, this is our only chance to save Castle Mila." Feliks rises to his feet in his more human-like form. His tail fluffs up behind him, huge and orange. "Unlock this and everything will become clear. I've watched you for years and I know how brave you are – you can do this."

My chest swells as I feel more sure of myself. I slide the key into the keyhole, and turn it.

A loud, clear *click* resonates through the attic and into my body. I feel it rippling through my flesh and echoing in my bones. Then a blinding light rushes over me and I close my eyes and draw back, still clutching the key in my hand.

"It's all right, Olia. We're safe." Feliks nudges me gently and I peep my eyes open. As they adjust to the bright light, I see a section of the dome has opened outwards, forming a door. Beyond it, I should see the roof of Castle Mila. But I don't. My jaw drops and I gasp at the sight of a whole other land.

CHAPTER TWELVE

THE LAND OF FORBIDDEN MAGIC

The land through the doorway is beautiful and shining, iridescent with colour. My eyes widen as I lean forwards and try to take it all in. The sky is pale blue and vast, but it curves, like one of the castle's domes. And the sun is a thin crescent, tiny and distant. Looking at it makes my mind twist. This place is nothing like my world.

Beneath the sky are rolling green and gold fields, full of swaying grasses and delicate, long-stalked flowers that I've never seen before. Scattered oak trees rise from the ground, huge and leafy, and an enormous ocean glistens to my left. There is no muddy, rocky or sandy shore. Gentle waves wash straight onto the fields with a rhythmic swishing, making the plants dance dreamlike in the ebb and flow. A wide, meandering river burbles to my right. Warm air, carrying the crisp scents of brackish water and ocean creatures, flows over me, and distant splashing sounds tickle my ears.

"This is incredible," I whisper, leaning even further through the doorway, half expecting the land to vanish and Castle Mila's roof to reappear. "What is this place?"

"This is The Land of Forbidden Magic." Feliks steps through the doorway and takes a long, deep breath. His fur fluffs up and a smile makes his moustache curl into a wave. "I've known about this place since it was created, but I've never been inside. For five hundred years I've searched for a way in, but without the key it's been hopeless. I couldn't even get near the hat because it was shielded by magic. But then you found a way." Feliks glances at me. "Your belief that you were going to get into Sun Dome and find something magical changed everything, Olia. Belief is one of the few things more powerful than magic." His eyes gleam as he offers me a furry hand. "Would you like to step inside?"

A huge smile grows on my face. I feel proud that I found a way here, and giddy with wonder. I grasp Feliks's hand gently between my fingers and excitement zips along my arm. Then I step through the doorway.

The air stretches and pops, like it did earlier in Sun Dome, and I get the same whiff of sun-baked stones and earth...then I'm standing in the dazzling land. Everything has a shining silver hue and with a twist of confusion, I realize the grass, the trees, even the water in the ocean and river, are covered with fine silver threads that are tangled together like a net. I feel the threads tingling against my bare feet and the sensation makes goosebumps rise on my skin.

This place is baffling, but *real*. A whole land, extending out from Aurora Dome. I've looked for magic all my life, and now I'm completely surrounded by it. I feel like whooping with joy.

There is a swoosh behind me and with a jolt of panic I realize the door has shut, blocking my view of home. I grip the key and the hat tight in my hands and remind myself why I'm here.

"So what do we do in this land?" I ask. "How do we stop the storm?"

"We talk to the cat. She will know what to do." Feliks points to a large green oak not far away on the ocean shore. I shield my eyes and peer at the tree. A golden chain is wound around its trunk and at the end of the chain, curled up on the ground, is a small, black cat, asleep.

"How will a cat know what to do?" I ask, following Feliks as he walks towards her. The air is warm and calm and I think of my home being torn apart by fierce cold winds and I wonder how this all fits together, and how a sleeping cat in a different world can help.

"Five hundred years ago, there was a witch called Naina. I knew her by reputation, and saw her from time to time when she visited the castle. She helped create this land, so she understands its magic better than anyone. Naina was chained to that tree and, while bound there, she transformed into that cat. I'm sure she'll be able to help us." Feliks looks back at me and smiles, although I notice he's fiddling with his coat buttons nervously.

Still, Feliks feels so much like home it's comforting to have him with me and I trust that he'll help me do what's best to keep everyone I love safe. I miss Rosa, my parents and Babusya already, and the worry about them feels like one of the wriggly caterpillars that sometimes eat into the apples in the grove. I wish my family and friends were here, so I knew they were safe, and so we could share this adventure.

The land that stretches ahead makes my mind twist with all its impossibilities. The domed sky above refracts the light in odd ways, making strange-shaped rainbows flash at the edges of my vision.

For a moment, I think I see more domes beyond the one above, but then I'm distracted by the river to my right. Water flows in different directions, depending on where I look at it. And the ocean to my left moves unnaturally, changing shape as I turn my head, so it's always in view. A golden fishtail, as big as a whale's, rises from the waves and glistens in the light. It's speckled with what look like huge jewels: emeralds, rubies and sapphires. I stare at the tail in awe as it splashes back into the ocean. "What was that?"

"Could be a wishing pike." Feliks barely glances up. "Or maybe the wizard Volga in his fish form. We'll see many magical spirits in this land and we simply don't have time to stop and discuss them all if we're going to save the castle."

"But how and why is there a whole land filled with spirits here? I now know there is magic in and around Castle Mila, but nothing like this!" I quicken my pace to keep up with Feliks and my footsteps disturb what I think are pale green butterflies resting in the long grass. But as they flutter into the air spraying water droplets, I realize they're tiny winged fish spirits. "This place is incredible!" I gaze after the fish spirits. Everything feels so surreal, and yet real too.

"It is incredible," Feliks agrees, but there's a frown creasing his face. "Your ancestor, the Princess Ludmila, created this place five hundred years ago with the hat she stole from the wizard Chernomor."

"This hat?" I lift the floppy green velvet and stare at it, wondering how it could be used to create a whole land.

"Yes. The hat was much more powerful back then,

capable of folding vast areas in or out of the world, to make them seen or unseen. Ludmila folded everything in here out of the real world, and hid it beyond Aurora Dome."

"But why?" I walk around a marshy puddle, staring at a rabbit-sized, newtlike spirit, which is basking in the water. It has six legs, spotty blue skin and two bright green horns.

Feliks shifts into a fox to leap over the puddle. "There was a rivalry between your royal ancestors and the wizard Chernomor that was in danger of escalating into a war. Ludmila feared the wizard would use magic against her, so she forbade its use and banished Chernomor and hundreds of magical spirits here. It became known as The Land of Forbidden Magic."

"But she didn't send you here?" I look at Feliks in confusion.

"I helped care for Castle Mila, so I was useful to her. But she banished so many others that she nearly used up all the magic in the hat. Eventually, she sealed the land shut. It carried on existing beyond Aurora Dome, but she hid the hat so that no one could get in or out." Feliks growls the last words and his bushy eyebrows fall, making his eyes darken like Lake Mila beneath the storm.

I look around again. I didn't think this place could feel any more wondrous, but knowing that we really are the first to come here in five hundred years sends a thrill through me, and I wish once more that I could share this with my family and friends.

We reach the oak tree. The cat is still asleep, curled up at its base. Feliks clears his throat loudly, but the cat doesn't stir. "Excuse me, Naina," Feliks says finally. "We need your help with a matter of great urgency."

My thoughts swing down with a bump as I remember how urgent our mission is. Time is ticking away. At least a quarter of an hour has already passed since we left the castle at eleven o'clock – maybe longer. We only have until the harvest moon rises at six o'clock to save our home and I still have no idea how to do that. I look down at the cat. Hope that she will help us lifts and swirls like dandelion seeds inside me, and I hold my breath as I wait to see how she will respond.

CHAPTER THIRTEEN

KOSHKA

The cat opens her eyes a slit. They're a fiery amber colour and her pupils are needle-thin. "I'm not Naina any more," she snarls angrily, but it's so wonderful to hear another animal talk that I smile. "Naina the witch was chained to this tree five hundred years ago. She and her magic faded away soon afterwards. All that's left now is me, Koshka the cat. And in case you hadn't noticed, I'm still bound to this tree, so I'm in no position to help you, urgently or otherwise."

"Apologies, Koshka." Feliks bows slightly and his ears dip forwards. "But we can free you, if you'll help us."

Koshka's eyes remain narrow as she stares at us, and her tail flicks back and forth in irritation. "You're

Castle Mila's *domovoi*, aren't you?"
She glares at Feliks. "And you're
with a human child." Koshka spits out
the word *human* as if it tastes bad. "So
I cannot trust either of you."

"After being chained up by Ludmila,
I understand you feeling like that."
Feliks looks at the heavy gold metal
around Koshka's neck and his eyes well
with sadness. "But Olia is very different
from her ancestor."

"Why was Ludmila so cruel to you?"
I crouch down, so that I'm not towering
over Koshka. "To chain you up for all
those years…" I feel hot with shame
that one of my ancestors could be
so heartless.

"Humans are always
most cruel when
they're scared."

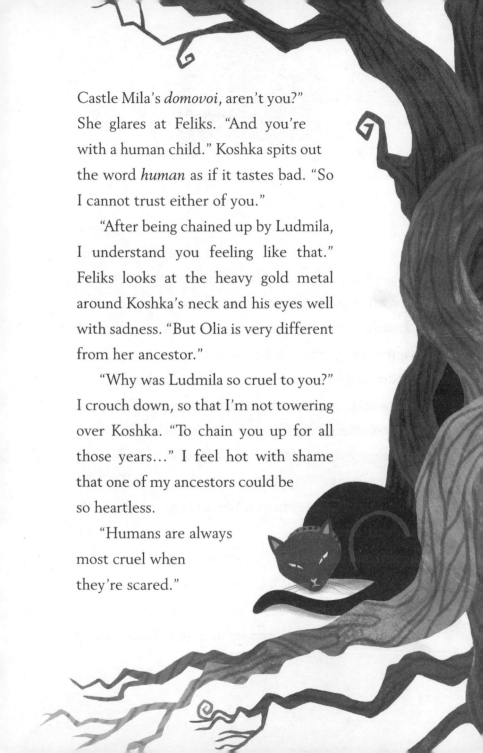

Koshka stretches her long, slender body all the way to the tips of her claws, then rises to her paws. She paces back and forth, her chain glinting in the light. "Ludmila feared me because I understand the magic of this land. I helped her create this place, but she worried that I might undo it all, because while I wanted a safe space for magical spirits, she only wanted a prison. So she chained me up and sealed the land shut. She betrayed me and all the spirits she either tricked or forced into here. This is what humans do – lie and deceive. They're not to be trusted."

"My family and friends are honest and kind," I say, hoping that somehow I'll be able to convince Koshka to help us. "So not all humans are like that."

"In my experience they are." Koshka twitches her whiskers disdainfully. "That's why I'm happy to be a cat now. I don't want to look like a human or live with them ever again."

I turn to Feliks, an idea sparking in my mind. "Can we free Koshka, then let her decide if she wants to help us or not?"

"But what if she chooses not to?" Feliks looks

horrified at the thought. "We need her. Only Koshka understands this land."

"Then I guess we'd have to figure it out for ourselves." I bite my lip nervously and glance back at Koshka. "I hope she helps us. But we can't blackmail her into it, and we can't leave her chained to this tree." I look closely at the chain around her neck. There are no fastenings on it. "How do we remove this thing?"

"Use the hat." Koshka looks at the hat in my hands and lifts her chin in a gesture that makes me feel like she's challenging me to do it. "Unfold the chain. Turn it back into the magic that made it."

The hat warms my fingers. Somehow, in my heart, I know exactly what to do, and as long as I don't think too hard it makes sense. I stow the key safely in my pocket and focus on the hat. I hold it open with one hand and place my other hand on the chain around the tree.

"Are you sure you want to free Koshka without her agreeing to help us?" Feliks's fur bristles anxiously.

"Absolutely," I say. "Ludmila should never have done this and, as her descendant, it feels like my responsibility to undo it. I'd also like to show Koshka that not all humans are bad."

Feliks sighs but nods in agreement. I close my eyes and feel the magic trembling in the chain. I imagine it flowing along my fingers, up my arm, through my chest, down my other arm and out of my fingers into the hat. I open my eyes. The chain has faded so much it looks like a ghostly imprint, and I almost squeal with excitement. *I'm using magic!* I close my eyes again and imagine the chain disappearing completely. My fingers throb with warmth and when I look this time, the chain is gone and the hat's lining is glowing brighter. A huge, proud smile spreads across my face as I tuck the hat away into my pocket.

"Well done, Olia." Feliks nudges my elbow. "You have a talent for magic."

Koshka stares at me. She moves her head all around, then stretches her neck and yawns. There is a gleam of gratitude in her eyes, but she doesn't say anything.

"Please, Koshka," Feliks says softly. "We really do need your help."

"What is it you want?" Koshka licks her lips as her

gaze shifts into the shimmering distance beyond the river.

"My home, Castle Mila, is being destroyed by a storm." My words rush out as I remember the fierce winds and the smashed dome. I wonder what state the castle is in now and what my family are doing, and my chest tightens because I have no way of finding out.

"A great deal more than your castle is being destroyed." Koshka's amber eyes flare.

"What do you mean?" My mind flits back to Babusya telling me the storm could destroy even more than she could explain.

"For five hundred years the magic here has been building and tangling, forcing open cracks in the land. Small streams of magic have seeped out into your world before. You might have seen them as glowing winds. But over the last few days I've felt much bigger rifts opening, and magic flooding out. That will be causing the storm threatening your castle. But I'm more concerned about this land and the spirits who live here."

I glance around at the calm sky, the gently swishing grass alive with tiny fluttering fish spirits, the rolling waves of the ocean and the soft burble of the river. "But it all looks so peaceful," I whisper.

"Less than an hour ago, the ground shook so much that I thought the oak was going to fall on top of me." I follow Koshka's gaze to the tree's roots and a cold wave of fear splashes over me as I notice some of them are lifted from the ground, above freshly rumpled earth. "Soon this whole land will be completely torn apart and everything and everyone in it will be lost. The magic will blast into your world and raze your castle too."

"Oh no." I feel dizzy, overwhelmed by the enormity of what is at stake. Not only Castle Mila, but this whole beautiful land filled with hundreds of spirits is in danger too.

Feliks rests a hand gently on my arm. "We can change this, Olia. That's why we're here, remember."

I slip my hand into my pocket to get strength from the fabric patch I made. I think of Rosa, and how I want to be the kind of big sister who would protect her family and anyone in need. The patch makes me think of the blanket too, and how it shows that everything is linked: my family and our castle, stretching back into the past, onward into the future, and out into the village and fields around Mila. And now I know that it stretches into this incredible, magical land too. What I do here will affect the future of more than my world and somehow, like the stitches between patches, I have to hold it all together.

"What can we do?" I rise to my feet. "To save *everything*."

"You must cut off the beard of the wizard Chernomor." Koshka slinks away from the tree. "Follow me and I will lead you to him. You can save this land and your castle, then leave me in peace."

"Cut off what?" I look from Koshka to Feliks, my thoughts more tangled than ever.

"I'll explain on the way," Koshka calls back impatiently.

"Shall we?" Feliks raises his furry eyebrows and his whiskers twitch questioningly.

A flock of winged fish spirits flutter past and dive into the ocean. The six-legged newtlike spirit dashes after them, snapping at the bubbles they leave in their wake. And the huge jewelled fishtail crests and splashes in the distance, making a star-shaped rainbow in the domed sky. It's all so beautiful, and astonishing, and absurd.

I take a deep breath to fill myself with courage, then step forwards. "Whatever it takes to protect my family and save our home and this land, we must try."

Chapter Fourteen

Chernomor's Beard

Feliks and I catch up with Koshka on a field that gently slopes towards the river. She's creeping through the long grass, shaking her fur every time it gets damp.

"How will cutting off Chernomor's beard stop this land from being torn apart?" I ask, feeling dazed by the strangeness of my own question.

"Nearly all of Chernomor's magic is in his beard." Koshka growls at a tiny tentacled spirit that rains water droplets as it floats past. "Before he was banished here five hundred years ago, Chernomor's beard was cut off to remove his power. But since then it has been growing back and, with it, all his evil magic."

"Evil magic?" I frown. I've always thought of magic as some kind of force or energy, neither good nor evil.

Koshka stops and pushes some grass aside with her paws, revealing fine silver threads running beneath. "Do you see these?" She scratches at the threads with her claws. "They're tendrils of Chernomor's magic and they've been spreading over this land. Each year they get worse, and now they cover everything."

I kneel down and touch the glowing silver tangle. It thrums with warm vibrations. "But why is this evil?" I ask.

Koshka scratches harder until a dense mass of the threads shifts aside revealing a small, narrow crack in the ground beneath. "See that?" Koshka's eyes flame with anger. "Chernomor's magic has been growing so out of control that now it's forcing this land apart and allowing magic to escape into your world. That's why you must cut off his beard."

The silver tendrils shift and wriggle back into the crack. I stare at them, mesmerized by their movement but horrified at what they're doing. Then I stand and scan the view. The silver glow of Chernomor's magic is everywhere. "Does Chernomor realize his magic is endangering this land and my home?" I ask.

Koshka shrugs. "He's an evil wizard with a long history of doing nefarious things."

My eyebrows draw together as I think that Koshka didn't exactly answer my question.

Feliks nudges the silver tangle on the ground with his boot. "So if we cut off Chernomor's beard, these threads will disappear, and this land and our home will be safe again?"

"Yes. The land will stop cracking apart and magical winds will stop storming into your world." Koshka lifts her chin, but her confidence doesn't seem to reach her eyes and her gaze slides away from us.

"Won't his beard just grow back again?" I ask. Koshka's plan doesn't feel very permanent.

"Eventually." Koshka flicks her tail and carries on walking towards the river.

I glance at Feliks, hoping he can somehow reassure me that this is the right thing to do. But he's hopping on one leg as he tries to shake off the threads that have now tangled over his boot. He barks in frustration, shifts into a fox, then leaps away from the tangle and bounds after Koshka.

A rumble like thunder sounds in the distance and the ground shakes. Scores of spirits dash out of the grass and rush towards the water in panic. My heart races. *This land really is breaking apart.* I feel an urge to run home to the safety of Castle Mila, but with a sharp pang I remember the castle isn't safe any more. It's being torn apart too. And if I don't do something fast both my home and this land will be destroyed, and I'll lose my chance to return to my family and friends altogether.

The ground stops trembling and I sprint to catch up with Feliks and Koshka. "Where is Chernomor?" I ask, eager to get to him as quickly as possible.

"In his fortress," Koshka replies. I shudder as I remember the faded painting in Sun Dome, of chilling silver eyes staring out from a red fortress.

"How long will it take to get there?"

"It depends on the journey." Koshka leaps over a muddy patch. "This land is made of different domes. We're in Water Dome now, where river and ocean spirits live. Ludmila chained me up here because she knew I hate the wet." Koshka hisses at a small volelike spirit with silver scales and it dashes away. "You need to get some things from Fire Dome, then we can go to Earth Dome, where Chernomor's fortress is."

"What things?" I ask, looking up at the domed sky. Again I see a hint of more domes beyond it, although they're difficult to make out, as they shift and shimmer in the light.

"Armour." Koshka bounds a little as she picks up her pace. "And the Giant's Sword."

"Armour and a sword?" My eyes widen in panic. "But I'm not a warrior! I can't use a sword!" I look down at Feliks. "Is this how you *endeavour to keep me safe?*" I use Babusya's words on purpose.

Feliks glances at my clothes. "Armour is better than pyjamas for protecting people."

"The Giant's Sword is the only blade that can cut through Chernomor's beard," Koshka explains. "And only *you* can use it."

"Me?" My voice cracks. I suddenly feel like I'm far out on Lake Mila and my limbs are cramping so tight I can't swim. "Why me?"

"Only someone with royal blood can wield the Giant's Sword." Koshka stops walking and stares at me intently, her eyes so bright they look aflame. "So if we're going to do this, we need you."

I shift uncomfortably. I don't understand how being descended from some long-ago monarchs should make me more able to use a sword than anyone else. "What's Chernomor like?" I ask nervously. "Would I have to fight him to cut off his beard? I've never fought anyone and I don't want to, especially not with a sword." My stomach twists and writhes at the thought of it.

"Chernomor is old and tired. He spends most of his time asleep. There's a chance you could cut off his beard without even waking him." Koshka's gaze is steady but my stomach still squirms.

"It doesn't seem right to attack someone when they're asleep. And what if he does wake?" I look down at my knitted cardigan, pyjamas and bare feet, and shake my head in despair. "There must be another way. I'm not the right person for this. I can't face an evil wizard and cut off his beard with a sword."

"You are the *only* person who can," Koshka says sternly.

A wave of homesickness crashes over me and I fight back an urge to build a blanket fort to hide in, like I used to do with Mama when I was little and scared of noises in the dark. I want to go home to where I am just Olia – a daughter, sister and friend – not someone with royal blood fated to wield a giant's sword. Tears well in my eyes and I struggle to blink them away.

Feliks reaches up and touches my hand with his soft, furry fingers. "I promised your Babusya I would help you stop the storm and get you home safe, Olia."

"Thanks, Feliks." I squeeze his hand back. If he made a promise to Babusya, I know in my heart he'll do everything he can to keep it. I remember too how Babusya said my actions have the power to change everything. Maybe I didn't choose this role, but now isn't the time for doubts.

Cutting off a wizard's beard in a tangled land is a strange way to stop a storm, and the thought of armour and a sword makes me feel as wobbly as the castle's block flooring. But with Feliks by my side, I feel able to try.

We draw close to the river and the grass thins, revealing more of the silver threads beneath. They tingle with warmth, but cold mud oozes up between my toes and I shiver, wishing I'd brought my boots with me.

A splashing draws my gaze. Two spirits have risen in the middle of the river. One looks like a young girl, although she appears to be made of water, and the other looks like some kind of frog-man. He has green skin, webbed hands and a wide face mottled with algae. "Who are they?" I ask.

"The female water spirit is a *rusalka*, and the male spirit a *vodyanoy*." Koshka grimaces. "I've never trusted water spirits. Ludmila banished them here because she believed they lured people into deep and dangerous waters."

"Did they?" I ask nervously.

"Probably not on purpose. Many humans are just foolish enough to follow them."

The green-skinned *vodyanoy* stands tall and proud, looking down on the *rusalka* and talking to her in a loud, croaky voice. Droplets of muddy water spray from his wide, toothless mouth with every word. The *rusalka*, who barely comes up to his shoulder, is scrunching her faint, reedy eyebrows in a frown and chattering fast in a torrent of bubbling sounds. I don't understand what they're saying, but it's clear that the *rusalka* and the *vodyanoy* are arguing.

All of a sudden, the *vodyanoy* puffs up and his eyes burn red as he glares at the *rusalka*. He plunges his webbed hands deep into the water, then sweeps a tidal wave of wet mud straight at her. It hits the *rusalka* full-force and she stumbles backwards. As the liquid mud runs off her, small clods of dirt and flecks of brown-green algae are left swirling inside her watery body.

The *rusalka* looks down at herself, clenches her watery fists, then flings herself at the *vodyanoy*. They blur together in a mass of rushing water, bubbles, mud and green skin. The *vodyanoy* shrieks, a shrill and piercing sound that hurts my ears, as he's dragged beneath the surface by what looks like hundreds of watery arms.

I panic, thinking the *vodyanoy* is going to drown, and I race into the river, wanting to save him. For a moment I wonder if I'm being foolish, like Koshka said, but all my life my parents and Babusya have taught me to help people in need, so I can't stand by and watch him struggle for his life. Cold water splashes everywhere and soaks through my pyjamas, and I slip and skid on the slimy mud of the riverbed.

"Leave them, Olia!" Koshka shouts after me. "They're always fighting. It's not worth getting involved."

Feliks rushes after me, but I move ahead of him and I'm soon waist-deep in the water, right next to the churning currents of the *rusalka* and the *vodyanoy*'s fight. I've had to break up so many quarrels between Dinara and Luka over the years, I act without thinking. I grab one of the *vodyanoy*'s flailing webbed hands and pull with all my might, until his red eyes and algae-speckled cheeks rise from the water.

One of his eyes meets mine and glows a brighter red. His wide mouth grins and his slimy webbed fingers tighten around mine. Tiny claws creep out from the tips of his fingers and scratch my skin…and then, with a thump of horror, I feel myself being pulled down into the river.

CHAPTER FIFTEEN

CASCADIA

I thrash around, trying to free myself from the *vodyanoy*'s grip and keep my head above the water. "Stop! What are you doing?" I splutter. "I'm trying to save you!" But the *vodyanoy* pulls harder and I slip deeper into the water. The *vodyanoy*'s other hand reaches for me, but I bat it away as I struggle, wishing I'd never rushed into the river. I've made a terrible mistake.

The watery arms of the *rusalka* curve over us and splash down, slapping so hard against my skin that it stings. Water rushes between my hand and the *vodyanoy*'s, then it swells into the shape of the *rusalka*'s hand and pushes, until finally the *vodyanoy* releases me and sinks beneath the surface. The *rusalka* disappears with a splash. I stand still, my heartbeat racing as I scan the ripples for signs of the water spirits' return.

"Olia!" Feliks shouts. He's standing in the shallows, his face crumpled with concern. "Are you all right? I can't swim. Can you please come back here?"

Koshka mewls in agreement. "Get out of the water, Olia. Water spirits aren't to be trusted."

I wade back towards them. The skin on my hand burns and I frown at the tiny claw marks. "I was only trying to help the *vodyanoy*," I grumble, trying to rub the pain away.

"Don't rub the wounds, you'll make them worse." The *rusalka* rises in front of me and splashes my hands apart. I stare at her in shock as she drapes a spray of long, feathery leaves over the marks on my skin. "Hold those there for a few minutes. They'll clean and soothe your cuts."

Straight away, the burning sensation lessens. "Thank you." I look into the *rusalka*'s watery face. Flecks of mud and tiny fish swim inside her. Her eyes are huge, dark whirlpools and long, reedy hair flows from her head, down her cheeks and over her watery body.

"Why would you want to help a *vodyanoy*?" the *rusalka* asks. Her voice is like a bubbling, trickling brook, but I realize she's speaking my language now, instead of whatever language she was using with the *vodyanoy*.

"It looked like you were trying to drown him." I step out of the water to where Feliks and Koshka are waiting for me. My clothes are soaked, and now the fight is over and I've calmed down, I'm shivering with cold.

"That was noble and brave of you." The *rusalka* smiles, revealing a row of rounded teeth like pearls, and I flush with pride. "But you can't drown a water spirit." She laughs and a tiny white cloud rises from her mouth. "We were only arguing over space. He shouldn't have been in my territory."

My flush of pride is replaced by a feeling of foolishness. "I didn't know that," I mumble, staring down at my wet clothes. They're going to take ages to dry. "And I didn't think he'd try to pull me under."

"He can't help himself." The *rusalka* has followed me and is lying in the shallows now, her head and shoulders above the surface. "*Vodyanoy* love to show off their underwater realms, especially to humans, as you're all so easily impressed. And he hasn't seen a human in five hundred years. None of us have. Are you from Castle Mila?"

I nod, take the leaves off my hand and check all the things in my pockets are still safe.

"We must move on," Koshka urges and my stomach knots as I think of time racing away. "Fire Dome is on the other side of the river, and we need to find a safe place to cross."

"Thank you for helping my friend." Feliks nods politely to the *rusalka*.

"Yes, thank you," I echo, trying to wring some of the water out of the bottom of my cardigan. "But Koshka is right, we are in a hurry."

"Let me help you get dry before you leave." The *rusalka* lifts a hand and I feel my clothes tingling with warmth. Tiny droplets of water lift from the fabric, flow towards the *rusalka* and disappear into her hand. In a few moments I'm as dry as if I never went into the river.

"That's amazing," I exclaim, thinking how brilliant it would be if me, Dinara and Luka could do that after swimming in the lake.

"Cascadia." The *rusalka* rises from the river and steps onto the bank. She's shorter than me, about as tall as my shoulder. "My name is Cascadia." She holds

out her watery hand and I touch it tentatively with my own, worried that my hand might pass through hers. But she feels solid, even though she looks like liquid.

"My name is Olia, short for Magnolia, after my grandmother's favourite flowers," I say, thinking how happy it would make Babusya to see me talking to a water spirit.

"May I ask you something, Olia?" Cascadia draws her hand away from mine, leaving a thin layer of water and a few slimy weeds behind. "Have you seen a *rusalka* like me in Lake Mila?"

I think back to all the times I sat on the kitchen window sill when I was younger, staring down at the lake, hoping to glimpse the water spirit Babusya told me she heard singing. If I ever did see anything, I've either forgotten, or convinced myself it was my imagination. "I'm not sure, I'm sorry."

Cascadia's eyes swirl with sadness and I'm overcome by an urge to make her smile again. "My grandmother told me she heard a water spirit singing though, several times."

Cascadia's eyes light up and she smiles so wide I see her teeth again, and a tiny shrimp nestled between them. "That must be my mother! We were separated when Ludmila banished me here."

"I'm so sorry." I shake my head in disbelief at Ludmila's cruelty, ashamed once again that I'm related to her.

"Oh, but my mother is trying to sing me home! Is there a way? How did you get here? Can I go back with you? I haven't seen my mother in five hundred years, and I'm so fed up with this place, and of fighting with the *vodyanoy*. To go home to Lake Mila and my mother is all I dream of."

"Of course you can come back with us," I say, eager to reunite Cascadia with her mother and return to my own family too.

"No, she can't." Koshka scowls.

"If you're thinking I'll dry out on the journey, I won't." Cascadia waves her arms around, sending tiny droplets of water raining down, which makes Koshka scowl even more. "I'm fine for hours out of water."

"We're going to Fire Dome first, to get armour and

a sword, then we're going to Chernomor's fortress." My heart pounds as I remember everything I need to do to stop the storm.

"Olia is going to cut off Chernomor's beard to stop his magic breaking this land apart." Feliks's tail swishes with pride as he steps towards Cascadia and holds out his hand. "I'm Feliks, and perhaps you know Koshka?"

"You are noble and brave!" Cascadia glances at me before shaking Feliks's hand. "All the water spirits have noticed the cracks getting bigger and the earthquakes getting stronger." Cascadia shudders, sending ripples through her watery body, then she turns to Koshka and darkens like Lake Mila before a storm. "I've seen you chained to the oak. The *vodyanoy* says you helped Ludmila create this land that imprisons us, so you are a betrayer of your own magical kin and not to be trusted."

Koshka shakes her fur nonchalantly. "Well, I don't trust anything made of water."

"That's fine. I've always thought trust should be earned." Cascadia laughs out another cloud, and the sheer beauty of it makes me feel warm with happiness. I can understand why people might follow *rusalki* into the water.

"I'll come with you," Cascadia says decisively. "I'll be able to help, and there's nothing for me to do here besides argue with the *vodyanoy* anyway. Then, after you've cut off Chernomor's beard, you can help me get home to my mother." Cascadia splashes on her toes excitedly. Her enthusiasm reminds me of Dinara and I wish she and Luka were here to see this land, and to help me. "I know where you can cross the river safely." Cascadia skips off along the riverbank, and beckons us to follow.

I glance down at Feliks. "Could you tell me the time, please?" I ask, worried how much longer we have to stop the storm before it destroys my home.

Feliks expands another clock from his pocket. This one is shaped like a mermaid, with a ticking tail. She's holding a pearl with a clock face on it, and both its hands are pointing straight up. "Midday." Feliks shrinks the clock and tucks it away. "An hour gone already." His eyebrows draw together. "We've got a plan to stop the storm and are about to enter the next dome. But there is still much to do and only six hours left before…" Feliks's voice trails away but unsaid words about the countdown to the castle's destruction seem to shout in my ears.

I jog after Cascadia, with Feliks by my side. Koshka frowns in disapproval, like one of the portraits of my royal ancestors, but she follows too and soon we reach a bend in the river where the muddy bank is scarred with strange tracks.

"The water here is only ankle deep." Cascadia splashes into the river, sinks, then rises up again in a different spot.

"Are you sure?" Koshka peers at the water suspiciously.

"I'm happy to carry you across," I offer, feeling brave because I've been in the river once already, and also because Cascadia helped me I feel like we can trust her. But Koshka backs away from me. "Or I'll walk ahead, so you can see how deep it is," I suggest, stepping into the water. Feliks remains by my side, his black boots gleaming in the wet. The water is as shallow as Cascadia said it would be, and we soon reach the opposite bank.

As I step out of the water the air stretches and pops. I smell hot stones, then everything in my vision warps for a moment. "We just crossed through a magical boundary, didn't we?" The domed sky looks different, as if it has changed shape, and the distant crescent of sun is now facing the other way. The ground is covered in charred grass that prickles against my bare feet. "This must be Fire Dome," I say, trying to sound calm and confident although my nerves are thrumming as I wonder what kind of spirits might live here.

Koshka steps onto the bank next to me and shakes the water from her paws with disgust. Then she looks up and a small smile twitches at the corners of her mouth. "It's good to finally leave Water Dome. I suppose I should thank you, Olia, for freeing me from that tree." Koshka says each word as if it scratches her throat.

Feliks stares at Koshka in shock, as Cascadia splashes out of the water and swings her arms to create a small but perfectly formed heart-shaped rainbow.

"I heard a gracious word from the cat is as rare as a rainbow in Fire Dome."

"You're welcome, Koshka." I smile, trying to still my quivering worries as I scan the scorched landscape around us. "Now, where is the armour and sword that I need?"

CHAPTER SIXTEEN

FIRE DOME

"You'll find armour at the base of those cliffs." Koshka nods to a dark row of rocks on the other side of the field. "And the sword isn't far away."

"What burned all this?" I ask, fear creeping into me as I walk across the crispy, ash-filled grass.

"All kinds of fire spirits and fire-breathing spirits live here." Cascadia splashes her hands together, sending water droplets into the air. "But you don't need to worry, because you have a watery friend to keep you safe."

I look at Cascadia, surprised and thankful that she used the word friend. I miss my lifelong friends from home, especially Dinara and Luka. Exploring is always better with them than alone. But it's nice having new friends to help me here. Feliks is like a part of home; he makes me feel protected and surer of myself. Koshka understands the land, and without her we wouldn't have a plan to stop the storm. And Cascadia makes me feel like I could be noble and brave – plus she wants to be reunited with her family, just like me. Despite the dangers ahead a glow of gratitude warms me and I feel a smile lifting my face.

The glowing threads are everywhere, tangling into hundreds of cracks in the ground. Some are just a few inches wide, but others are so big I have to stretch my legs to stride over them, and Feliks has to shift into a fox to leap from one side to the other. The sight of the land, so broken apart, sends a rush of determination through me, to stop Chernomor before this gets any worse.

"Look, firebirds!" Cascadia cheers excitedly and I look up to see a flock of bright orange birds whoosh out of a cave in the cliffs ahead. Each one is as big as a peacock and just as beautiful, with long trailing feathers that shine and waver like flames. As they flap over the field I notice chunks of metal glinting amongst the blackened grass, reflecting the birds' light.

"Is that armour?" I ask, picking up my pace, even though the seared ground makes my bare feet hurt. I start to spot pieces of armour everywhere. The grass is littered with items in all shapes and sizes. There are helmets bigger than my whole body and others that could fit into the palm of my hand. Dented iron breastplates lie amongst torn leather ones, and there are swords, spears, and bows and arrows abandoned everywhere.

"What happened here?" I ask, the blood draining from my face. It looks as if we're in the middle of some kind of battlefield.

"Many of the spirits in this land fought against their banishment, so they arrived dressed for combat." Koshka hisses at a small hedgehog-like spirit hiding in a bronze gauntlet. Its spikes burst into flames and it rolls away like a fireball across the charred grass. "But once the land was sealed shut, most spirits abandoned their armour and weapons here." Koshka's tail waves slowly as she looks around. "There must be something here to fit you, Olia."

Feliks glances down at my feet, which are red and scratched and streaked with ash and soot. "We should look for boots in your size too."

"That would be good." My feet are cold and sore and I'm longing for the woollen socks Babusya knitted me. But my muscles tense as my gaze roams over the armour. It all looks so heavy and cumbersome, made for warriors – not me.

"Over here!" Cascadia rushes to a sprawling pile of iridescent fabric. "What about this?" She holds up a shimmering grey-gold breastplate that looks the right size. "It's *rusalka* armour, light but strong, and imbued with protective magic. Made from the scales of a wishing pike."

"It's perfect." I try to sound sure, despite the uneasy feeling the armour is giving me.

"It smells of water spirits." Koshka sniffs at the *rusalka* armour and backs away from it with a look of disgust on her face. "But it will help keep you safe from Chernomor and other dangers. There are many kinds of spirits in this land, and not all of them are friendly."

"Like the Immortal Cloak." Cascadia's waters churn and darken.

"What's that?" I ask nervously.

"Olia doesn't need to know about the cloak," Koshka snarls at Cascadia.

"It's a living cloak that belonged to a spirit of life." Cascadia flicks water at Koshka and continues. "Ludmila tried to banish them both, but they got separated and only the cloak is here. It's lonely without the spirit, and lives up in a floating tower in Air Dome. Every so often it swoops down, takes a spirit into its folds and whisks them away." Cascadia's eyes are huge and fearful, making goosebumps rise on my flesh. "The Immortal Cloak has taken three *rusalki* from the river over the years. It kept them prisoner for decades, forcing them to polish cursed gold in the hope that might bring back the spirit of life, who always loved shining treasure. But that will never work, because the spirit isn't in this land. By the time the *rusalki* returned to the river they were as tiny as raindrops." Cascadia shakes her head sadly.

"Will this armour protect me from the cloak?"

I look at the breastplate in Cascadia's hands hopefully.

"Nothing can protect you from the cloak," Cascadia whispers ominously.

"That's enough," Koshka snaps. "These are just stories to scare feeble spirits. Olia, if you do see the darkness the cloak brings, which is highly unlikely, you simply run and hide."

"All right." I push thoughts of dangerous spirits from my mind. "Can you help me put the armour on?" I step closer to Cascadia, not wanting to waste any more time, and she lifts the breastplate high then lowers it over me. It flops loosely against my cardigan, but when Cascadia tightens up a set of straps down my back the armour pulls snugly against me.

Feliks passes me a pair of calf-length boots of the same material and a small helmet with two fins sticking out of the top. The helmet is so light that I barely feel it on my head, and though the boots are slightly too big for me, they're smooth against my skin and comfortable when I walk.

I look down at myself and see a warrior dressed for battle, and I wonder what my family and friends would think if they saw me now. Would they be proud or scared for me?

"Are you going to find some armour?" I ask the others.

"My fur is all the protection I need. Like your armour, it's imbued with magic." Feliks shifts into a fox and ruffles his bright orange coat.

"And I've learned plenty of defensive moves from fighting with the *vodyanoy* for the last five hundred years." Cascadia lifts a hand and a bubble extends from her fingers, forming a kind of watery shield around her.

"That's amazing." I lift a finger to touch the bubble, expecting it to waver, but it's as solid as glass.

A deep rumble sounds from somewhere beyond our sight. It escalates until the ground trembles. I hold Cascadia's bubble shield for support, and Feliks edges closer to me. "What was that?" I whisper, as the rumble subsides and the ground stills.

"You mean, *who* was that?" Koshka pads away in the direction of the noise. "His name is Golov and you need to ask him for the Giant's Sword."

My legs wobble with trepidation at the thought that the horrifying noise is coming from a living thing who I must talk to. I creep after Koshka, holding my breath, not knowing what to expect. Feliks and Cascadia follow me, and soon a huge, round mound rises in front of us.

The mound is rumbling and we slow as we draw close to it. I frown as I try to make sense of what I'm seeing. The mound is a head. A giant head, three times taller than me. With no visible body. It's just a head, lying on the ground, snoring. I stop and stare at it in awe, wondering if it does have a sword, and how I should ask for it. Fears jitter through me and I realize that inside this armour I'm still only Olia and I'm scared. But I try to stand tall, like a warrior, think of Rosa to give me strength, and step forwards to face the giant head.

CHAPTER SEVENTEEN

GOLOV

The giant head is so massive, my eyes are only level with its lower lip. But aside from its size, the head looks human. It's wearing a burnished gold helmet, plumed with a still-proud brown-and-white feather that is bigger than me. A thicket of messy, brown hair tumbles from beneath the helmet; a matching moustache sits beneath a huge, pink, bulbous nose, and a beard crawls down the enormous chin, sprawling over the ground like brambles.

The head is asleep. Wind surges past me as air rushes into the bulbous nose. There is a thunderous snore, then a deep groan rumbles from the mouth. The ground shakes and damp, warm breath swirls around me.

"Is his body buried under the ground?" I whisper. "Did Ludmila do this?" Anger and shame flare through my veins again at the cruelty of my ancestor.

Koshka shakes her head. "Ludmila didn't do this to Golov."

I breathe a sigh of relief, then spot hundreds of round, orange eyes, about as big as my own, peeping out from Golov's brambly beard. "There are creatures in his hair!" I exclaim.

"They are Golov's owls," Koshka whispers back to me. "He always kept owls when he had his body, and now they stay with him, nesting in his hair and bringing him food."

"Golov doesn't have a body?" My eyes widen in shock. "He really is just a head?"

Golov stirs at the sound of my voice. One of his snores rises into a yawning groan, then his eyes pop open. Cavernous black pupils dilate. Green irises swell, and for a moment I'm mesmerized by the swirling patterns in them. But then Golov's mouth opens as wide as the old west entrance of the castle and he roars so loudly that his breath blasts into me

like a punch. I skid backwards, stumble and fall onto my knees.

Shielding my face with my forearms, I look around for the others. Feliks is to my right, leaning into the gust of breath with his boots dug deep into the ground. Cascadia is to my left, huddled inside a bubble shield. I don't see Koshka until I look behind me. She's skidded into a jumble of rusty armour and is rising back onto her paws with a vicious scowl on her face.

"Go away!" Golov bellows and another surge of his storm-breath blasts into us. Cascadia's bubble shield wavers and she frowns with the concentration of trying to hold it together.

"Please," I shout over Golov's roar. "We only want to talk to you for a moment."

"I'm sleeping." Golov's eyebrows fall and scores of owls fly from them straight towards us. Beaks and claws flash and I duck down further to shield myself. Wings stroke the air, feathery bodies swoop past me, high-pitched screeches strike my eardrums, and claws graze the *rusalka* helmet covering my head, making me grateful to be wearing it.

Cascadia bursts into a flurry of tiny bubbles and I scream as they tumble down and disappear into a puddle.

"She's fine." Feliks nudges me reassuringly. "That's what *rusalki* do when they feel threatened."

I stare down into the puddle and see Cascadia's face staring back up at me like a reflection. "Is it safe yet?" she mouths.

The owls circle around and swoop back into Golov's eyebrows. His eyelids droop and fall and he smacks his giant lips together, like Babusya does when she's sleeping. I feel an urge to creep away before Golov wakes again, but the thought of the sword keeps me rooted to the spot. Koshka stalks back to me and curls around one of my ankles.

"Where does Golov keep the sword?" I whisper.

"Under his head."

"How can I get *under* his head?" I stare at Golov's huge sleeping face. His hair and beard spread from it so thickly that I can't see if he has a neck or not, or any way to sneak under his chin.

"There is no way under. You must ask him to move." Koshka nudges me forwards.

I shake my head and sigh. Nothing makes sense in this land. *How can a disembodied head move?* But, flaring with an urge to get the sword without wasting any more time, I decide to ask Golov.

I edge closer and move to the side of his mouth, in case he tries to blow me away again. I root myself firmly down, like I do when I'm climbing the roof back home and call Golov's name as loudly as I dare.

"Go away!" he thunders without opening his eyes.

"I'm sorry to disturb you, Golov, but this is important. I need to cut off Chernomor's beard to save this land and my home from being torn apart, and Koshka says I can only do that with the sword under your...under you."

Golov opens one eye and peers at me with an interested but slightly mocking look. "You think you can defeat my brother, little one?"

"Chernomor is your brother?" My voice trembles with the thought that Chernomor might be as big as Golov.

Golov's head rocks forwards slightly, in what I assume is a nod. "Chernomor is my brother. And he did this to me – a giant! So how are you, little one, going to defeat him?"

"Your own brother cut off your head?" I stare at Golov, disbelief and dismay sweeping over my skin like cold lake weeds.

Golov's face twists with anger and pain. "I trusted him. I *loved* him. And he deceived and wounded me in the most barbarous way. Do you see, behind me?" Golov raises his eyebrows and the owls inside them flutter with the movement. I lean around Golov, craning my neck to look behind him. There is a bramble-covered mound not too far away, shaped something like a body, although it's impossibly long, extending far into the distance.

"Is that your body, under the brambles?" I stare at it, amazed. If the long mound was attached to Golov's head and he stood up, he would be almost as tall as Castle Mila.

"Yes." Golov groans and his eyebrows fall again. "How I miss my body!" His enormous eyes fill with water and for a moment I think Golov is going to cry huge tears, but then his bulbous nose purples with anger and he inhales sharply, as if he's about to roar again.

"Wait!" I shout. "Maybe I can help you? Is there anything that can be done?"

Golov blinks away the tears in his eyes and stares down at me. "Perhaps. But you're a tiny, magicless human child, and what I need is beneath my brother's fortress. You are no match for Chernomor. With a flick of his beard, you'd find yourself sailing through the air so fast you'd burst every dome in this land."

I draw my shoulders back, determined not to let Golov's words scare me. "Koshka says Chernomor is old and tired. If you give me the sword, I'll cut off his beard, then he'll have no power. And then I can help you." I stare right into Golov's eyes, feeling all of a sudden stronger.

Golov's gaze turns on Koshka. "That cat is not to be trusted. She worked with Ludmila to create this land and trap her own magical kin inside it. She's a traitorous turncoat."

Koshka stares back at Golov, her mouth drawn into a thin line and her whiskers twitching irritably.

"I'm trying to save this land and everyone in it," she growls. "If Chernomor's beard is not cut off soon, his magic will tear us all apart."

"Who knows what lies you're telling, or what your real motives are?" Golov's owls flutter as his nose purples even more. I feel an argument rising in him like a storm, and panic tears through me that Golov is about to open his cavernous mouth and blow us away for good, like the winds blowing away my home.

CHAPTER EIGHTEEN

THE GIANT'S SWORD

Golov opens his mouth to roar. I brace myself, step right in front of him and lift my arms to get his attention.

"Koshka made a mistake working with Ludmila, but now she wants to help the magical spirits that live here. And she's telling the truth – I know for a fact that my home and your world are in danger." I point at the silver threads spiderwebbing through the black grass. "These strands of Chernomor's magic cover everything, and beneath them are cracks in the ground."

"A large rift opened yesterday." Golov rocks forwards slightly. "It nearly shook me over. My owls say it's not far from here, near the feet of my body."

I peer around Golov again. At the far end of the brambly mound there is a dense tangle of silver, glowing bright. "Your brother's magic is clearly linked to the land splitting apart." Babusya's note flutters into my mind, telling me to *look from all angles* but there's no other explanation that makes sense to me.

Golov sighs and his hot breath whirls around me. "If you truly believe using the sword will help you save this land and your home, I will give it to you. I don't like it anyway, with all its bad memories. My brother used the sword to cut off my head. It is the only sword that can cut through our magic."

"So Chernomor is a giant, like you?" I tense with fear at the prospect of needing to defeat someone so huge.

"He wishes he was!" Golov booms with laughter so loud that my legs shake. "Chernomor is tiny. Tinier even than you. We're the children of a giant and a wizard. I got all the giant, and he got all the wizard. Chernomor was always jealous of my size – that's why he did this to me." Golov stops laughing and frowns.

I think how awful it must be to have a brother or sister hurt you. Dinara and Luka argue sometimes, but they're also fiercely protective of each other – the same way I feel about Rosa. It's terrible that Golov doesn't have that with his brother and I wish again that I could do something for him. "You said there is something beneath Chernomor's fortress that could help you."

"There is, little one." Golov's eyes light up, like the gas lamps along Castle Mila's corridors at night. "Under my brother's fortress is a pool and a well. The pool contains the waters of death and the well contains the waters of life. I need a little of each. The waters of death can reattach my head to my body, and the waters of life can bring my body back to life."

"I want to help." I slide my hand into my pocket to feel for the key, wondering if we'll have enough time to find the waters and bring them back to Golov, as well as face Chernomor. The metal flits between my fingers, as if it is there and then not there, and I pull it out in alarm. The key is faded, glowing much weaker than before.

"Oh dear." Feliks looks at the key and deep, furry folds wrinkle his forehead. "That doesn't look good."

"Will it still work? Should we leave now? But what about the storm?" My voice rises in panic. "Golov, I'm sorry but we won't have time to help you. This is our key home, and it's fading away." I stare in horror as the wards on the end of the key – the bits that make it turn a lock – completely disappear.

"But I can help with that." Golov smiles and owls hoot in his moustache. "If you put me back together, I'll give you the ring my father gave me. He hoped it would make me more wizardly, as it strengthens magic. The ring will make your key solid and ensure that you can get home."

I look at the faded metal in my hand, trying to still panicked thoughts of becoming trapped in this collapsing land. I could rush back to the doorway now, but I don't know if the key would work – and I need to stay here to save my home. "All right, Golov. I'll do my best to bring you the waters, if you fix this key. I have to see my family and friends again."

"We have a deal." Golov's smile widens, plumping his cheeks into huge pink mounds. "Oh! To have my body again, after all these years!"

Golov looks so excited that a smile grows on my own face too. It would be amazing to put him back together, and knowing he can fix the key is such a relief. "So, about the sword…" I hesitate, unsure how I can retrieve it from beneath his head.

"Move me!" Golov bellows and the owls roosting in his hair surge to life. They flap up and away, but this time they're all clutching bundles of Golov's hair in their claws. Slowly, with a great groan, Golov's head rises from the ground. His face contorts with discomfort as his hair is tugged and the skin of his scalp is pulled. His brown, brambly beard is so long that it dangles down from his chin like the huge curtains in Castle Mila's old theatre. "Go! Get the sword!" Golov yells when his head is higher than mine. "The owls can't hold me for long."

I rush into Golov's beard, pushing the hairs away with my arms. They are thick and scratchy and smell something like wet dog. To distract myself from them,

I hold my breath and pretend I'm diving into the lake with my friends to look for the legendary axe that built the castle. And just as I'm wondering how I'm meant to find anything in this dark tangle, there is a glow ahead.

"Hurry!" Golov booms and a lurch of movement sends his beard hairs swaying.

Heart racing, I wrestle forwards and spot the shining hilt of a sword poking out from a knot of hairs on the ground. I lean down and grab it and my whole arm shudders with the power of its magic.

The sword is much heavier than I expected it to be, but I turn around and drag it out, rushing and stumbling with the fear that the owls might drop Golov's head on top of me. As I see light through his beard up ahead, my gaze is drawn upwards even though I don't really want to see Golov's head from beneath. But there is only a glow where Golov's neck would be – a golden glow of what I imagine is the magic keeping him alive.

I exhale with relief as I emerge from his beard, dragging the sword behind me. When I'm a safe distance away from Golov, his owls drop him to the ground with a thunderous thud.

"Owwww!" Golov howls. His eyes roll angrily and with a flutter the owls disappear deep into his hair and beard. Golov's gaze turns on me, and the severity of his expression makes me stop still. "That blade has caused much heartache in its time. Make sure you use it wisely and only for good. It's a dangerous thing in foolish or impulsive hands."

I look down at the sword and gulp back a lump that forms in my throat. When I started this journey, my only thought was to stop the storm to protect my family and home. But now I feel responsible for preventing an evil wizard from tearing apart a land full of spirits, taking Cascadia home to her mother, and reuniting a giant's head with his lost body. There is so much I want to fight for, yet I'm still not sure whether I'm strong and brave enough to do it.

The sword's blade is as long as one of my legs and as wide as my palm. It's covered by a leather sheath, but I sense its sharpness through the leather, like pointed fangs behind soft, wolfish lips. Even if this sword wasn't magical, it would scare me. I've never held anything that could cause so much damage, and all of a sudden I wonder whether it's right to use a weapon like this at all, even if I am trying to use it for good.

CHAPTER NINETEEN

EARTH DOME

"Good luck, little one." Golov yawns and I stumble forwards as air gusts into his mouth. He closes his eyes and, like Babusya when she's tired, starts snoring immediately.

Cascadia rises from her puddle and wobbles back into shape. "You were so brave, Olia." She looks down at the sword in my hands and her eyes whirl wider. "And you got the Giant's Sword! The only blade that can cut through magic."

I shift uncomfortably. The sword is huge in my hands. "I'm not sure I want to use it. Maybe we should talk to Chernomor – perhaps we could persuade him to stop breaking the land apart. He might not even realize he's doing it."

"You can't persuade an evil wizard to do anything!"
Koshka hisses. "You heard Golov. Chernomor cut off
his own brother's head. He's heinous and merciless.
The *only* way to save this land from his magic is to
cut off his beard. Now hurry. Earth Dome – and
Chernomor's fortress – is this way." Koshka bounds
off airily, disturbing a small copper-coloured weasel-
like spirit, who roars fire at her before scampering
away. Cascadia flings a handful of water at Koshka's
singed fur and Koshka yowls in indignation before
walking on more cautiously than before.

At home, the most dangerous thing I've ever done
is slide down the bannisters, or climb onto the roof to
watch birds, or into a fruit tree to pick apples. Here,
spirits breathe fire, and a giant's head gave me a sword.

"Are you all right, Olia?" Feliks looks into my eyes
and his gaze draws the truth right out of my mouth.

"I think someone bigger, braver and stronger
should be doing this, Feliks," I whisper. "This sword is
heavy and dangerous. I really don't think it was meant
for me. I'm not wise or good, like Golov said I should
be. Only this morning, in the Great Hall, I was foolish

and impulsive. You saved my life in that fall, and Dinara…" Guilt squashes my chest as I picture her bandaged wrist and think how much worse it could have been. "And then at the river, if it hadn't been for Cascadia, the *vodyanoy* would have pulled me under."

"You're welcome!" Cascadia bubbles from nearby.

"I'm a magicless human child," I say desolately. "How am I going to face Chernomor?"

Feliks waves me closer, and I crouch down so we're eye to eye. "You're certainly not magicless, Olia. Perhaps you don't remember all the magic you've seen in your life, but I do. You've always felt the threads of magic running through the world. As soon as you could smile, you'd smile at me and all the spirits who live in the fields and lake and woods around the castle. You charmed all of us with your curious, happy nature, and by the time you were three you were playing games with tree spirits and water spirits."

Faint images form in my mind: a branchlike arm curling, as if beckoning me into the grove; a woody eye, winking; chasing bubbles that rose out of the lake;

and a voice like Cascadia's, laughing. "Why can't I remember all this properly?" I sigh.

"It's hard for humans to keep their belief in magic as they grow older. You want to understand things, so you build ideas of what the world is in your minds, then reject anything that doesn't fit into that." Feliks taps his chest. "But you keep it all in your heart, Olia. And it's still there, when you need it. That's why it's important to look and think with your heart. This morning, I watched you fold a key from only a little magic, and unfold Koshka's chain. You do understand magic, and you know how to use it. All you have to do is believe."

A knot of worry begins to unravel, loosening all my muscles.

"Also..." Feliks's blue eyes twinkle. "I've seen you be big, brave, strong, wise and good many times. And I've seen you be small, fearful, foolish and impulsive too. You can be all kinds of things, even in one day."

"So how can I make sure I'm the right thing at the right time? What if I get it all wrong? I've already made so many mistakes today."

Feliks puts his tiny, furry hands over mine. "The truth is you'll probably do some bits right and some bits wrong."

"What if that's not enough to save everyone?" I whisper.

Feliks raises his eyebrows. "Shall we find out?"

I take a deep breath. Whether I like it or not people are depending on me. "Of course, all I can do is try my best. Thanks, Feliks, for the nice things you said and for helping me. And for all the other things you've done that I've probably forgotten about." I smile, even though my heart aches for those lost memories. Feliks doesn't reply, but his moustache curls into a big wave as he smiles back.

"You two are so sweet." Cascadia splashes her hands together then looks at the sword, which I'm still holding awkwardly. "Would you like me to strap that to your hip?"

"Or I could shrink it into my coat pocket, if you like?" Feliks offers. "My shapeshifting magic is very useful for that. You wouldn't believe some of the things I have in here." Feliks taps his pocket. "Your great-great-grandfather asked me to shrink the banqueting table during the revolution, and it's still in here, disguised as pocket fluff – although I imagine the food on it is spoiled by now."

"Could you shrink the sword away? That would be wonderful, thank you." I feel lighter, as if the weight of the blade has disappeared already.

"No problem." Feliks takes the sword from my hands and slides it into his pocket and, like the paper bag full of *bulochki*, it disappears easily inside.

My stomach rumbles at the thought of food. "May I have one of the *bulochka* Babusya made, please?" I ask as we follow the path Koshka took across the burned, silver-threaded field. An army of antlike spirits scurry back and forth to a nest in the ground, their abdomens glowing like hot embers and smoke rising from their mandibles. And a staglike spirit gallops across the far side of the field, his hooves and antlers aflame.

"Of course." Feliks expands the paper bag of *bulochki* and passes it to me.

My stomach jumps at the sweet, buttery scent

that wafts from the bag and reminds me of Babusya. I open the top and offer it around. Feliks takes a *bulochka*, but Cascadia and Koshka both shake their heads. I take one out for myself and bite into the soft roll swirled with creamy poppy-seed filling. It's so delicious that I murmur with satisfaction, and my mind swims with thoughts of home…

Babusya in the kitchen, baking bread and warming soup for lunch. Mama, humming her favourite lullaby. Papa's face all furrowed as he tries to work out a riddle from one of his puzzle books. Rosa wrapping her tiny fingers around mine and staring into my eyes. But then the winds storm into my thoughts, and with them a paralysing fear for my family. Mama said she, Papa and Rosa would be back at the castle by lunchtime, but with the storm still raging, I don't see how that's possible. I don't know where they are or if they're safe…yet I'm here, munching *bulochki*. Guilt squeezes my belly.

"What time is it, Feliks?" I ask.

Feliks licks the last crumbs of his *bulochka* from his fingers and brushes down his beard. Then he expands a life-size, wooden, owl-shaped clock from his pocket and looks at its ticking wings and clockface eyes. Its beak suddenly bursts forwards on a spring, making Feliks flinch. "One o'clock." He shrinks the clock back into his pocket and I stiffen at the thought of another hour gone. Time is flying by, too fast. Now there are only five hours left until the harvest moon rises.

"How far is the fortress?" I ask, passing the paper bag back to Feliks so he can shrink it into his pocket.

"You're about to see it." Koshka blurs as she steps through a shimmer in the air ahead and I realize we've reached the boundary into Earth Dome. I experience the now-familiar stretch and pop of the air, then step onto the soft green grass of a field broken apart by wide cracks which are crammed with silver threads.

A multicoloured woodland lies ahead of us. Tightly packed trees are alive with whispering red, orange and purple leaves. Huge black-and-white flowers trumpet into the domed sky, attracting insects that shine like metal and click like pebbles bumping together.

The thin crescent of sun is now lying on its back, like a smile, and the smell of ripe fruits and damp moss drifts towards us on a pink-tinged breeze, along with a sweet whiff of pine that reminds me of my bedroom walls in the morning. Strange melodic birdsong soars through the air, punctuated by the occasional shriek of some distant, unseen spirit.

It's beautiful and breathtaking, but my nerves flutter as my gaze is drawn upwards to a huge, red, square building, rising from deep inside the woodland. "That must be Chernomor's fortress." My voice trembles at the thought of the task ahead.

"Yes." Koshka stares at the bright red walls, thickly webbed with silver threads and her fur lifts and shivers. What look like rectangular windows are almost completely covered with glowing tangles, and more tendrils tumble down from sturdy crenellations and turrets on the roof.

I push back my sleeves. I was brave enough to face Golov. Now I need to be brave enough to face his brother.

CHAPTER TWENTY

DUB

I take one last look at the position of Chernomor's fortress before stepping into the shadows beneath the trees. The glowing silver threads are thick on the ground, tangled into great, spongy mats. They coil around roots and trunks, creep up into the canopy like vines, then fall and sway, shining and sparkling like dew-coated spidersilk.

Small red and yellow mushroom-like spirits are quietly squealing as they dance on bouncy pillows of blue moss, while tiny mouselike spirits with a single, pointed horn are scurrying in and out of holes in low, curly logs. High in the canopy above, hundreds of spirits flutter and crash, some of them tiny as bees, others bigger than wildcats.

The woodland is spectacular, and I have to focus hard on not getting distracted, as I want to keep the position of Chernomor's fortress in my mind's eye. Koshka is prowling near my ankles, while Cascadia skips around, drawing water out of hollows in tree trunks with a wave of her fingers. She sighs with satisfaction and swells taller.

"Are you all right, Feliks?" I ask. His gaze is flitting around and his orange fur is quivering.

"Fine. It's just..." Feliks looks up at me apologetically. "There is a particular reason why I tried to find this land for five hundred years. I should have told you before, but I didn't want you to think I wasn't here to help you save the castle, because I am. But I also need to find my wife, Mora."

"Your wife?" I exclaim in surprise. "Is she in this land?"

"She was banished here by Ludmila." Feliks's eyes dim with melancholy. "And I think she would have settled in this dome. She's a *kikimora*, another kind of house spirit, kind and loving. A little taller than me, and where I am like an orange fox, she is like a black shrew. Ludmila blamed Mora for her nightmares. I tried to explain *kikimora* are misunderstood: they feed on nightmares, they don't cause them. But Ludmila wouldn't listen. She separated us and sent Mora here. No matter how much I begged, she wouldn't free Mora or let me join her. So I haven't seen Mora in five hundred years. Every day, I've tried to find a way into this land, and I've felt so useless..." A tear wells in one of Feliks's eyes and rolls into the fur of his cheek. "I should have done more to find her, and to protect her in the first place..."

My heart aches as I try to imagine what Feliks has gone through. It's been a wrench to be in a different world from my own family for just a few hours and Feliks has been separated from his loved one for five hundred years.

Anger at my ancestor sears through me and I clench my jaw to stop myself from saying something horrible about Ludmila. I lean down and brush the tear from Feliks's fur instead. "We'll find Mora," I say firmly, meaning it with all my heart. "And we'll bring her home."

I look around, half expecting to see a shrewlike house spirit watching us from the shadows...but something huge and heavy crashes through the canopy instead, making my heart nearly leap out of my chest.

The ground shakes as whatever it is thumps down somewhere close by. My legs wobble and I reach for a tree trunk to steady myself. "What was that?" I whisper, fears flapping in my chest like a trapped bird. I peer between the trees, but I can't see anything apart from branches bending and leaves blustering around. The woodland shudders with creaks and groans and my pulse races. "What's happening?"

"The tree spirits are fighting." Cascadia backs up against the tree next to me. "*Leshiye* are very territorial, and this woodland is far too small for them. We should stay out of the way until they pass."

Feliks shifts into a fox as he moves beside me, Koshka slides behind my legs, and we all stare in the direction of the rumpus. I flinch as a tree, taller than the tallest spruce back home, blasts through the smaller trees. It's moving with purpose, like it's walking.

My eyes widen as I see it's a kind of giant tree-man, with two thick trunk legs and rooty feet. His long branch-arms are dragging something, and I flinch again as he swings the thing high and releases it into the air.

As the thing zooms past, I realize it's another tree-man, a much smaller one – a tree-boy perhaps. He slams into a large rust-coloured cedar and crumples to the floor with a groan. The cedar behind him rocks, and a huge crack immediately opens in the ground beneath it, longer than the kitchen back home and wide enough for me to fall into. I stare in horror as the crack lengthens.

"Stay out of my woodland!" the larger tree-man yells in a creaking, crashing voice. I glimpse his face, high in the canopy. His eyes are knots of wood; his nose a large, rounded burr; and his mouth a jagged crack oozing globules of thick, gooey sap.

I press my back against the tree behind me and hold my breath, not wanting the giant tree-man to hear or see me.

"That's Vysok," Cascadia whispers. "The tallest of

the *leshiye*. The little one is Dub."

The smaller *leshy*, Dub, rises to his feet. He's almost twice as tall as me, but looks tiny next to Vysok. He blinks his barky eyelids and stares at the crack in the ground in front of him with a mixture of confusion and concern. Then, brushing fallen leaves from his limbs, he stares up at Vysok. "Where do you expect me to go?" Dub says, so slowly and calmly it reminds me of Luka, which makes my heart twinge. "This is the only woodland here."

"I don't care!" Vysok roars.

"But I'm *leshiye*, like you." Dub shakes his head sadly. "You know we need to live with trees. For five hundred years you've been throwing me out of this woodland, and I've been sneaking back in. Why can't we come to some agreement? I only need a small amount of space. Let me have this thicket here, between the cedar and the edge of Earth Dome." Dub glances behind him, towards the narrow strip of woodland that thins into the cracked green field beyond.

"No!" Vysok roars again and steps forward, raising one of his huge trunk legs as if to kick Dub.

An urge to defend Dub charges through me and I rush between the *leshiye*. "Stop!" I shout, lifting my hands into the air.

Vysok leans down and glares at me with a knotty eye. His mouth widens into a grin and a huge blob of sap drops onto the ground near my feet. My limbs tremble; I felt brave when I ran out but now I feel it seeping away. Even so, I try to stand firm because I want the fighting to stop. "Please don't hurt Dub," I beg.

Laughter creaks from Vysok's mouth and another blob of sap drops to the floor. "Are you going to stop me?" Vysok reaches down with his long branch-fingers, and I back away, fear pounding inside me.

"Leave her alone!" Feliks snarls and leaps forwards. He shifts from fox to man in mid-air, and flying-kicks Vysok's fingers away from me with his shining boots, before landing between us with a thud.

Koshka darts in too, hissing and spitting at Vysok, angrier than I've ever seen her. Then Cascadia surges in like a tidal wave. Her watery body is cloudy, swelling with tiny bubbles. She grows taller, stretches towards

Vysok and flashes her pearly teeth at him, revealing a small, angry-looking crab between them. "Leave us alone, or I'll drain every drop of water from your body." Cascadia lifts a hand and mist rises from the leaves around Vysok's face and flows into her palm.

Vysok twitches with discomfort and backs away. "I was only defending my territory. There's no need for threats like that, *rusalka*." Sap bubbles round Vysok's mouth as he grumbles the last word contemptuously. Then he turns and thunders away into the depths of woodland, the ground shaking with his every step.

"Thanks, Cascadia." I sigh with relief as Vysok disappears. "And you too, Feliks and Koshka."

Cascadia exhales a small white cloud. "We're lucky he left. I'm no match for him really, and he knows it. It's always better to stay out of the way of *leshiye*." Cascadia turns to Dub and the crab between her teeth swims away, across her cheek.

"This looks bad." Dub leans over the crack in the ground. His face is framed by slender yellow leaves and red berries. He looks just like one of the rowan trees that grow on the eastern edge of the spruce grove back home.

I walk over and peer into the crack too. It's more of a crevice, almost as wide as one of Castle Mila's corridors and so deep I can't see the bottom. Koshka said that Chernomor's magic was forcing the land apart, but here writhing silver threads are rapidly tangling into the space, filling the damage caused by Vysok throwing Dub. The ground judders and I take a step back as the crevice widens further. Maybe the threads are making it worse after all. "This is bad," I agree. "We've seen cracks on the way here, but nothing this big." I turn to Feliks and Koshka. "The magic escaping through this will be tearing at Castle Mila, won't it?"

"Yes," Feliks says sadly, putting his hand over his heart. "I can feel it, when a dome falls. The storm must be raging."

I wince as my own heart seems to drop and smash, like the dome I saw crashing onto the roof before we left. I want to know how many other domes have fallen, but I'm too scared to ask, knowing how much the loss of each one will hurt.

Koshka moves closer to me and curls her tail around my ankle. "The only way to stop these cracks getting worse is to stop Chernomor, and we're running out of time. If we don't do it soon, the land will be torn apart for ever."

"Torn apart?" Dub retreats from the crevice as slowly and gently as he can on his huge, rooty feet. "But then what would happen to the *leshiye* and the trees and the other spirits who live here?"

"If this land is destroyed, we'll all be destroyed with it." Koshka frowns and icy tendrils slither down my spine.

"Do you know the quickest way to Chernomor's fortress?" I ask Dub. "I'm Olia and this is Feliks, Cascadia and Koshka. If we can get to Chernomor in time, we can try to save this land and everyone in it."

"If there is anything I can do to help you, I will." Dub points to a narrow trail, thick with silver threads. "The only way to the fortress is through the stone maze, and the entrance is that way. I will show you."

"Maze? You didn't tell me about a maze!" I turn and glare at Koshka.

"Well, you know now," Koshka says haughtily and bounds off down the trail.

"But we don't have time to find our way through a maze!" I shout after her in frustration.

Dub leans down and rests a few branch-fingers gently on my shoulder. "Are you any good at riddles, Olia?" His bark-mouth curves into a smile. "Because I know one that can show you the way straight through the maze."

I think of all the riddles I've solved with Papa, our faces close together as we pored over his puzzle books in the warmth of the kitchen. "I am pretty good at riddles." Hope whispers through me and my confidence swells with each step I take towards the maze.

CHAPTER TWENTY-ONE

THE STONE MAZE

"What is the riddle that will lead us through the maze?" I ask Dub as we weave along a trail that is as winding as one of Castle Mila's corridors.

"It's a riddle told by *vily* – the tiny winged warrior spirits who built the maze." Dub sweeps a low-hanging larch branch aside, revealing a smooth, dark-green stone wall that rises so high it seems to merge with the sky. Silver threads are trailing from it like cobwebs and tiny glowing hummingbirds are darting in and out of small holes high above us.

"This must be the maze," I say, feeling bubbles of urgency fizzing and popping. After what Feliks said about the storm raging and domes falling, I want to get to Chernomor faster than I could slide along the third-floor corridor.

Dub continues walking alongside the wall. "I've never been inside it, but I know there's an entrance here somewhere."

"But what's the riddle?" Cascadia splashes next to Dub impatiently.

"I overheard a *vila* singing it to his children once. He said all young *vily* must learn the riddle, because it contains three answers that lead swiftly to the waters of death beneath Chernomor's fortress. The pool there is the only place where blood flowers grow, and *vily* need their nectar to survive." Dub's brow creaks into woody knots. "I've often pondered the riddle, but I've never been able to solve it."

I raise my eyebrows, eager to hear it.

Dub clears his throat with a noise like branches knocking together, then recites earnestly:

"Wordless whispers lift your wings
over sunshine stores with soundless rings,
and the voiceless path that always sings."

I repeat the riddle quietly, trying to commit it to

memory and think of any similar ones that I've solved with Papa. I feel like I should have at least some idea what the answers might be, but right now my head is so full of rushing thoughts and worries that I can't focus.

"Here's the entrance." Dub stops and pulls a thick tangle of glowing threads away from the wall, revealing an archway beneath. I step towards it but the threads quickly writhe back, blocking it again.

"Use the Giant's Sword," Koshka urges, curling around my ankles. "It's the only thing that can cut through them."

I frown at the thought of the sword, but we need to get into the maze. "All right. May I have it please, Feliks?" I straighten my back and brace myself as Feliks expands the sword from his pocket and passes it to me.

The hilt is warm with magic, but I shiver as I slide the blade free from its sheath. The metal shines so brightly that my eyes sting, so I look back to the archway, tangled over with glowing threads. Golov's words echo through my mind, about how dangerous the sword is, and my mouth goes dry. "Will this hurt Chernomor?" I ask.

"No. Do you feel a haircut?" Koshka rolls her eyes, but her expression seems honest.

With both hands, I lift the sword. It wobbles, so I grip it more firmly, then slice down. There is a crackle and a sizzle, and the threads shrivel back as if burned, freeing the entrance and revealing hundreds of fine cracks in the dark-green wall around it. The archway trembles, a crack widens and a few tiny fragments of stone rain down.

I stop still and hold my breath, thinking that I've done something wrong and made the entrance unstable. But then the trembling stops and all is quiet again. I sigh with relief as I return the sword to its sheath: I used the blade and nothing bad happened.

If cutting off Chernomor's beard is like cutting through these threads, then it might not be too difficult after all. *As long as he's asleep.* If he's awake, I don't think I could confront him with a weapon. I give Feliks the sword to shrink back into his pocket, silently hoping that Chernomor is as sound a sleeper as Babusya after her morning walk.

I lean into the archway. The silver threads are wavering either side of it, already trying to stretch back across the entrance. Inside is a long, dark-green stone tunnel with side passages to the right and left: some are low and wide, some high and narrow, and there are a few circular openings midway up the tunnel walls too. "There are so many choices," I whisper. "How do we know which way to go?" My gaze flits around in confusion. Finally I notice three large, curved tunnel openings just a few paces away that each have a small symbol etched neatly into the stone above them. "What are they?" I ask, pointing at the symbols.

Everyone gathers closer together and looks through the archway at the symbols. The first is a circle with a dot in the middle; the second a spiral, whirling round and round; and the third, a circle with a crescent inside it.

"I think they could be *vilanese* runic symbols." Feliks moves forwards. "Mora's grandmother was a *vila*. She had similar symbols carved on small stones that she used for fortune telling."

"Perhaps one of them is the solution to the first part of the riddle," I suggest. *"Wordless whispers lift your wings.* Do you know what any of the symbols mean?"

"Possibly, but I need a closer look. Shall we go inside?" Feliks's ears twitch nervously.

I nod and step into the cool dark of the tunnel. The only light comes from the archway behind us and the silver threads glowing on the walls. The others follow me, Dub creaking as he stoops low to fit through the archway. The ceiling is higher inside the tunnel, but not high enough for Dub to stand upright, so he hunches over, reminding me of the trees that were weighed down with apples in the fruit grove back home.

We pass a couple of small side passages with cold, musty air swirling out of them. Then we reach the curved tunnel openings. Feliks rises onto his boot toes and cranes his neck as he struggles to read the runic symbols high above him. "Would you like a lift up, so you can see them better?" I ask, weaving my fingers together and offering them to Feliks like a step.

"Please, allow me to lift all of you." Dub holds out one of his thick barky palms and it creaks as it grows larger. I thank Dub, step onto his hand, and Feliks and Cascadia jump up beside me.

"I can see fine from here." Koshka backs away.

Dub curls his branch-fingers so they make a kind of fence to prevent us falling, then lifts us close to the symbols above the curved openings. Feliks pulls a tiny pair of half-moon pince-nez spectacles from his pocket, balances them on his furry nose and squints at the shapes. "I think this one represents the sun." Feliks touches the symbol on the left lightly, which is the circle with a dot in the middle. "And I think that one represents the moon." Feliks points to the symbol on the right, which is the circle with a crescent inside.

I peer at the symbol in the middle – the spiral whirling round and round. Inspiration spins through me as I think of the storm back home, whooshing around the domes, and I remember a riddle that me and Papa worked out a few weeks ago, just before Rosa was born. It was about *wingless fluttering* and *mouthless muttering*, and its solution might also work for the

first line of this riddle. "Does this symbol represent the wind?" I ask, trailing my finger along the smooth, carved line.

"Yes. How did you know?" Feliks removes his pince-nez and slides them back into his pocket.

"Because I think that's the answer. *Wordless whispers lift your wings* could mean a breeze or wind. It's similar to a riddle I solved with Papa." Even though I'm as sure as I can be, the prospect of making a mistake, taking the wrong tunnel and ending up lost in this maze, unable to save anyone, sends a cold wash of fear through me.

"Of course it is." Dub's mouth creaks into a wide smile. "You're clever, Olia."

"It's an easy riddle." Koshka rises to her paws and steps forwards, startling a large molelike spirit who was hidden in a circular side passage. The mole flashes huge metallic claws and rapidly digs away through a stone wall, making me wince at the loud scraping noise.

The maze shakes and I wonder if the mole is breaking the land, the way Dub did when he was thrown to the ground, or if these tremors are being caused by Chernomor. Whatever the reason, the thought of an earthquake striking while we're in here is terrifying. "Come on, let's hurry." I jump down off Dub's hand.

Feliks shifts into a fox and leaps down beside me, and Cascadia splashes down in a wave, rippling with excitement. "With the riddle to help us, we'll reach the fortress faster than bubbles fly to the surface!"

I jog into the middle tunnel, hoping Cascadia is right, but almost immediately two small side passages branch off to the left. And further down the tunnel I glimpse more and more openings. "There must be another carved symbol somewhere." I stop and scan the walls desperately because without more clues to show us the way, getting through this maze will be impossible.

A deep groan creeps from a low archway ahead of us. Then there is a rapid scuffling noise followed by an abrupt and ominous silence. My heart pounds as I remember Koshka's and Cascadia's talk about dangerous spirits.

Feliks draws closer to me. "We're part of a group now, Olia," he whispers. "Me, you, Koshka, Cascadia and Dub. We'll protect each other."

"The best way to stay safe is to keep moving." Koshka pushes her head against my ankles. "I think we should continue along this tunnel until we find another symbol."

"All right." I glance round at my friends, and the sight of them helps to still my pitter-pattering fears. "But we all need to keep a close lookout." Everyone nods in agreement and we walk on.

The tunnel twists and winds into deeper darkness. Minute after minute ticks away as I peer at the walls above and around every side passage until my eyes ache, not wanting to miss a clue, and trying not to imagine what perils might lie around the next corner.

CHAPTER TWENTY-TWO

SINGING GOLD

Inside the maze, the air grows colder and I shiver. Whispers swish from every passage and faint light from the glowing threads makes everyone look ghostly in the shadows. "What time is it, Feliks?" I ask, frustrated that we can't move faster because we need to search for symbols at every opening.

Feliks expands a hummingbird-shaped clock from his pocket. A small fish in its beak is ticking as it flaps and wriggles, and a clock face on the bird's belly glows as if it's been painted with moonbeams. "Two o'clock," Feliks replies and my heart flaps like the fish in the bird's beak. Time seems to be zooming away, faster and faster, completely out of my control.

In only four hours, this land will break apart, all

the spirits here will be lost, and my home will fall – unless I can get through this maze and find enough bravery to confront Chernomor.

"I found a symbol!" Cascadia squeals with excitement and points to a carving above a large rectangular side tunnel. It's the whirling spiral that means wind. We look around for more symbols, but that's the only one.

"It's the same symbol that was correct at the last junction, so I guess we follow it again?" My voice is a question, but time is tick-tocking away, pushing me on, so I lead the way into the tunnel. It quickly narrows and soon Dub is struggling to move without scuffing his branches against the green stone walls.

I sigh with relief when the tunnel widens, then opens into a roofless courtyard. High above us is a square of pale blue sky and I take a deep breath of the fresher air.

"Only two choices this time." Koshka looks from one side of the courtyard to the other. There is a large wooden door on either side. Both doors are made from plain dark wood, and a small symbol is carved into the centre of each.

Feliks moves to the door on the left, slides his pince-nez from his pocket and peers through them at the shape. It looks like an arrow with two heads, one above the other.

Dub groans as he stretches to his full height. "These tunnels aren't designed for *leshiye*," he grumbles, straightening his back.

"What was the next line of the riddle?" Cascadia asks.

"*Sunshine stores with soundless rings.*" I frown. I can't remember any similar riddles in Papa's books, and I wish he were here to help. We always solved new riddles *together*. "Does anyone have an idea what the answer might be?" I ask.

"Soundless rings could be the rings you wear on your fingers," Koshka suggests, licking her paw. "And they often shine in sunlight."

"So do bubble rings." Cascadia breathes in sharply and a ring-shaped bubble forms inside her mouth and then floats gently upwards, until it sits on her reedy hair like a crown. "My mother used to blow bubble rings in Lake Mila for me to swim through." Cascadia smiles at the memory and her bubble crown pops.

"What about a ring of mushrooms?" Dub rests his long branch-fingers against the centre of his trunk. "I like mushrooms. Especially the ones that look like reindeer horns. They're tasty."

I step next to Feliks, who is now peering at the carving on the door on the right. It looks like the symbol for the sun – a circle with a dot in the middle – but has something like a crown on top of it too. "Do you know what it means?" I ask.

"I think it might represent treasure or gold. But I'm not sure."

"Lots of jewellery rings are gold." Koshka slinks towards the door. "This could make sense."

"What about the arrow-like symbol?" I glance over to the other door.

"I'm sorry, I don't know that one." Feliks removes his pince-nez.

The ground judders, like it did when the crevice opened in the woodland. My eyes widen in panic and I look around, half expecting the ground to split open right here.

A boom, louder than thunder, sounds in the distance and echoes through the maze. "That was another rift opening, wasn't it?" I shudder at the thought of the ground ripping apart and even more magic storming out to Castle Mila. Whether it's Chernomor causing this quake, or *leshiye* fighting, or burrowing molelike spirits with metallic claws, or some other spirits I haven't seen yet, I need to stop this. And in a rush to do something to help, I push open the heavy door in front of me.

"Wait, Olia!" Feliks steps between me and the door. "We don't know if this is the right choice."

"But we need to hurry! I'll just take a quick look. Perhaps it will give us another clue." I peer around the door and a cold breeze whispers into my ears.

"Olia," the breeze sighs, and my skin tingles. "Olia," it says louder and I push the door open wider.

"I have a bad feeling about this." Feliks grabs the straps on my armour and tries to pull me back. "Please don't go in there. Take another moment to think about the riddle."

I hesitate, uncertain, but then *something* yanks

me forwards so sharply I stumble through the doorway. I gasp at the sight of a mound of gold coins ahead, as tall as one of the apple trees in the grove. A thrill gusts through me, so fast and strong that it blows away all my uncertainties, and I walk towards the mound.

I hear the others calling for me, but they sound far away.

"*Gold,*" the breeze whispers, louder than any of them. "*Gold, to save your castle.*" I pick up speed, even though I know in my heart gold isn't the answer to saving my home. Cold, sharp fear digs into my chest as I realize too late it's some kind of magic pulling me on. I made a mistake opening the door, and now I'm not in control of my actions.

"*Gold,*" the breeze whispers again and I step onto the mound of coins. Each coin has a head engraved on it, bald and wide-eyed, like a skull. All the coin heads open their mouths in unison and sing to me, "*Gold, to polish and shine! Gold, to make everything fine!*"

I stare down at the singing coins in horror. My stomach flips and I groan with the effort of trying to stop my legs from carrying me onwards, towards the top of the mound.

"Olia! Stop!" I hear Feliks's soft, growling voice again, Cascadia's bubbling call, Dub's deep sonorous tones and Koshka's urgent yowls. They all sound so far away and I can't turn my head to look for them, though my heart is urging me to. I want to return to my new friends, who have been helping me on this journey, but my body won't cooperate. Tears of frustration sting my eyes as I begin to feel more and more helpless and alone.

My hand reaches for a coin on the top of the mound. It's bigger than the others and the head engraved on it wears a tall, spiky crown, like the leaves of a pineapple. "*Goooooold!*" the coin-head sings in a resounding, operatic voice, its mouth wide open. My fingertips touch the coin's shining surface. Then there is an icy gust of wind and everything goes dark.

"Run!" Koshka meows from far away. "Hide!" But before I can do anything, thick, heavy fabric falls over me and tightens around my body.

CHAPTER TWENTY-THREE

THE IMMORTAL CLOAK

The heavy fabric wraps around me so closely that it completely blocks my vision and I struggle to breathe. I feel myself being lifted into the air, then spun, faster and faster. Air rushes around me like a whirlwind. I try to scream and call for help but my voice is muffled by the endless folds of fabric.

My heart bolts and I try to wrestle free, but my arms are pinned tight to my sides. I hurtle along so fast my head pounds. Then I land with a thud on a cold, hard floor and the fabric flutters away.

I open my eyes, but it's darker than the most hidden staircase in Castle Mila. I can't even see my hands in front of me. But I know that I'm not in the maze any more. The air feels different – thinner, and so cold it prickles against my skin. All is silent, grim and threatening.

"Hello?" I whisper and my voice echoes back to me, reedy and scared. Tears well in my eyes. I shouldn't have opened that door. We hadn't solved the riddle properly, or figured out what the symbol on the other door meant. If only I'd taken longer to think about it instead of rushing foolishly ahead.

Something light and soft brushes against one of my hands and I scramble away from it in horror, until my back is pressed hard against a cold stone wall. I peer into the darkness, my heart knocking like the woodpeckers who nest near the east side of the castle.

Slowly my eyes adjust, and I make out folds of fabric hovering in front of me. It's a cloak, floating in the air, moving on its own. It must be the Immortal Cloak – the one that Cascadia warned me about. A corner of fabric extends towards me, rumpled into a vague handlike shape. But I clench my fists, draw them against my chest and shake my head. Cascadia said the Immortal Cloak kept three *rusalki* prisoner for decades. I must get away from the cloak and escape this place. I don't have time to be trapped! I have to save the castle and this land, before it's too late.

The cloak spins around and points into the darkness. Behind it, I see the treasure – the same huge mound of singing gold coins that was in the maze is now here, in this stone room. The cloak flies over my head and something floats down into my lap. I flinch as it lands, but it's only a cloth – a small, silky cloth, like the one my parents use to polish their wedding rings on their anniversary.

"Polish us. Make us shine," the coins whisper and the cloak rises, circles around the treasure, then spins and vanishes in a rush of air. I stare after it, my anger bursting like a touch-me-not seed pod exploding. I have more important and urgent things to do than polish whispering coins for a living cloak. I screw the cloth up and throw it onto the treasure mound. I need to find a way out of this room, and quickly.

The darkness makes it difficult to see, so I feel my way around, moving my hands over the stone walls and floor, searching for any openings, like I do when I'm looking for a secret door to one of Castle Mila's unexplored domes. But there is only smooth, unbroken stone. The coins whisper, louder and louder, over and over. "*Polish us. Make us shine. Gold, to make everything fine.*" Frustration and fear make my movements sharp and shaky. I'm trapped here in the dark, and time is running out.

I want to go home; have Babusya pull me into one of her bony, awkward, walking-stick-filled hugs, cuddle Mama, feel Papa's warm arm around me, and cradle little Rosa in my own arms. Every part of me aches with love and longing.

I sit down and focus on taking a slow breath in, like Luka does when he gets anxious. Getting upset isn't going to help. I slide my hand into my pocket, stroke the patch I made for comfort, and remind myself what I do have, hoping that will help me come up with an idea to escape. Besides my pyjamas and the cardigan Babusya knitted me, I have the *rusalka* armour and helmet, and the faded key back to Castle Mila.

I dig deeper into my pocket and my fingers close around the letter Babusya wrote me, and the green glass vial. It's empty, but staring at it fills me with purpose. I want to return home with the vial full of the waters of life Babusya asked for. And I need to return home having saved both the castle and this land. I made a mistake taking that door, but there is no time to dwell on it. Babusya said everyone makes mistakes. Now I must find a way to fix it.

I put my hand into my other pocket and pull out the floppy velvet hat. The lining inside shimmers with magic. I wish I could tell Babusya that I *see* it now. A smile grows on my face as I remember I can do more than see magic – I can *use* it. I did before. I folded the key to get into this land, and I unfolded Koshka's chain to free her. I can do it again. I can unfold these walls to free myself. I close my eyes, place one hand on the cold stone and keep my other hand on the hat.

The stone beneath my fingers warms and vibrates. I feel the magic that made it swirling and rising up through my arms, across my chest, then flooding down into the hat like a waterfall. The wall shivers and a few pieces of stone drop to the floor with a *plink-plunk*.

I close my eyes tighter and imagine the wall breaking apart, turning into glowing energy and zooming into the hat like a magical wind. Energy surges through me and I gasp as if I've been thrown into water. The wall shakes, harder and faster, until finally the stone splits beneath my hand with a loud *CRACK!*

A trickle of cold air from the other side of the wall brushes against my fingers and hope streaks through me. I open my eyes and yell at the wall, as loud as I can. "Break! Open! Let me OUT!" The room convulses, jolts, then the split in the stone beneath my hand is rent wide open. I stumble back as icy air and bright light flood in.

A domed blue sky is all around and I take another step back as I realize that I'm stood on the edge of a sheer drop. The opening in the wall leads outside, but this room is so high up, I can't even see the ground below. The sun is a distant upside-down crescent, frowning at me.

My heart plummets as I remember Cascadia telling me that the Immortal Cloak lives in a floating tower in Air Dome. So even though I've broken free of the room, I'm still trapped, high above the ground. Dread crashes over me as I realize I don't even know if there *is* a ground here and that I'm in a completely different dome from my friends, with no one to ask for help.

My head aches as I try to work out what to do. Awful plans swirl in my mind – like attempting to descend the sheer walls of the tower, or unpicking my cardigan to make a rope. I can't think of a single safe plan, and I clutch the hat, desperately trying to work out how I might use its magic to help me now.

Panic spurs my heart. While I'm trapped here, helpless, time is ticking, the land is breaking, the storm is raging, my castle is falling, and I don't know where my family and friends are, or if they're even safe.

I stare into the sky until my vision blurs, searching frantically for a way to get down from this floating tower so I can get back to trying to save two worlds. And that's when I see something large and dark hurtling towards me. The Immortal Cloak has returned... My heart leaps into my throat.

CHAPTER TWENTY-FOUR

TEFFI

The dark thing flying towards me draws closer and I back away into the room. But, as I look, I see that it's a creature, not the cloak. Feathered, with two wings open wide to catch the wind and four long, slim legs that are galloping so fast they're almost a blur. It's an enormous black horse, soaring swiftly through the sky.

Every time a hoof descends there is a burst of sound, as if the air is being thumped away. The horse lifts its head and makes a loud braying noise. My muscles tighten with fear until I spot the familiar shape of Feliks standing on the horse's back. His orange moustache and beard are trailing in the wind.

"Feliks!" I shout. A smile beams across my face at

the sight of my friend and I realize this is my way to escape.

"Hurry!" he shouts back. "There is no time to waste!"

The horse slows, then hovers steadily in front of me, its wings curved in two arcs, its legs still beating the sky. Feliks beckons me again with a wave and I stare at the horse's back, which is covered in black feathers. I'll have to jump over a sheer, endless drop to reach it. I take a breath to fill myself with courage, aim carefully, then leap.

Feliks grabs my hands and pulls me safely onto the horse's back. I collapse down, my legs bent either side of the horse above its wings, and clutch its feathered neck, which is as soft as Rosa's curls. My heart thunders. I've never ridden a horse before, let alone a flying one.

The horse lifts its wings high, then sweeps them down, and beats its legs faster. It rises, then banks and swoops away. I sit up and stare at the tower I was trapped in: an enormous blue cylinder, almost the same colour as the sky, somehow floating impossibly

in the air. I try to ask Feliks how he knew where to find me and rode here on a flying horse. But the thump of the horse's hooves on the sky and the wind rushing past whip my words away.

The horse circles down through damp, cold air until we pass through an ear-popping, vision-blurring boundary, and emerge into the sky of Earth Dome. The multicoloured woodland is far below, Chernomor's bright red fortress rising from the centre of it, surrounded by the dark-green maze.

"Brace for landing!" Feliks yells. The horse lowers its head and folds its wings into its body, and we zoom down, faster than I slide down the bannisters of the castle, before landing with a clatter of hooves on stone. We're back in the courtyard where I opened the wrong door. My face flushes at the thought of my mistake and the time it's cost us.

"You're safe!" Cascadia splashes her arms around me as I slide off the horse's back.

Dub grins widely as he gently touches my shoulder with a branch-finger. "We were worried about you."

Koshka looks up at me, her eyes wide with a

mixture of relief and concern. "While you've been gone, we've heard several more rifts opening, and felt the ground shaking and shifting."

Worries crowd around me and tangle with my shame and guilt, until I feel like I'm being suffocated by the Immortal Cloak again. "I'm sorry. I shouldn't have opened that door. If it wasn't for Feliks, and the horse…" I turn to thank them.

"This is Teffi." Feliks leaps off the horse's neck. "She's one of a flock of flying horses that live with a Yaga, a type of witch, at the edge of Earth Dome."

Teffi lowers her soft, downy face to Feliks and he strokes her snout gently, murmuring something that I don't understand in a quiet, whickering voice.

"When we saw the Immortal Cloak take you, I knew you'd be imprisoned in the floating tower." Cascadia's waters whirl with anger. "We didn't know what to do, so Koshka and I listed all the flying spirits we could think of who might help."

"As soon as they mentioned flying horses, I knew what I had to do." Feliks expands a wrinkled apple from his coat pocket and offers it to Teffi. "One of my cousins is a stable spirit. He taught me to speak horse, so I called out, and Teffi came."

"Could Teffi fly us over the last bit of the maze, so we get to the fortress sooner?" I ask hopefully.

Koshka frowns and shakes her head. "The outside of Chernomor's fortress is locked up tight with magic. The only way in is through the underground tunnels of the maze. But once you've cut off Chernomor's beard, his magic will fade. Then we can escape through the fortress doors."

Teffi whinnies something to Feliks and he nods. "Teffi says she'll return with her flock and meet us in the gardens outside Chernomor's fortress so we can make a quick getaway after we've faced him."

"Thank you, Teffi." My voice wobbles as I grapple with the realization that we'll have to escape rapidly from an evil wizard, who is likely to be extremely angry with us. I've been clutching onto the idea that Chernomor will be asleep when we find him but as we draw closer to his fortress, I'm going to have to prepare myself for the fact that he might be awake. "What time is it, Feliks?" I ask, wondering how long is left before I have to confront the wizard once and for all – someone so terrible, he cut off his giant brother's head. The thought of him makes my skin run as cold and clammy as the eel that got caught on our line the last time Dinara, Luka and I went fishing.

Feliks expands a large, dark-wood pendulum clock from his pocket. Leaping over its face is a horse, mid-flight, with a rider on its back, dressed for battle. "Just after three o'clock," Feliks says, as the pendulum swings heavily back and forth on the end of a long chain.

"Less than three hours…" My stomach lurches with the movement of the pendulum, which seems to speed up with every swing. It doesn't make sense, just like time doesn't make sense in this place. It's slipping away from me, too fast.

"We can't be far from the fortress – we can do this." Cascadia rushes over to the door on the opposite side of the courtyard.

I follow her, noticing again the symbol carved in the wood that looks like an arrow with two heads… or…it looks like how I used to draw spruce trees in chalk on the walls of my parents' workshop when I was little. "It's a tree!" I exclaim, realizing that could be the answer to the riddle too. *"Sunshine stores with soundless rings.* The solution could be a tree, couldn't it – 'rings' could mean the growth rings in the trunk? And that symbol looks like a tree."

"I should have got that." Dub groans. "I'm not very clever."

"Of course you are." I glance back at Dub before pushing the door open. "It's just difficult to think when everything is falling apart around us."

Dub smiles as he hunches over, ready to duck through the doorway. Feliks shrinks his clock, then whispers something to Teffi. She opens her wings and beats her hooves, first against the stone floor, then against the air. She rises, neighs loudly, then gallops up and away.

"Thank you!" I shout again as she disappears into the sky. Cascadia waves, showering us all with tiny raindrops. Then I walk through the doorway into another dark-green tunnel. It's riddled with side passages, some of them huge. We're going to have to stay alert so we don't veer off course.

The tunnel splits into two ahead and I'm not sure which way to go until I spot the tree symbol again, carved above the right fork. "This way," I say, peering into the darkness, hoping there isn't anything down there that might snatch me away like the Immortal Cloak did. I guess somewhere, at the end of this tunnel, we'll need to solve the final line of the riddle to reach Chernomor's fortress. "I can do this," I whisper to myself. "For Rosa, and my family and friends."

"And for our castle." Feliks glances up at me and his moustache curls into a wave.

"For my mother!" Cascadia bubbles beside me. "And Lake Mila!"

"For all the spirits in the land." Dub's deep voice echoes along the tunnel.

"For some peace and quiet." Koshka flicks her tail in irritation.

"For home," I say a little louder, thinking that is what links us all: a desire to protect and return to the things that make us feel safe and complete.

We walk together, deeper into the maze. Thoughts

buzz in my mind like a swarm of hoverflies, and I try to make them settle. I remember what I said to Feliks after I got the Giant's Sword: that I thought someone bigger, braver and stronger should be doing this. And I remember Koshka telling me that I'm the *only* person who can use the blade.

I'm relieved and glad to be back with my new friends, but this also feels like something that I alone am responsible for doing. Two worlds depend on me being strong and brave and good enough. But inside, I feel as unsteady and uncertain as the floorboards in Sun Dome that broke and fell away beneath me.

Babusya enters my thoughts, with her twinkling eyes and huge white hair, telling me that if I believe I can do it, then I will. I look down at Feliks, who is trotting alongside me as a fox, and remember him telling me that belief is one of the few things more powerful than magic. And I think to defeat Chernomor maybe I must be more than strong and brave. I must believe in myself too.

CHAPTER TWENTY-FIVE

VILY

We move as fast as we can along the tunnel, past side passages that hiss and whisper and growl. When the tunnel splits, we find tiny tree symbols to guide us. Without the riddle giving us a shortcut we'd be wandering, hopelessly lost in here, until the land fell apart around us.

The floor dips steeply and water drips from the ceiling – big, fat drops that make me shudder when they land on my skin. Cascadia loves them. She gathers them up and sighs with satisfaction as they sink into her body.

A rumble in the distance makes the walls vibrate, sending more water droplets raining down, and the thought of another crack opening up in the land makes me burst into a run. A circle of light appears ahead and I decide to sprint towards it, imagining that I'm racing along the corridors of Castle Mila during the morning chase, to distract me from the trembling.

I emerge into a second courtyard, larger than the last one and sunk deeper into the ground. The others are close behind me. Five arched tunnel openings lie ahead, each one with a runic symbol above it. This must be where we solve the final part of the riddle. At the thought of Chernomor fear storms through my body, but spinning amongst it are feathery seeds of hope that soon this will all be over and I'll be able to return to my family.

Feliks puts on his pince-nez to examine the symbols.

"*A voiceless path that always sings,*" Dub recites as he stretches to his full height. He tilts his head at the runic symbols, then offers his hand to lift us up towards them.

"Thanks, Dub." I clamber onto his palm next to Feliks and Cascadia, and he sweeps us up to the symbols. The one on the left looks like waves on an ocean. The next one is bumpy, like a fluffy cloud.

Then there is a zigzag line, followed by two upright wavy lines, and finally two horizontal flat lines.

"They all look watery." I move my fingers over the symbols. "An ocean...a cloud..."

"I believe you're right." Feliks points at the zigzag line. "I think this one represents ice."

"*A voiceless path that always sings*," Dub repeats, his face deeply wrinkled in thought. "Do you think the answer might be a river?" he asks timidly.

"Oh! It could be." I smile, feeling in my heart that Dub is right. "Yes, I believe it is."

Cascadia nods, and Koshka mewls in agreement from the floor.

Dub's mouth curves into the widest smile I've ever seen on his face, his leaves rustle with pride and the berries around his face blush redder.

I look at the two remaining symbols – two upright wavy lines and two horizontal flat lines. "Either of these could represent a river." I turn to Feliks again. "What do you think?"

"I'm not sure." Feliks adjusts his pince-nez, so they're closer to his eyes.

"Maybe we should split up to take a look down both tunnels," Cascadia suggests.

"No, we should stick together," I say, thinking about what happened the last time I made the wrong choice. "What do you think, Koshka?" I call down to her. "Which symbol do you think is a river?"

"I don't know." Koshka paces back and forth between the two tunnel entrances, her tail whipping around.

"What about you, Olia? What do you think?" Feliks asks and I stare at the symbols.

"I think the upright wavy lines represent a river, and the horizontal ones a lake," I say finally, "but I'm guessing." I frown, wishing I could feel more certain.

The walls and the floor of the maze shake. Dub lurches sideways, almost dropping us, but manages to regain his balance and lower us safely to the floor.

Koshka bounds towards the tunnel with the upright wavy lines above it. "Come on, let's see if you're right."

"But I could be wrong," I protest. "Going into that tunnel could be another massive mistake." Even though the ground has stopped shaking, my legs still feel wobbly and doubts are jumping like frogs in my stomach.

Feliks removes his pince-nez and looks up at me. "Why do you think that symbol is the river?" he asks.

"I think the wavy lines show a river's movement, and the flat lines the stillness of a lake. In my heart, I feel that's right. But how can I be sure?" I pull Chernomor's hat out of my pocket. "Maybe I can use this?" I turn to Koshka. "How can I use the hat's magic to find out if I'm right?"

"You can't." Koshka shakes her head. "The hat can only be used for folding and unfolding magic."

A groan rises in my throat. "Then I don't know what to do."

"If you feel that's the right tunnel..." Feliks taps his chest, over his heart. "Then I'm happy to follow you in there."

Cascadia and Dub echo an agreement.

"But what if I'm wrong?" I say again.

"Then we'll face it together." Feliks beckons me towards the tunnel as the maze quivers around us. His faith and friendship make me feel like I'm wrapped in the family blanket.

I look up at the symbols once more, then take a step into the tunnel. There is no whoosh of ominous, icy air. No whispering winds or singing coins and no dark cloak falls over me. I sigh with relief. "All right, let's go this way," I say more confidently.

Feliks pads by my side as a fox, Koshka creeps close to my ankles, Cascadia follows us, and Dub ducks into the tunnel last. As his branches block out the light from the courtyard, something small and sharp pricks into my neck. I yelp in shock.

I lift my hand to my neck and feel something sticking out of my skin, about as big as a needle. I pull it out, wincing at the pain, and stare at a tiny silver arrow with a drop of my own blood on its tip.

Before I have a chance to say anything, hundreds more tiny arrows zoom out of the darkness. Most ping off my armour and helmet, but a few of them pierce the backs of my hands, which I've lifted to shield my face. Another arrow hits my neck, and several tear through my pyjama trousers and stick into my knees and thighs.

"Ouch!" I yell. "Stop!" I try to turn away from the

arrows, but they're flying from every direction. Feliks is batting them away as if they're mosquitoes.

"It's the *vily*. They're attacking us!" Dub creaks as he backs off. Koshka takes cover behind my legs, and Cascadia crouches beneath a bubble shield.

"Stop!" I yell again, as another tiny arrow pierces my hand. "We're not here to fight, we only want to get to Chernomor's fortress."

Another barrage of arrows blasts into me and I duck, trying to make myself a smaller target.

"Find another way!" A high-pitched voice echoes out of the darkness ahead. "You're not coming past our pool. It's for *vily* only."

Feliks steps in front of me, holds up his hands and speaks in a language I don't understand. His voice is high-pitched, like that of the *vila* who spoke to us, and his words are melodic. I stare at him in shock, before remembering Feliks said Mora's grandmother was a *vila*. He must have learned some of their language from her.

The attack stops, then out of the darkness hundreds of tiny winged spirits emerge. They're about as big as sparrows, human-like, but with sharp-toothed smiles and glowing, yellow eyes. Every one of them is carrying a tiny bow loaded with an arrow, poised to attack.

Then another spirit emerges, much bigger than the *vily*, who looks something like an old woman and something like a shrew. She stands taller than Feliks, but shorter than me, and has silky, black fur, rounded ears on the top of her head, and a pointed snout with whiskers extending on either side. She's wearing a long rust-coloured coat that looks similar to Feliks's, and a smooth tail escapes from beneath it. "Feliks!" An enormous smile spreads across her snout and Feliks rushes forwards.

"Mora! My Mora!" Feliks sings, leaping onto Mora and wrapping himself around her in a huge furry hug. "Finally, I've found you!"

My heart swells as I realize that this is Mora, Feliks's wife, and finally they're together, after five hundred years apart. Tears pool in my eyes, out of happiness for them, but also with longing for my own family too.

CHAPTER TWENTY-SIX

MORA

"I never thought I'd see you again." Mora squeezes Feliks so tightly he gasps for air. She strokes the fur on his cheeks and tears well in her round, black eyes.

Feliks's tail wraps around Mora's and he smiles so wide his moustache almost touches his ears. "I knew I'd find you, but I didn't think it would take so long. I've been searching for a way into this land for five hundred years. If it wasn't for Olia..." Feliks turns to me. "She found Chernomor's hat and used it to unlock the door, but we don't have long here."

"The land is breaking apart and our castle is being destroyed by fierce winds." I try to keep my voice even, but the worry for my family, somewhere in the middle of the storm, has grown from a wriggly caterpillar to a quake of huge moths.

"How long do we have?" Mora's whiskers twitch and her eyes widen with fear.

From his pocket, Feliks expands a heart-shaped clock that ticks with a beating sound, and his face becomes sombre. "Four o'clock. Only two hours left."

Another rumble shakes the tunnel walls and the *vily*'s wings flutter faster as they flit around in panic.

"We need to go." I step forwards and stand as tall and strong as I can. "Koshka believes that slicing away Chernomor's magic will save the land and stop the storm." I frown as I hear myself say "Koshka believes" and I try to work out what I truly believe. Is it really Chernomor causing all the devastation? Doubts about Koshka's plan are squirming inside me. I've seen Chernomor's threads filling the growing cracks in this land, but will cutting off his beard really fix it all? And even if it does, won't his magic just grow back again?

My frown deepens as I think of the crevice we saw, and of the magic surging into my own world. I do believe Koshka wants to stop the destruction, and she understands this land better than me. She's also helped keep me safe so far. No matter what angle I look at it from I can't seem to figure out another explanation. It tugs at me though, like one of Castle Mila's roof domes that I can't find a way into.

The *vily* chatter in their high-pitched voices and lower their bows and arrows. "We'll help you get to Chernomor." Mora beckons us with a lift of her snout and a twitch of her ears. "This way." She keeps hold of Feliks's hand, and their tails remain entwined as she leads us deeper into the tunnel. The *vily* follow, fluttering around me, Koshka, Cascadia and Dub. They seem to like Dub especially, and many of them fly down to sit amongst his branches and leaves.

I pick the tiny arrows out of my hands, legs and arms as I walk. They scratch like thorns and are as sticky as the goosegrass burrs that latch onto my clothes when I walk between the spruce grove and the lake at home, clinging to my fingers when I try to flick them away.

"Sorry about the attack. The *vily* are very defensive of the pool." Mora glances back at me apologetically.

"Especially since these shocks have been shaking the tunnels. The water level has decreased, and we've all been very worried about the blood flowers. Look." Mora points ahead, to where the tunnel widens into a large spherical cave.

A pool of water lies in the centre of it, so dark and still it looks like a mirror reflecting a starless night. A sudden heaviness falls over me. I feel my eyelids drooping and fight an urge to sink down to the floor to rest. Forcing my eyes to open wide I stare at the clusters of small blood-red flowers that are glistening as they float at the edges of the pool.

It's all beautiful, but so eerie that goosebumps rise on my flesh. Mora dips her smooth pawlike hand into the water, lifts a tube-shaped blossom and shows it to us. "These are blood flowers. They usually glow much brighter and are more swollen with nectar."

"That water gives me the shivers." Ripples roll through Cascadia's body as she looks into the pool. "Apart from the flowers, there's nothing alive in it. And it's too quiet. Water should be noisy." She splashes her hands together.

"The waters of death are always quiet and still." Mora leans down to place the blood flower back into the pool.

"May I take a small amount of this water for the giant Golov, please?" I ask. "I promised I would try to get some of the waters of death and some of the waters of life, to reunite his head with his body. In exchange he's going to fix our key home – we can't get back without it."

Mora uses the blood flower in her hand to scoop up a little of the water. She seals the tube-shaped blossom by pressing the edges together, then passes it to me.

I hesitate for a moment and Mora smiles reassuringly. "Neither the water nor the flower will harm you. The waters of death are only dangerous if you drink them. And as a balm, they only have healing properties. A few drops will seal Golov's head back onto his body. I'll show you where the waters of life are too."

I take the flower and follow Mora to a far edge of the cave, where a short, stocky well is set into the floor. I lean over it and hear water rushing far below. A fresh, cool breeze rises from the opening, whipping away the sleepiness that came over me at the pool of the waters of death.

"That's more like it!" Cascadia holds her hands over the well and strokes her fingers through the fine mist dancing in the air.

"I have a vial." I pull the one Babusya gave me out of my pocket. "Would I be able to get enough for two people?"

A *vila* flies out of Dub's branches, sweeps the green glass vial from my fingers and swoops down into the well. She emerges a moment later with it full of glowing water and passes it to me. "Thank you." I smile, thinking of how I can keep my promise to Golov, get the key fixed, and give some of the water to Babusya for her rheumatism too. But first, I must face Chernomor. I gulp back the fears rising from my stomach. "Where do we get into the fortress?" I ask.

"This way." Mora leads us into a low, wide tunnel. It slopes steeply upwards and ends abruptly with a trapdoor in the roof, which reminds me of the one into Astronomer's Dome. The air seems to thicken uncomfortably as I wonder if that dome still exists or if it has fallen in the storm. "This is a secret hatch that leads straight into the fortress. Chernomor won't be expecting anyone to come through here, so we have a good chance of sneaking up on him." Mora pulls the trapdoor down and masses of silver threads tumble from it. As they mound onto the floor, the task ahead of me seems to grow larger and more formidable.

"I'll never fit through there," Dub groans. He's already struggling to fit into the tunnel. His head is pressed against his chest, his arms and legs are bent awkwardly and his leaves are squashed against the walls.

"There is another way up into the fortress gardens, although you can't get into the fortress from there because Chernomor has sealed the main doors shut with his magic." Mora looks up at Dub. "The *vily* could show you the way though, and we could meet you there once Olia has removed the wizard's power."

"All of you could go with the *vily*. I don't want to put any of you in danger." I glance round at my friends, trying to gather all the bravery I have. "I can face Chernomor alone and meet you afterwards."

"I'm coming with you." Feliks gives me a stern look that reminds me of Babusya.

"And me." Mora squeezes Feliks's hand tighter. "I don't want to leave Feliks ever again. And I have a special skill that might be helpful."

"I'm coming too." Cascadia smiles, and a whirligig beetle whizzes over her pearly teeth.

"And I'm staying with you." Koshka steps closer to me, and curves her whole body round my ankle.

Gratitude for my new friends warms me, like one of Papa's secret spice sachets added to milk. But I'm still scared and full of uncertainties. I've never faced an evil wizard before and I have no idea what to expect.

I don't even remember using magic before today and now I need to defeat the most powerful spirit in this land. *What if I'm not able to cut off his beard? What then?* I can't even face the possibility.

Dub's bark brow rumples with concern. "Are you all right, Olia?"

"I will be, once I've done this and I can go home."
My voice wavers.

Dub leans close to me and whispers softly, "It's all right to feel scared." He holds out one of his long branch-fingers and I take it and squeeze gently, glad of something to stop me shaking. "Fear helps keep us safe. It doesn't mean you won't succeed."

I lean into Dub and hug his whole arm. His leaves rustle around me. If I close my eyes, I could almost be in a tree in the grove back home. "Thanks, Dub," I say, realizing he's right. I can't get rid of my fears, but I can fight past them. And I must, for everyone I love, new friends and old.

"Thank you for doing this," Dub replies. "And once you have...when you go home afterwards..." Dub pauses and the berries around his face blush. "Can I come back with you? My father lives in the spruce grove near Castle Mila, and I haven't seen him for five hundred years. I miss him, and I miss our home. I don't want to stay in this land, spending all my time being thrown out of the woodland by Vysok, sneaking back in, and being thrown out again..."

"You can't," Koshka snaps and I stare at her in shock.

"Why not?" I ask. "If Dub doesn't want to stay in this land, he should be free to leave."

"And me." A wave rolls through Cascadia and she swells taller. "I want to go home and be with my mother in Lake Mila."

"And Mora is coming home," Feliks says with a resolute growl. "And the *vily* too."

Mora nods. "The *vily* want to return to the spruce grove like Dub, and I want to live with Feliks again."

"We have to help everyone get home," I say. "I've missed my family so much today, I can't imagine how awful it must feel to be separated for five hundred years."

"No one can go back through the doorway except you and Feliks." Koshka lifts her head obstinately. "Everyone else's magic has linked together and become a part of this land and if they leave they'll tear it apart. You've seen the cracks and what the winds are doing to Castle Mila as the magic escapes. Well imagine those winds a thousand-fold more powerful." Koshka's eyes blaze yet they make me feel cold. "Any spirits

246

leaving this land would release a tempest of magic, destroying the land and the castle for ever. So we all have to stay here."

"Why didn't you tell us any of this before – like when Cascadia said she wanted to return home to her mother?" Anger lashes into my words and my doubts about Koshka's plan widen like a crevice in a quake. *If everything is linked, how can I be sure it's only Chernomor's magic that is destroying the land? And if my friends here can't leave, what will happen to them now?*

"I said Cascadia couldn't go home but you were all too busy making friends to listen to me," Koshka says bitterly. "Besides, there was no time for explanations. And there isn't time now. We must focus on the immediate danger, which is this land being wrenched apart."

A deafening crack sounds right above our heads, and fragments of the tunnel roof rain down. Most are gravel-sized, but I flinch away from a chunk as big as my hand, and my heart vaults into my throat. Koshka is right: we have to stop this devastation and save everyone's lives before anything else.

"Quickly." Koshka leaps through the trapdoor above us. "We must find Chernomor immediately."

I feel like the meadow grass flattened by the storm as I look from Dub to Cascadia to Mora. "I have to help you get home but…" My words dissolve on my tongue because right now I can't think how to.

"Don't worry, Olia. Focus on facing Chernomor and saving the land. That's more important than anything else right now. Hundreds of spirits live here, and you must think of your own family too." Dub smiles, but his leaves rustle sadly, and one of them falls to the floor.

"I *will* get you home," I say firmly, hugging his arm once more. "I'll cut off Chernomor's beard, then I'll find a way. You'll meet us in the fortress gardens?"

Dub nods and I turn and clamber up through the trapdoor after Koshka, trying to ignore my clashing emotions and concentrate on what I must do next. Nobody can go home until our worlds are safe, so I prepare myself to face the evil wizard who is tearing everything apart.

CHAPTER TWENTY-SEVEN

THE FORTRESS

I emerge through the trapdoor into an enormous square hall, wider and taller than the Great Hall of Castle Mila. Koshka is waiting for me, her tail flicking impatiently. My heart drums as I gaze at the walls, the floor and the ceiling. They are bright red beneath a web of silver threads. Cracks are everywhere, brimming with Chernomor's glowing magic. *Why would he break apart his own fortress?*

Feliks and Mora leap up beside me, as a fox and an oversized shrew, then shift into their more human-like forms. Cascadia splashes up like a wave. I hear Dub in the tunnel below, creaking as he moves away, and the *vily* fluttering and chattering amongst his branches.

"That way." Mora points to a doorway almost blocked by a silver tangle on the other side of the hall, and we walk towards it. Threads are mounded around us in the ghostly shapes of chairs and tables, and they shroud the tall rectangular windows, so the room is filled with an ethereal, silvery light. "Chernomor lives alone and has been asleep in his bedchamber for a hundred years at least," Mora whispers.

I bite my lip nervously. If Chernomor stays asleep, then I think I can do this… "May I have the sword?" I ask Feliks.

Feliks expands the sword and passes it to me. The weight of it makes my feet sink deep into the matted threads on the floor. I feel their magic pulsating, even through my boots. We reach the doorway and I slide the blade from its sheath and swish it through the thick tangle blocking our path. The threads shrivel away from the blade, revealing a spiral staircase ahead. It, too, is covered with silver threads, which cascade down the steps like a glowing, curving waterfall.

"Chernomor's bedchamber is at the top of the stairs," Mora says, her whiskers twitching nervously.

I lead the way up, cutting back more threads as I go to make it easier for us all to walk. It's satisfying at first, watching them sizzle away, but further up the stairs the threads seem to increase in power and soon my arm is aching from moving the heavy sword back and forth. And the higher we climb, the faster the threads grow back when I cut them.

I keep hold of the sword, but give up swinging it, and clamber awkwardly up the last few stairs, my feet getting caught in the glowing silver tangle. Cascadia struggles as her watery feet get trapped amongst the threads, and Koshka, Feliks and Mora all falter with every step.

It's a battle to reach the top of the stairs. And when we get there, I hesitate. There's a red door in front of us, almost completely webbed over with threads, and a low, soft snoring rises and falls behind it.

Koshka steps next to me. "If you're quiet, he probably won't even wake." She nudges me on.

Feliks looks up at me, his ears tilted forwards. "You can do this, Olia."

"I can do this," I whisper back, thinking about my

251

family surrounded by the storm. I don't know what lies behind this door or what Chernomor is really like, but I must find out. I lift the sword high and slice down through the threads covering the door. A large gold handle is revealed and I grip it before the threads grow back. With a deep breath I push the door open. It moves slowly, and only with a great deal of effort, because silver threads are piled up behind it in huge hummocks.

I creep inside, wobbling over the threads. The room is so tangled with them it takes me a while to spot Chernomor. He's a tiny, thin and ancient man,

not much bigger than Feliks, wearing a golden robe and hat and lying on an enormous bed. Long, silver hair flows from his head, his eyebrows, his cheeks and chin. It tumbles off the bed and transforms into the glowing threads that fill the space and escape down the stairs to cover the whole of the land. *How can someone so small and frail be causing so much devastation?*

Chernomor's closed eyes are set deep in a pale, wrinkled face. His nose and mouth are almost hidden behind his beard and moustache. His fingers, poking out from beneath his golden sleeves, look weak and brittle. It seems inconceivable that he's the brother of a giant, and could have injured Golov in the way that he did.

Koshka nudges me again and my mouth goes dry as I step closer. My feet sink deeper into the thick mass of threads and I reel, unsteady. The sword slips in my hand and I try to grip it tighter, but my palms are sweating. The sword falls again and its tip sizzles through threads and clinks against a tiled floor beneath.

Chernomor groans and stirs in his sleep.

"Do it now," Koshka urges from behind me, "cut off his beard."

I lift the sword with both hands, hold it steady, then slide it gently between Chernomor's chest and his beard. All I have to do is slice upwards, and Chernomor's beard will be severed. Koshka says that will make this land and my home safe. I could do it. Chernomor is asleep, there is no fear stopping me. But Babusya's note is buzzing in my mind again: *Remember to look from all angles, see with your heart and believe in yourself,* she wrote. And when we were in the grove, she said things depend on how you look at them and where you're standing. *What if I'm missing something?*

I remember the crevice that opened when Dub was thrown to the ground, and how Chernomor's magic webbed across it and filled the gap. And when I first used the sword to cut through the threads blocking the entrance to the maze, the archway trembled and I thought I had made it unstable. An avalanche of doubts tumbles through me, like a roof dome falling, and I stop still. "What if this is a mistake?" I whisper.

"It's not," Koshka hisses. "You must cut off his beard to remove his magic. You've seen how his threads are tearing the land apart."

I pull my shoulders back, trying to gather the courage I need to say what *I* think and believe. I feel so unsure of myself that it takes more bravery to speak up than it would to cut off Chernomor's beard. "His threads are all over the land," I say finally, "but we don't know for certain it's them tearing everything apart. And you said everyone's magic has linked together here, Koshka, so I don't know what all the consequences of doing this might be."

I think back to when the thread trailing from the family blanket caught on my fingernail this morning, and the blanket started to unravel. "It's like we're all part of a patchwork," I continue, "and I worry that if I slice through some threads, or cut away a piece, the whole thing might fall apart." I look around for Feliks. He's stood behind me, his ears and whiskers twitching nervously. "I'm just not sure this is the right thing to do."

Feliks stops fidgeting and taps his fingers over his chest. He's reminding me to see and think with my heart. I close my eyes and try to still my thoughts. My mind isn't making sense of this plan.

There is so much at stake – my family and friends, our castle, my way home, this whole land. And there is also the freedom of Cascadia, Dub, Mora, the *vily* and the other spirits too. All of us linked, our futures depending on this moment.

If I cut off Chernomor's beard, the spirits here will still be trapped and his magic will just grow back. I feel like I'm trying to solve a puzzle with Papa, but we don't have all the clues. "There must be another solution," I whisper.

"Olia, listen to me." Koshka curls around my ankle. "You must do this. It's the only way."

I open my eyes again and frown. I'm stood holding a blade over a tiny, sleeping old man. Tears well in my eyes. "I'm sorry. I can't. In my heart, I believe this is wrong."

"Olia, you *must*!" Koshka hisses again, louder. "This is your one chance to save everything." Her tail is thrashing back and forth and she shoves me forwards with her head. I stumble slightly, my hand wobbles, and the sword slips and bumps against Chernomor's chest. And his eyes pop open.

CHAPTER TWENTY-EIGHT

CHERNOMOR

Chernomor's silver eyes widen. The threads around him glow brighter and fly upwards, straight towards me. Some wrap around my hand and try to wrench the sword from my grasp. The fine strands cut into my skin and I yell in pain, but squeeze the sword tighter, not wanting to lose it.

Thousands of threads circle my body and close over my armour. I feel myself lifting off the floor and struggle to break free, but more strands gather around me, crushing my body.

"Help!" Feliks cries behind me and I turn my head to see him pinned against a wall. He's almost completely encased in silver threads, wrapped up as if caught in a spider's web. Koshka is beside him, a yowling blur of struggling limbs within a tangle of silver. Cascadia has tried to shield herself inside a bubble, but threads have wrapped so tightly around her she isn't able to flow between them and her waters are crashing and frothing in panic.

My muscles tighten. I wish I could help my friends, but the more I try to lift the sword the more Chernomor's threads cut into my skin. I wish I'd sliced off his beard when I had the chance, but now it's too late. My gaze darts around as I frantically try to think of something I can do. Silver threads are spreading over Feliks's eyes and mouth and he's gasping for air. Koshka has stopped thrashing and her one amber eye visible through the threads is burning with desperation. Cascadia is losing her shape, and swirling smaller and smaller.

Chernomor rises slowly, lifted by the glowing strands around him. "What are you doing in my fortress?" His voice is like the crackle of lightning, and fear charges through me. He glares at Koshka, his eyes intensely bright. "You, witch! You're not welcome here. It's all because of you we're trapped in this land. You're a traitor."

"That was five hundred years ago!" I protest. "And Koshka was only trying to help the spirits, as she is now!"

One of Koshka's paws twitches uselessly against the threads tightening around her. I struggle to break free to help her, but I can't move.

Chernomor turns on Feliks. "And you, castle *domovoi*. You protect the castle that traps us all here."

Feliks tries to shift into a fox to escape, but he's stuck tight and his eyes glisten with tears.

Then, all of a sudden, a dark flash, no bigger than a sparrow, bursts from the mass of threads near Feliks's hand and slams into Chernomor's chest. Chernomor falls back with a wheezy cry and his eyes close.

"I can make him sleep, but not for long," the spirit on Chernomor's chest says in a high-pitched voice, and I realize it's Mora, only she's as tiny as a *vila* now.

The silver threads holding me relax enough for me to wriggle against them. I twist my hand around, even though it makes the threads dig deeper into my wrist. The sword in my hand sways, and I swing it right and left. It moves only a fraction at first, but the threads holding it scorch back and fall away, and then I'm able to move it more. Finally, I'm swinging the sword all around me and stepping free of the silver threads.

Feliks gasps weakly. He's completely encased in silver threads and I can't see him or Koshka or Cascadia at all.

"Olia! Cut off Chernomor's beard!" Mora cries.

My heart and my mind race. I don't know whether to rush to Feliks and my friends and cut them free, or turn to Chernomor and slice off his beard.

"Please!" Mora squeals. "Feliks can't breathe."

I'm still scared about making the wrong choice, but Chernomor has just proved how dangerous he is so I slide the sword beneath his beard again.

"Hurry!" Mora begs.

The others are still and silent and I remember how they've helped me, and saved my life. Cascadia, Koshka and Feliks all jumped forwards to defend me from Vysok. And Feliks rescued me from the floating tower. They've all helped me get safely through this land. Now I must save them.

I flick the blade up without another thought, and slice through Chernomor's beard. All the silver threads in the room crackle and shrivel back. And only a few short hairs remains on Chernomor's chin. Feliks and Koshka drop onto the floor, gasping for air. Cascadia lands with a splash, then rises, her body rippling and wavering back into shape. Relief washes over me. My friends are alive and safe again. I did it – I was strong and brave enough to cut off the evil wizard's beard!

Mora grows to her usual size, but remains sat on Chernomor's chest. He's still asleep, and now that all his threads of magic are withering back, he looks tiny and harmless.

"How did you shrink like that and make him sleep?" I ask Mora.

"*Kikimora* can make themselves smaller to creep through keyholes at night. And we can bring sleep, so we can drink nightmares. But I can't keep him like this much longer. We should leave now, before he wakes. Even though his beard is gone, he might have some magic left in him, and he won't be happy we did this."

A rumble sounds in the distance. The whole

fortress shakes and a crack in the floor widens. My heart plummets as I glance at the others. "If it was Chernomor's magic breaking the land apart, why are the quakes still happening?" All of a sudden, guilt for what I did to Chernomor bites into me. I needed to save my friends, but I wish I could have thought of another way. And I wish I knew, for sure, exactly how everything connects together.

"That was probably just an aftershock." Koshka shakes her paws free of the remaining threads. "Olia, you made the right decision. You saved everyone in this room and everyone in this land. And your castle and family will be safe now too."

I want to believe Koshka – that I've done the right thing and protected everyone I love. I look at the threads wrinkling into nothing, the last few sparks and crackles of their magic dying in the air and I wonder what my family are doing now. It must be sometime between four and five o'clock. Is the storm still raging, or could they be in the castle preparing for the feast? Perhaps that is too much to hope for after everything that has happened.

Feliks shifts between forms before settling on his human-like one and smoothing down his coat. Chernomor groans in his sleep.

"You leave first," Mora whispers. "And I'll follow."

Koshka slips out of the room, followed by Cascadia. Feliks hesitates in the doorway until Mora creeps off Chernomor's chest and joins us. I pass Feliks the sword and he shrinks it back into his pocket, then we pick up speed as we descend the stairs.

Hope blooms as I see that sunlight is flooding into the fortress through newly revealed windows as the silver threads fall away. There are beautiful, swirling patterns on the floor tiles and bright paintings of flowers on the walls.

Cascadia bubbles with delight and Koshka flows down the stairs with a purr rumbling in her chest. Feliks and Mora have their tails entwined and relieved looks on their faces. So I bury my doubts, leap onto the bannister and slide the rest of the way down like I do at home, letting my thoughts rise with this moment of success.

I have the waters of life and death for Golov, so I

can put him back together and use his ring to make the key home solid again. I've done everything except think of a way to get Cascadia, Dub, Mora and the *vily* back through the doorway. But maybe I can even do that on the way home, and still get back before the harvest moon rises in time for the feast, if it is going ahead.

"The fortress gardens are through there." Mora points to large double doors as I land at the bottom of the stairs. I rush to them and push them open.

Dub is stood in the middle of a colourful garden, smiling widely as *vily* flutter around him, weaving in and out of his branches excitedly. "All the threads have gone! I knew you would do it, Olia. And I hear hooves on the wind."

Feliks's eyes light up as we step outside and he brays loudly into the air. From somewhere high above, the flying horses bray back. "Teffi and her flock are coming." Feliks looks up at me. "They can take us to Golov, then back to the door so we can get you home quickly." He smiles, but it doesn't reach his eyes.

"We *will* find a way to bring Mora home with us." I put my hand on Feliks's shoulder and squeeze gently.

"I'm not sure how yet, but we will. Maybe Golov will be able to help? Or that magic ring he has?"

"Perhaps." Feliks doesn't sound confident.

The hoofbeats draw closer and Cascadia looks up eagerly. "I've never ridden a flying horse." She splashes her hands together with excitement.

"I'm too big and heavy to ride a flying horse." Dub creaks sadly.

I turn to Feliks. "Dub's right, isn't he? The horses won't be able to lift him."

"Don't you hear the footsteps?" Cascadia smiles.

I tilt my head and listen. As well as the rapid thunder of hooves in the air, there is a slow, rhythmic thumping that is shaking the ground. "What is that?" I ask.

"The flying horses live with a Yaga." Cascadia ripples with a mixture of excitement and nervousness. "And Yaga live in houses with chicken legs."

CHAPTER TWENTY-NINE

DEDA YAGA

The air explodes with the sound of hooves and a flock of at least twenty flying horses appears in the sky above us. I recognize Teffi, with her black feathers, flying amongst horses of every colour – not just white and grey and brown, like horses in my world, but blue and gold and scarlet.

I shield my eyes and gaze up at them in wonder. Then a huge dark shadow swoops into view and the horses bank away to make room for it. My breath catches in my throat, because it's a house. An enormous house, walking on impossibly long, thin legs.

"Move out of the way!" Cascadia grabs my shoulders and pulls me back. Mora and Feliks rush to our side and Koshka darts behind my ankles. Dub moves too, but he's slow and cumbersome and I gasp as a huge, black chicken foot lands on the floor with a bone-shaking thump, barely missing Dub.

I stare at the scaly foot in awe. It's so big it could have crushed all of us beneath it, and the shiny black claws on the end of its toes are longer than my whole arm. My gaze drifts up, following the legs to where they connect with the house, higher above us than the hawks hunt over the meadows back home.

Because the house is directly overhead, I can't make out much of it, but I can see it's made of wood as dark as ebony. Thin white things dangle from the house's underside, clattering as they sway back and forth, and I shudder when I realize they're bones.

Another enormous black foot swings forwards and hovers above us, then the house leans over, as if to get a better look. My jaw drops as the house comes fully into view. It's not as big as Castle Mila or Chernomor's fortress, but is at least five times bigger than any of the houses in the village back home. It has three floors and a single domed roof, and what seems like hundreds of tiny round windows that blink as I stare.

More bones, bright white against the black wood of the house, dangle from window sills and eaves, swaying and rattling. The arched front door creaks open and a man emerges, leaning on a walking frame made of bones.

He looks older than anyone I've ever seen, with deeply wrinkled skin and clouded, rheumy eyes. A huge black hat, with skulls and flowers emblazoned on it, is balanced crookedly on his head. And a long black coat, far too big from him, billows around his bony limbs. He smacks his lips together, making the long white hairs tufting from dark moles on his cheeks and chin sway.

"That's Deda Yaga," Cascadia whispers, as the bones of his walking frame rattle and clump across a large oval veranda that extends from the front door like a huge black tongue. "Ludmila banished him into this land because he knows death magic."

"Death magic?" I echo, a shiver running through me.

"It's nothing to be scared of," Feliks says. "Death magic only involves helping the dead leave the world peacefully and return to the stars."

"Oh." I can't take my eyes off Deda Yaga. I've never seen anyone look so old and weak in body, yet have so much strength radiating from inside them. He peers over the edge of the veranda and his pale eyes seem to look right into my soul. "If he's trapped in this land," I whisper, "who is helping the dead back in Mila?"

"There are other Yaga in the world," Koshka explains. "Although I suppose they'll have had more work to do because this Yaga is trapped here."

I frown as I think about all the consequences of Ludmila creating this land. It's a beautiful, wondrous place, but it should never have been made, and spirits should never have been trapped in here against their will, away from their homes and loved ones.

"Star-filled greetings!" Deda Yaga calls down in an ancient, gravelly voice. "Teffi tells me you would like a lift to Water Dome, where you've opened the door to Castle Mila?"

"Yes, please!" I shout. "But we need to stop by the giant Golov first. I have the waters of life and death to put him back together." My cheeks warm with a small flush of pride and excitement.

"The *leshy* can ride with me on the Yaga house's veranda. The rest of you can ride on the horses." Deda Yaga sniffs and grunts something which I think is an instruction to the house. The other clawed foot darts down so fast it creates a whirlwind. It wraps around Dub's trunk and lifts him into the air before he can wave farewell. Then he's deposited on the veranda of the house, where he sits, dangling his rooty feet over the edge and beaming down at us, the *vily* still fluttering excitedly in his branches.

Teffi swoops down with two more horses: a bright green one and a yellow one, both softly feathered with calm, gentle faces. They all land with the drum of hooves on earth and Feliks greets each of them with a nose rub. "Why don't you and Koshka ride on Teffi?" Feliks suggests, looking at me. "I'll ride with Mora, and, Cascadia, are you all right riding alone?"

"Of course!" Cascadia splashes up onto the green horse's back and it shivers as she lands. Feliks and Mora leap onto the yellow horse, and I give Teffi a gentle pat and climb up onto her smooth, feather-coated back.

Koshka stiffens and her whiskers twitch with disdain, but she jumps onto Teffi's back behind me. I lean forwards and wrap my arms around Teffi's soft neck as she lifts her head high and opens her wings. All three of the horses drum their hooves again, first on the earth, then the air, and they lift us into the blue sky and fly towards the rest of the flock.

With one giant step and a rattle of bones, the house lurches away from the fortress gardens. Its clawed foot lands on top of the maze, then it takes another giant step into the woodland.

Teffi and the rest of the flock zoom after the house and I press my whole body into her back and hug her tight. Her heart is thundering in her chest, matching the rhythm of the hooves pounding around us. I've never moved so fast or felt so exhilarated, and I swell with so much wonder, I feel as big as Deda Yaga's house.

We fly over the multicoloured woodland and I see the shimmering edge of Earth Dome. Beyond it, I can see the curved skies of Air, Fire and Water Dome, each with their own crescent sun. The domes sparkle like silver, with rainbows of colour arcing over them.

They remind me so much of the domes of Castle Mila that tears well in my eyes. But I'm so nearly home, I can almost smell the pine-log walls.

Chernomor's threads have disappeared from the land below, making everything look more colourful, but all the cracks have been fully exposed too. There are thousands of them: thin ones linked like spiderwebs over the ground, and long, deep chasms that extend as far as I can see. I didn't realize how much the land had broken, and worries jump and flip inside me. *Is magic still storming out to batter my home?*

I turn and try to ask Koshka if the rifts will heal, but she's clutching onto Teffi with her claws splayed and her eyes are wide and scared. She doesn't even acknowledge me. Then we fly through the boundary into Fire Dome and I hold on tight as my vision blurs and the air pops.

"There's Golov!" I shout as the view clears and I spot his head directly below us.

The house with chicken legs, which is walking ahead of us, jerks to a stop and folds its legs beneath itself, coming to rest with a clatter of bones beside

Golov's head. Teffi and the other horses swoop down and land in a circle around the house.

Cascadia laughs as she splashes down from the green horse. Mora and Feliks leap down from the yellow horse, their tails still entwined. Dub and Deda Yaga are sat on the house's veranda, but rise to their feet as I jump down from Teffi's back.

"Are you all right, Koshka?" I ask. She's sat stone-still, apparently unable to retract her claws from deep in Teffi's feathers.

"I don't like heights," she whispers so quietly I barely hear her.

"Would you like a lift down?" I offer Koshka my hands and, to my surprise, she leans forwards so I can pick her up. Her soft fur is cold with fear. I can't resist giving her a stroke to warm her up, before placing her carefully on the ground. She fluffs up her fur, flicks her tail and walks away towards Golov.

"Golov," I shout, but he doesn't reply. He's fast asleep, snoring.

I fumble in my pockets and my fingers fall on a soft, cold wisp of something. I pull it out and stare at what is left of the faded key in horror. There is barely anything of it, just a small rod of faint, flickering metal. I quickly find the blood flower and the green glass vial and hold them up right in front of Golov. Then I shout again, louder. "Golov! I brought you the waters of life and death." I need him to wake so I can put him back together, then he can fix the key.

Golov's eyes open slowly at first, but his eyelids whip up when he spots the flower and the vial in my hands. A smile spreads across his face, so wide that it disturbs the owls nesting in his eyebrows and hair and they flap and flutter. "You got them," he whispers, although his voice is still so loud it stirs a wind between us.

I nod and Golov's eyes well with tears. "I never thought this day would come. I'm going to get my body back." He roars with excitement and I wobble backwards.

"So how do I use them?" I ask, turning the blood flower and the vial over in my hands.

"Use the waters of death first." Golov leans his head forwards and licks his huge lips. "Sprinkle a few drops on my head and a few drops on my body, then wait. When my head has rejoined my body, sprinkle a few drops of the waters of life over me."

I open up the tube-shaped blood flower and step closer to Golov. "This won't hurt, will it?"

"No matter if it does, little one, it will be worth it." Golov lifts his chin slightly and his enormous beard rustles like brambles in a storm. "Pour it under my chin."

I reach into his hairs, tip the blood flower, and let a few drops of the water inside fall onto Golov's skin. They sink into his flesh and disappear. "Is that enough?" I whisper, but before the words have left my mouth Golov falls still and silent.

CHAPTER THIRTY

THE WATERS OF LIFE
AND DEATH

"Is Golov okay?" I stare at the giant's lifeless face and panic speeds my heart. I whip my gaze around to Koshka. She's sat behind me, watching everything with her amber eyes narrowed. "Is this supposed to happen?" I ask.

Koshka tilts her head to one side in thought. "It's been a long time since I used the waters of death. I think you need to sprinkle some drops onto his body next, as quickly as possible. The magic in the water doesn't last long."

Feliks appears at my side and holds out a hand for the blood flower. "I'll do it," he offers. "I can run faster than you."

I thank Feliks and carefully pass him the blood

flower. He seals it shut, slides it into his pocket, then shifts into a fox and races away to the brambly mound behind Golov's head. I watch nervously as he sprints up onto what I think is Golov's chest, shifts his form, then sprinkles some water near where Golov's neck might be.

From the corner of my eye, I see Golov's face greying. His veins are darkening and hardening – they protrude like ropes beneath the skin on his chin and cheeks, and my stomach rolls with worry.

"Golov looks terrible." I turn to Koshka again. "What if I've done something wrong? The waters of death don't sound like something that would put a person back together."

"He'll be fine, Olia. Don't worry." Mora steps closer to me and gently rests a paw on my elbow. She looks so calm and genuine that my worries begin to ebb away.

Deda Yaga, with Dub by his side, rattles closer. "It isn't Golov's time to return to the stars." He smiles, revealing a single brown tooth protruding from his gums.

Feliks runs back to us as a fox, then shifts form again. "Look, Olia, it's working."

For a moment I don't notice anything different. Golov's face is still grey and unmoving, his body still covered in brambles. But then I notice the ground shifting. Earth and brambles slide from the mound, revealing worn leather clothing beneath.

A groan rumbles from Golov's head and it tilts backwards, further and further, until – with a great *bang* – it falls over. Hundreds of owls take flight from Golov's hair, screeching, hooting and flapping their wings in confusion. I stare as Golov's head keeps moving. It skids, faster and faster, towards his body, owls trailing in its wake. Then, with a disturbing *crunch* and a flash of golden light, the two connect.

Golov's head doesn't wake, and his body is still littered with earth and brambles. There's no movement to suggest he's alive, but he's in one piece.

"Sprinkle him with the waters of life." Koshka nudges my legs. "Quickly. He's vulnerable like this, with his head connected to a body that's been dead for hundreds of years."

Koshka's words set me sprinting towards Golov. His face is turned to the sky now and his owls are circling over him. I open the vial of the waters of life and wonder whether I should climb up onto Golov, or sprinkle some on his ear, which is the highest place I can reach from the ground. Worried I'll fall off him if he wakes, I decide to go for his ear and let three small drops fall onto one of his earlobes.

The droplets roll off Golov's skin and drip to the ground. I frown at them in annoyance. The waters of death sank in so I assumed the waters of life would do the same.

I seal the vial shut again, then jog away from Golov's head towards his body. I pass his neck, then scramble up onto a moss-covered shoulder. There, I open the vial again and drip three drops of the water onto a flat area near his collarbone. The drops pool together and shine in the light, but don't sink in.

"Am I doing something wrong?" I shout back to Koshka, but before she can respond, the mossy shoulder twitches beneath me and I fall to my knees.

It twitches again, and I seal the vial and tuck it back into my pocket, then slide off Golov's shoulder.

Golov inhales a great gust of wind and his huge chest expands. Landslides of earth and brambles crash down and I turn and run, my pulse racing.

"Olia!" Feliks shouts. He's halfway between me and the others. "Hurry! Give Golov plenty of room."

I race all the way to Feliks, then turn back around and watch as Golov opens his eyes. He groans and moves his head from side to side. Then he smiles, which makes his cheeks plump up and turn pink. The dark veins sink back beneath his skin and his grey tinge fades. His owls shriek with delight.

"I'm…" Golov moves his head again, now lifting it off the ground and looking down at his body. His fingers twitch. His arms rise up, sending brambles flying and earth scattering. "My body!" A laugh quakes through Golov's chest and more earth, moss, burned grass, brambles and briars crash down.

The ground shakes as Golov scrambles to his feet. He doesn't have complete control of his limbs, and he slips and falls several times like a newborn fawn, but all the while he's laughing, a great booming laugh, and there's so much joy in his face I find myself laughing too.

Finally, Golov stands, almost as tall as Castle Mila, and roars victoriously into the sky. "I have my body back. My body!" He pats himself all over, lifts his arms and legs and wiggles his hands and feet. I notice a ring glistening on the smallest finger of his left hand and my heart soars, because that must be the ring that can fix the key so I can finally get home.

Golov turns around, looks up at the sky and across the fields, then back up at the sky again. "I can move!" he shouts and owls swoop all around him. Then he jumps up and lands with such force that the whole land reverberates with shock waves and I'm shaken off my feet. He hops from one foot to the other, spins around and leaps into the air. "I can dance," he yells and bursts into an echoing, happy song in a language I don't understand.

I turn to Feliks and find him singing along with an enormous smile on his furry face. "I know this song," Feliks explains. "I sang it to Mora on our wedding day.

It's about rebirth and being together, and the beauty of that."

Mora snuggles close to Feliks, and they sing the song together.

"I can feel!" Golov booms. "My legs! My arms!" He spins around once more and the last of the earth, grass and brambles on his body splatter to the floor around us. I put my hands over my head to protect myself, but I am beaming with happiness for him.

Golov leaps into the air even higher, then lands with a deafening crack...and the ground splits wide open. My breath freezes in my chest as the land tilts all around us. In one split-second movement, Golov slips and disappears into the crack. Then everything around us skids towards it too: abandoned armour, dark rocks, brambles, burned ash-filled grass, glowing ants, clods of earth...

I fall onto my back and slide towards the widening chasm ahead, my heart in my throat. I hear Feliks and Mora shouting beside me, Cascadia splashing, Dub creaking and the bones of the Yaga house rattling.

Everyone is sliding into the massive rift in the land.

I desperately reach for the hat in my pocket, but the world skids past in a blur. My elbows and the backs of my legs burn as they grate over sharp, gravelly rocks, and with a terrifying crush of icy dread I realize that I'm going to crash down, somewhere deep and dark, and even if I survive the fall, I'm not going to be able to save any of us from inside a chasm.

CHAPTER THIRTY-ONE

THE CHASM

My breath is thumped out of me as I land on hard, rocky ground at the bottom of a hole that is almost as deep as the Great Hall is high. My fall from Sun Dome comes rushing back to me as I look down at myself like I did this morning, to check that I'm okay. My pyjama sleeves and trousers are shredded, the skin on my arms and legs is stinging with grazes, but the *rusalka* armour has protected my chest and back.

The earth walls shake and blackened mud rains down. Thunder rumbles, and my heart feels crushed as I realize it's the sound of the land breaking apart. "No!" I shout, scrambling to my feet and looking around for my friends. This can't be happening. Not now, when I was so close to getting home.

I spot Feliks and Mora clinging onto each other tightly, shaking with fear. Koshka is skidding down towards us, her descent slowed by her claws digging into the muddy walls.

Further along the chasm lies Golov, in one piece but crumpled in a heap, one of his legs stuck in a smaller rift in the ground. The house with chicken legs is behind him, with its legs splayed at an odd angle and its house-body tilted steeply to one side. Dub is leaning over nearby, his branch-arms creaking as he tries to lift Deda Yaga to his feet. *Vily* are fluttering all around them.

I scramble over to help. Deda Yaga has tumbled forwards and his bone walking-frame has skidded away from him. "Are you all right?" I kneel beside him and put a hand on his cloaked, bony shoulder.

Deda Yaga coughs and struggles to stand. I pull his walking-frame close, trying to ignore what it's made of, and help him put his hands on it and rise to his feet.

"Is everyone else all right?" I look around. "Where's Cascadia? And the flying horses?"

"I'm here." Cascadia rises from a puddle near Feliks and Mora. "And the flying horses bolted into the sky."

"Are you all right, Golov?" I shout over another rumble as I clamber towards his head across rocks and mounds of mud. His owls flutter around him and a few of them pull some of his hair back, so that I can see his eyes. They're closed. "Golov!" I shout as loud as I can into one of his ears. "Wake up! Please!" He groans and stirs, and I sigh with relief.

Golov wriggles awkwardly, trying to right himself. His foot is wedged tight into a crack, and the more he pulls it, the more the ground shakes and the more mud rains down.

"Stop!" I shout finally. "You're making the ground split more." I try to think what to do. We all need to get out of this chasm, before the sides collapse and we get completely buried in mud.

"Can the house help?" I call back to Deda Yaga.

"The house is wedged tight and can't move at all." Deda Yaga shakes his head, his deeply wrinkled face even more folded with concern as he looks at it. The house stares back at him with its hundreds of window eyes all round and scared. It creaks as it jerks against the chasm walls, but only a few bones jangle with the tiny movement it can make.

"I thought the land would stop cracking open once you cut off Chernomor's beard." Cascadia splashes over to me, her waters dark and stormy. "But this is worse than ever." She wobbles as another rumble shakes the earth.

Feliks yells in pain and I turn to see him clutching his chest. "What's wrong?" I rush to his side.

"I feel the castle being torn apart." Feliks slides out a small, cased pocket watch and opens it up. On one side is a gently ticking clock face, and on the other side are tens of tiny drawings. A sketch of Mora is in the centre, and around her are sketches of dark-haired children. I spot Babusya and Papa when they were young, and Rosa and I, amongst what must be our ancestors when they were young too.

"Oh, Feliks." My heart aches as it hits me how Feliks has always been part of my family, always protecting and caring for us, even when we haven't seen or remembered him. My gaze drifts to the clock face. It's five o'clock, only an hour until the harvest moon rises and the castle falls. Tears sting my eyes. I thought I would be home by now, preparing to celebrate the castle's birthday with my family and friends. Instead I'm stuck in this chasm, in a land falling apart, while the storm takes away my home. Everything I tried to do has failed and everyone I love is still in danger. I feel my anger flame, igniting a burning desire to do something.

"Koshka, what's going on?" I demand. She's landed next to Feliks and is sat looking small and lost.

"I don't know," she says quietly, staring at her paws in shame. "I thought the silver threads of Chernomor's magic were tearing the land apart. But maybe..." She glances up at me, her amber eyes glistening. "Maybe I made a mistake. Maybe the cracks in the land weren't to do with his magic after all."

My heart gallops like a flying horse's hooves. "So getting the sword, finding our way through the maze and cutting off Chernomor's beard was all for nothing?" My voice rises.

Koshka winces away from me. "You're angry..."

"Yes. No. I'm…" I try to breathe out the fire that rages inside me, and crouch down next to Koshka. "I'm worried, about all of us and all the spirits in this land, and my family and whether I'll ever be able to get back to them." Tears pool in my eyes and I try desperately to blink them away. "We need to find a way out of this chasm, then figure out why the land is still being torn apart." I look at everyone, hoping someone has an idea.

Golov's face twists in frustration. "Every time I wiggle my foot, I put us all in more danger."

"The house can't move at all," Deda Yaga repeats, moving towards its veranda and shaking his head sadly.

"I could call the flying horses back," Feliks suggests.

"But what about Dub and the house and Golov? They're all too big to be lifted by the horses." I think hard. "We need to find a way to free Golov's foot. If we can do that, he's tall enough to lift us all up and climb out of here." I slide the magic hat out of my pocket and walk over to Golov's foot. "Do you think I could unfold some of the earth trapping his foot?" I ask Koshka.

"Maybe…" She pauses. "But it might rip the chasm even wider. And unfolding anything in this land will send even more magical winds back to your world."

"Is that what happened when I unfolded your chain?" I ask, horrified. "Did it send winds back to my home? You should have told me! You should have told me everything. That's what friends do!" I close my mouth and clench my jaw because berating Koshka isn't going to help us now.

Koshka lowers her head again. "The magic released from my chain would have gusted back into your world, but it wouldn't have been a massive amount. Unfolding a whole chunk of land would be very destructive though," she says nervously.

The chasm shakes again, causing Cascadia to splash down into a puddle. Golov yells in pain as his foot is crushed more, and his owls screech and wheel in panic.

"Maybe I should prepare a feast," Deda Yaga suggests as the shaking subsides. His bone walking-frame rattles as he climbs up the steps onto the house's veranda.

"A feast?" I call after him in confusion. "What for?"

"If we're all going to die here, then we'll need a party to celebrate our lives before we go." Deda Yaga glances back at me. His eyes are shining and a gummy smile creases his face.

"We're not going to die here!" I yell, angry at Deda Yaga for suggesting it. "Come back here and help us think of a plan to get out."

Deda Yaga's eyes widen in shock, then his smile grows, revealing his single brown tooth. "You're very determined to live," he mutters as he totters back down the veranda steps.

"Of course I am! Aren't you?"

"I love life," Deda Yaga replies. "But I love guiding the dead too. And I've been trapped in this land for five hundred years, where there are no dead to guide. Forgive me if I got excited about the prospect of guiding again for a moment."

"If you help us get out of here and return home then you wouldn't be trapped any more!" I say, frustrated.

"That would be nice." Deda Yaga sighs wistfully. "I've missed guiding. And sunrises. Ludmila folded tiny slivers of the sun in here, but no moon and no stars. I've missed sunrises, sunsets and the night so much. But I don't know what to do." Deda Yaga shrugs his bony shoulders and my heart sinks.

The hat tingles in my hands. "Using the hat is the only plan I can think of to help us escape." I walk over to Golov's foot. "I have to try. I'll just use it a little and see what happens. It's better than sitting here doing nothing."

"Are you sure?" Feliks asks, still clutching his chest. "What if Koshka is right and it makes everything worse – both in this chasm and back at the castle."

Thoughts of Babusya, my parents and Rosa rush into my mind. I don't want to put them in more danger by making the storm worse, but I must get home before the hour is up. I'll have to trust they're keeping each other safe, and do what I can here. "I'll start slowly and see what happens," I say decisively, putting one hand on the chasm wall above Golov's boot and my other hand on the hat. Then I close my eyes.

The magic in the earth pulses beneath my fingers. It warms and swirls and flows along my arm, through my chest and into the hat. The wall shakes gently, then more violently, and doubts crowd back into my mind.

"Olia." Feliks nudges me. "I'm not sure you—"

Feliks is interrupted by a boom like thunder and a landslide of mud and earth. Mora squeals and Dub moans and I jump back, fear coursing through me. I shouldn't have used the hat. I've made everything worse and now the walls of the chasm are collapsing around us. I shield my head with my arms and look around for the others, my eyes burning.

Then I hear a strangely familiar voice that sounds like the crackle of lightning.

"Give me back my hat!" Chernomor yells, and I turn to see him hurtling towards us, flying on the back of a giant swan.

CHAPTER THIRTY-TWO

FORGIVING

Chernomor's golden robe, hat and silver hair trail behind him as he rides on the neck of the enormous white swan. Its body is as long as my rowing boat back home and, as it draws close, it opens its huge black-and-orange beak and trumpets aggressively. I drop the magic hat in shock and the chasm walls stop shaking.

"Are you intent on wrecking this land?" Chernomor demands as the swan comes to land right next to me. I back away from them, scared of the swan's size and Chernomor's angry face. His silver eyes are glaring, too bright to look at. "First you cut off my beard, destroying all the magic I was using to hold this land together, then you use my hat to rip more holes! Give it back to me immediately, return to Castle Mila and leave us all in peace. Perhaps with my hat, I can repair some of the damage you've caused."

"The damage *I've* caused?" I stare at Chernomor in shock. "Your magic was holding the land together?" My eyes widen as Chernomor's words click into place in my mind. Why was it so difficult to look at the land from all angles? I think about all the cracks I've seen filled with silver threads and groan with the realization that they were trying to seal the cracks, not force them apart. I should have tried harder and seen what was happening sooner. "I didn't know... I'm sorry..." I stop, because Chernomor isn't listening to me. His gaze has drifted to Golov's boot and enormous body.

The wizard's face pales as he sees Golov's head. "Brother," he whispers, "you're whole again."

"You dare to call me brother after what you did to me!" Golov's face reddens and his eyes swirl a darker shade of green. I back away towards Feliks and the others, because I've felt the power of Golov's anger before. "I am whole again," Golov roars, "and once I get my foot free, I will wreak my revenge upon you!" The last word blasts from his mouth.

The swan beneath Chernomor beats its wings and honks angrily at Golov's nose in response. Golov's owls swoop towards the swan, their claws flashing and beaks gaping, and the swan snaps back at them. Then Golov opens his mouth and blows out a gust of wind that sends the swan flapping away so rapidly that Chernomor falls off its neck onto his bottom.

Chernomor shields his face with his hands. "Brother, I'm so sorry!" he shouts, his voice crackling and rising with emotion. "I'm sorry I cut off your head. I truly am."

"You will be!" Golov reaches a hand towards Chernomor, each one of his giant pink fingers almost as big as Dub. "I will squash you. No! I will pull your tiny head from your tiny shoulders and let you live in two pieces, like I did for hundreds of years." Golov's fingers draw closer to Chernomor and dread fills me.

"Stop!" I yell, racing forwards. I grab Chernomor's shoulders and pull him away from Golov. "There isn't time to fight. This land is falling apart! Please, Golov, we need to figure out how to get out of this chasm. Maybe your brother can help us."

"Chernomor won't help," Koshka grumbles. "He's an evil wizard whose greed and rivalry with your ancestors led to all of this—"

"And you're an evil witch," Chernomor interrupts, "who helped Ludmila create this land and imprison hundreds of magical spirits."

"I was trying to make a safe—"

"But you made a prison!" Chernomor interrupts Koshka again, but then his face softens and he sighs. "The point I was trying to make is that you aren't Naina the witch any more. You're a cat. Being trapped in this land for five hundred years has changed you, and it has changed me." Chernomor looks back to Golov. "Brother, please believe me, I'm sorry for what I did to you. I love you. You're my family and my home and I miss you."

Golov frowns. His owls flutter down and land in his eyebrows and hair and hoot softly. I feel a battle raging inside Golov. I think he wants to forgive Chernomor, but can't.

"I understand it must be hard to believe me," Chernomor says sadly. "But I am sorry, and have been since the day I cut off your head. Guilt and regret have been boulders on my chest, getting heavier with each passing year."

"Then why didn't you come and save me?" Golov roars again, so loud that Chernomor skids back. "Your fortress sits over the pool of the waters of death and the well of the waters of life. You could have put me back together any time you wanted. But you didn't!"

Chernomor flushes as red as Golov's cheeks. "I wanted to. But I was scared that, as soon as you were whole, you'd take your revenge on me."

The corners of Golov's mouth twitch as he suppresses a smile. "I would have."

Chernomor holds his hands out, as if he wants to hug Golov, despite his size. "Let me help you now, brother. I can free you from this chasm, if this girl returns my hat." Chernomor glances at me accusingly.

"My name is Olia." I clutch the hat tighter in my hands. "And I've already tried to use the hat to free

Golov, but it only made things worse. The walls of the chasm shook more."

"How long have you been able to use the magic in my hat?" Chernomor asks curiously.

"I only found it this morning." I think back to when I first used the hat's magic to make the key into this land. I still feel the excitement and pride that swelled inside me. Finding out magic exists, after spending my whole life looking for it, is amazing, incredible. The thought fills me with renewed hope that anything is possible. There must be a way to use the hat, not only to free us from this chasm, but to fix *everything* – the land, the storm and my home. Perhaps we could even use it to free the spirits who want to return to their homes too.

Chernomor reaches a hand towards me. "Please, Olia, may I have it back? I've studied magic for thousands of years, and with my hat I'm able to weave it intricately and masterfully. I can unfold some of the land around Golov's foot, and refold it in a way that won't cause any more damage."

I cling onto the hat, unsure whether to trust

Chernomor. I trusted Koshka and she got it all wrong. What if Chernomor does the same? "This is the only magic I have and it might be my only hope of protecting my family." I turn the floppy green velvet over in my hands and feel its warm tingle. "I never felt magic until I found this hat," I whisper.

"That's not true." Feliks looks up at me. "Remember what I told you before. You've always felt the threads of magic running through the world. As soon as you could move your fingers, you'd experiment with them. I've seen you fold sunbeams through the castle's windows and curl rainbows through drops of rain."

Papa jumps into my thoughts, saying that Mama and I are the kind of people who make rainbows out of rain.

"The hat channels magic, but you can see and feel magic without it." Feliks smiles. "Like your sister can."

"Rosa," I whisper, the desire to go home overwhelming me.

"Olia." Chernomor lifts his eyebrows and looks at me sincerely. "I promise, if you give my hat back, I will help get you home."

I close my eyes for a moment to think with my heart, and almost immediately I know what is the right thing to do. I offer the hat to Chernomor. "I'm sorry. Of course you should have your hat back. I'm sorry my ancestor stole it from you. And if there is anything you can do to get me home, I would be grateful. I miss my family more than anything, and I'm worried about them."

Chernomor takes the hat from me, and I feel a crackle of energy rush into the fabric. "Thank you, Olia. And I would like to apologize too, for my part in the events of the past. My behaviour was less than honourable. I let greed and petty rivalries consume me, and made threats of war against Ludmila that must have scared her. There is much I did back then that I'm ashamed of now. I hope we can learn from the mistakes of the past, move on and even try to fix some of them." Chernomor turns to Golov. "Will you let me free you, brother?"

"I'm not ready to forgive you," Golov says sulkily. "But if you free me, I promise I won't squash you or pull you apart."

Chernomor walks over to Golov's boot. He puts a hand on the chasm wall above it and holds out the hat with his other hand. The wall glows with sparks of golden light and Chernomor gathers them into his hand with graceful finger movements. He ushers them into the hat, then swirls them back out again and flings them at the cavern wall. It's like watching music being conducted or art being created.

The chasm walls vibrate gently, and slowly Golov's boot is revealed as the earth widens around it. The bones on the Yaga house sway and rattle as the house moves too, and I realize the whole chasm is widening.

In a few moments Golov and the house are rising to their feet and my heart soars, because I know this means we're going to escape from here. But I have less than an hour to figure out how to save my home and this land before they are smashed and lost for ever.

CHAPTER THIRTY-THREE

FALLING APART

G olov rises to his feet and his head lifts above the edge of the chasm. "Would you and your friends like a lift, little one?" he booms, reaching one of his hands towards us. I stand still, although part of me wants to run from his huge fingers. They scrape into the floor and he scoops up the whole chunk of rocky earth that we're stood on, and holds us steady as he climbs out of the chasm.

"We'll follow you!" Deda Yaga shouts from the house's veranda, and the house climbs out of the chasm too on its long, thin legs.

Golov stands tall and my breath is whipped away as we're lifted so high, so fast. The land and the sky blur past, then Golov's huge face appears right in front of us. "There are cracks everywhere," he says, his cheeks pale. "The land is crumbling."

I peer over the edge of his palm and feel like covering my eyes in horror. The charred fields of Fire Dome are fractured by wide splits, the ground broken and uneven. The staglike spirit I saw galloping earlier, with his hooves and antlers aflame, is lying down. His eyes are wide with fear, and only a thin line of smoke is rising from his antlers. A deep rumble reverberates through the ground below and Golov stumbles, making us all sway.

The sky suddenly fades to a dull, steely grey and the distant crescent of sun flickers like a dying candle, throwing warped shadows over everything. "What's happening?" I ask in confusion.

"The land's magic is flooding out through the cracks to Castle Mila. My threads were holding most of it in, but now they're gone..." Chernomor's voice trails away. Guilt squashes my chest and my mind spins as I wonder how we can fix this.

"Can you take us to the door back to Castle Mila?" Feliks shouts up to Golov. "It's in Water Dome, near the oak tree on the shore of the ocean."

Golov starts walking. He cups his hand slightly, so we're stood in the bowl of his palm, with his giant fingers rising up around us. He tries to hold us steady, but we still sway back and forth through the air and wind whips around us.

I sit down as close to the edge of Golov's palm as I dare and look out at the land, hoping to spot some kind of clue that might give me an idea of how to save it. Feliks, Mora and Cascadia sit beside me. Koshka curls up so close she's almost on my lap, although her back is to me, and I gently rest my hand on her for comfort.

Dub holds on to one of Golov's fingers and stares at the view whizzing past, with the leaves and berries around his face blowing in the breeze and *vily* sheltering in his branches. Chernomor stays beside Dub, frowning deeply at the cracks in the land.

With a sharp twist of confusion and a rush of panic, I notice Chernomor and Dub are next to Golov's smallest finger, and this is his left hand, but there's no sign of the ring I saw earlier. "Where's your ring?" I shout up to Golov.

But he doesn't hear me. He's stepping over cracks, his owls circling around his head. Every so often they swoop down to hoot at the house with chicken legs, which is walking alongside Golov, its bones rattling and clattering. The house is almost as tall as Golov's shoulder when its legs are fully extended, but it ducks and bobs as it steps and jumps over the vast web of cracks.

I shout at Golov again. What if he lost his ring back in the chasm? I pull the key from my pocket and my eyes burn as I hold back desperate tears. All that remains is a tiny fragment of faded metal, smaller than my little finger. There's no way it will work like this.

Golov and the house leap over a chasm deeper and wider than any I've seen before, and we see-saw, rock and stumble. When Golov lands on the other side, the ground shakes so violently that both Golov and the house nearly fall over. Golov's fingers tighten around us in a loose fist, so we lose our view of the land, but I can hear it cracking apart and my heart shudders.

"Hold on tight!" Golov booms as he breaks into a run. His feet pound the earth and the house's feet thump alongside him. Golov leaps again, I feel the stretching and popping in the air and know that we've moved into Water Dome. There's splashing below as we cross the river, then our movement stops and we're lowered gently to the ground.

Golov's fingers open and we all climb down onto the green and gold field where I first arrived into The Land of Forbidden Magic. The door home is hovering in the air – a ghostly imprint of roof shingles and a tiny firefly keyhole. The grass at my feet is the same green as Rosa's baby wrap, and the thought of going back to my family makes my heart reach for the door, but the key is barely there at all.

"Golov, where's your ring?" I ask again.

He looks at his hand and his face falls. "I...I..." He checks his waistcoat pockets, but I know he won't find it. I saw it on his finger before he fell into the chasm and, in my heart, I know that's where it is now.

"What can I do?" My voice cracks as I turn to Chernomor and hold up the tiny, faded key. "Can you fix this?"

Chernomor peers at what's left of the key. "I believe you can fix that yourself. It should be no problem for a human child who found a magic hat in the morning and was using it to unfold chunks of a chasm in the afternoon. Even if it was dangerously done," he adds with a stern look.

"How?" I ask. "Can I borrow your hat? Shall I try to refold the key?"

Chernomor shakes his head and I grumble in annoyance, like Babusya does whenever anyone tries to take charge of what she's doing without understanding that she's stronger than they realize... Little sparks of light flash in my mind. I'm stronger than I realize too. And belief is more powerful than magic.

I close my eyes and squeeze the key in my hand until it feels as warm as if it's been sitting on the stove in the kitchen back home. Then I open my eyes and look down at the key. It's complete, solid and glowing as brightly as the domes of Castle Mila before the storm. "I did it!" I beam. "I fixed it!" I whoop with delight and look at the faces of my friends. They're smiling back at me but their eyes are sad.

My face burns with shame. This land – home to hundreds of spirits – is falling apart, like my own home, but I've focused on getting myself back to my family.

The oak tree Koshka was chained to has fallen into a crack and lies at an odd angle, its roots exposed. The river isn't flowing at all. Its waters look like lead, and the *vodyanoy* is sitting on its bank, looking mournful. The waves of the ocean have stopped mid-roll and the giant jewelled fish I marvelled at when I first arrived here is lying on the surface, barely moving. Tiny winged fish spirits are trembling, terrified, in the grass.

My heart cracks like the land and I turn to Chernomor. "Can you fix the land now you have your hat back?"

Chernomor's eyebrows draw together. "This land has been breaking apart since Ludmila created it. Magic was never meant to be locked away, and it's always fought to escape. I tried holding the land together with the magic from my beard, but I don't have that any more. It's true I have the hat now, and once you've gone home I'll try to seal the land shut with whatever magic is left inside it. When my beard grows back, I'll use that too. I promise I'll do everything I can."

The ground shakes again and a crack opens between us and the door home.

Feliks nudges me. "You have to go, Olia," he says gently.

"But what about Mora, Cascadia, Dub, the *vily*, Deda Yaga and the house, and anyone else who wants to escape through the door too?" I ask.

"You must return home alone," Koshka says solemnly. "If any of us go through that door with you, the magic that bursts out will destroy everything."

"Koshka is right." Chernomor sighs. "Everyone's magic is linked to this land and if they leave through that door it will cause irreparable damage on both sides."

I look at my friends and my heart implodes. "I can't leave you all trapped here for eternity, away from your loved ones and homes. And you, Chernomor, forever trying to hold together a falling-apart land. There must be another way." I desperately try to gather all the clues, like I do with Papa when we're solving a riddle. "We must be missing something."

"The only way to save this land and stop the magical winds escaping is to seal it shut," Chernomor says firmly. "I'm sorry, but there is no other answer." The ground rumbles again and Chernomor gestures to the door. "You must leave now. I need to start work." He holds up his hat and it glows with magic.

Feliks leaps over the crack, lands beside the door and beckons me to join him. "Hurry, Olia. If you don't leave now, everything will fall apart and you'll lose your chance for ever." He expands a grandfather clock from his pocket. It's shaped like a magnolia tree and has carved, white-painted flowers all over it. A jewelled beetle is ticking on one of the flowers. "It's almost six o'clock. The harvest moon will be rising and the castle falling. You must go now. I promised your Babusya I'd get you home safely and time is nearly up."

"But…" I stare wide-eyed at Mora, Cascadia, Dub and the *vily* in his branches, Koshka, Chernomor, Golov and the house with chicken legs with Deda Yaga on its veranda. "I can't leave like this!" My eyes sting and my chest cramps with guilt as my gaze is drawn to the key. Because I don't want to leave everyone trapped here, but the truth is I don't want to miss my chance to go home either.

"Don't feel guilty." Feliks reaches his hand out to mine. "Cutting off Chernomor's beard wasn't the answer, but because of you he is awake and has his hat back, so he can seal the land shut and stop the storm. You've saved two worlds from falling apart."

Another rumble shakes the ground and Dub wraps a branch-arm around me, lifts me over the crack and places me beside the door. "Please don't be sad for us. You should go home to your family."

I hold the key tight in my hand. "But I want you all to be able to go home to your loved ones too. There must be a way..." I look around frantically, as if the answer might be right in front of me, written in a runic symbol or floating in the air. "Let's look at it from a different angle." I take a deep breath and try to see with my heart. I think about what is most important... and I realize that it isn't the land. Although Koshka tried to make it a safe space, Ludmila turned it into a prison. What is truly important are the spirits inside it, and they are what must be saved. "What if we don't save the land?" I ask. "What if we let it fall apart? Is there a way to get all the spirits out of here safely?"

Chernomor's already wrinkled brow rumples deeper in thought.

"Koshka said when I unfolded her chain, the magic went back into my world." Hope fizzes through me. "Can you unfold the land and all the spirits in here? Can you undo what Ludmila did five hundred years ago and free everyone?"

"It's possible..." Chernomor scratches what's left of his beard. "But..."

My heart soars. "Can you do it now? What will happen?" Questions spin through my mind and out of my mouth, but if Chernomor can free everyone safely, that is all that really matters.

"There is something you need to know, Olia." Chernomor's voice crackles like lightning and I shudder as a sudden chill curls around me. "If I unfold this land, then all the magic will rush out, causing a hurricane of epic proportions."

"Will it damage Castle Mila?" I whisper.

"Oh no." Chernomor shakes his head. "It will completely destroy Castle Mila. Nothing will remain."

CHAPTER THIRTY-FOUR

THE PLAN

I look down at the key in my hand and think of my home. My bedroom, overlooking the lake. Our warm and cosy kitchen, where I gather with my family every morning and evening. My parents' workshop, where I draw while they cut and nail wood. The long, slidy corridors and whooshy bannisters. The beautiful, mysterious domes that I dream of exploring with Rosa. And the Great Hall, used for almost every birthday, wedding and wake. "Is there no way to free everyone *and* save my home?" I ask, my voice trembling.

Chernomor shakes his head again. "If I unfold this land, the magic trapped here will hurricane out into the real world, flattening your castle and everything nearby."

"What about my family, my friends, the villagers…"
My voice rises in panic.

"You would need to get everyone away from the castle. Otherwise they would be in grave danger."

"So I can go through the doorway and warn them before you do the unfolding?" I ask. My heart is galloping like a flying horse, and a suffocating sense of loss is crushing me like the Immortal Cloak. I'm hopeful that everyone in this land can be free, but I'm devastated that it will mean losing my family's home… the magical castle that I wanted to share with Rosa.

"If you go now." Chernomor nods to the door. "Get everyone safely indoors, away from the castle. Then they'll be protected from the storm and your home falling, and they won't see this land merging back with the real world, or the spirits being freed and returning to their old places."

"My home falling…" I echo Chernomor's words in a whisper and my throat tightens. Castle Mila has been our family home for five hundred years. All our ancestors, Babusya, Papa, Rosa and I were born there. And, except for Rosa, we have all grown up there.

But now Rosa won't have a chance to remember it, let alone explore it... And where will we live? Where will all the villagers gather for celebrations? I suddenly feel as lost as a caterpillar on a leaf blown far out onto Lake Mila.

"We don't have to do this." Cascadia leaps over the split between us and splashes her hand onto my arm, making me jump. "Chernomor doesn't have to unfold the land."

"I want him to." I look into Cascadia's huge, watery eyes. "There are hundreds of spirits trapped in this land, and their freedom is more important than my home. But..." My worries threaten to spill over as another thought creeps into my mind. "Is it safe to release all the spirits? I know you wouldn't hurt anyone." I look at my new friends. "But what about the *vodyanoy*, who tried to pull me into the river, and the Immortal Cloak and the whispering coins and all the other spirits I don't understand? What if they hurt people? And what about the huge spirits?" I glance up at the Yaga house and Golov. "How will you fit into my world?"

"It was their world, too, before Ludmila banished them here." Chernomor shakes his head sadly. "Do you believe bears, wolves and vipers should be forbidden?"

My cheeks burn as I realize Chernomor is right. I can't leave any of the spirits behind because of my fears. I don't want to make the same mistake as Ludmila. "Everyone deserves freedom. And I'm sorry I said it was my world. It's *our* world, and we need to get everyone back there safely. But I'll go to protect my family and friends before we do this."

"Thank you, Olia." Dub's face creaks into a smile and the *vily* flutter in his branches.

"Thank you," Golov booms, his owls wheeling around him.

"Yes, thank you, Olia." Cascadia pulls me into a watery hug.

"Enough!" I laugh, shaking water off me. "You don't have to thank me. This is the right thing to do, it's what I want to do, and I believe it's what my parents and Babusya would want too, because all my life they've told me to help people in need."

Deda Yaga grins his gummy grin. "We'll see you on the other side." He waves and the Yaga house behind him winks one of its windows and rattles a few of its bones.

"Olia." Koshka looks up at me, her amber eyes wide. "I want to apologize for getting it wrong. I feel so guilty and ashamed." She looks down at her paws and my heart stretches out to her. I understand how she feels. All day, I've felt guilt and shame whenever I've made a wrong decision, but now I'm about to lose my home, I realize what's truly important.

"I felt guilty this morning, after I went into the Great Hall." I wince at the memory of my fall. Koshka looks at me in confusion. "That was the first of many mistakes I've made today," I explain. "I walked over unsafe floorboards, fell from a great height and hurt one of my best friends. But my grandmother, Babusya, just said, 'To live is to make mistakes.' I didn't understand her then, but I do now. Making mistakes means we're trying and doing and adventuring and learning. They mean we're living. I've made so many mistakes on this journey, but I've learned about this land, and about magic, and about who I am and who I want to be. I've realized that I can do more than I ever thought possible, but I should listen to my heart, and not rush into decisions…" I shudder as the Immortal Cloak whirls into my thoughts.

"So you forgive me?" Koshka's brow crinkles and she shifts nervously.

"I don't think it's my forgiveness you need." I realize that the person who has made me feel the worst about my mistakes today is myself. "It takes courage to do, but I think you have to accept what you did and forgive yourself." I smile at Koshka. "You were only trying to help. And because of you, we're now here, with a chance to free everyone. We've made friends, and I hope you've learned…" My smile widens. "I hope you've learned that maybe you can trust humans after all?"

"I helped Ludmila create this land because I had no family or friends. I trusted no one, and wanted to hide away from everyone and everything." Koshka's eyes well with sadness and regret. "But thanks to you, Olia, I feel like I may be building the first friendships

I've had in over five hundred years." She glances at the others before looking back at me. "I don't know about all humans, but you've earned my trust, Olia." Her mouth twitches into a small smile. "And your Babusya sounds wise...for a human," she adds, with a flick of her tail.

"You two would get on. I know you said you don't want to live with humans ever again, and I don't know where my family and I will live when the castle falls." I glance at the door, thinking how little time there is left. "But perhaps you'd consider a new home with us when you return to our world."

"I'll think about it." Koshka lifts her chin haughtily, but there is a gleam of gratitude in her eyes.

The ground rumbles and I grip the key tight and turn to Chernomor. "So how are we going to do this?" I ask.

Chernomor leaps over the crack and lands beside me. "You'll go through the doorway first, to warn everyone. But before you go, I'll show you how the unfolding works, so you know what to expect." Chernomor lifts his hat and steps closer to the door.

"I'll start here, where the boundary is weakest." He grabs the air to one side of the door and sparks of light flash around his fist. His face strains with effort as he pulls the spark-filled air towards him. It's as if he's pulling something incredibly heavy yet invisible into the hat.

Bright ripples form in the air; wavering golden lines that distort everything around them. They're so vivid I have to shield my eyes. Chernomor stuffs the waves into his hat and its lining glows brighter. Then he reaches out, grabs the air and pulls again.

This time there is a noise, like something damp tearing. A thin split opens in front of us and I glimpse a dark sky through it. "Is that the sky in the real world?" I ask. Excitement floods through me. I'm going home! Then a gust of wind pulls me towards the split and I brace myself against it.

"Yes. Through that split is the real world. The wind gusting into it is magic escaping from this land. I only unfolded a tiny piece, but as I unfold more, stronger winds will hurtle out. This land will get smaller, and all the spirits here will be drawn towards this split and escape through it. As they do, the split will get larger. In the real world, you'll see it as a shining tear in the sky above Castle Mila. When all the spirits are free, I'll come through last. Then there will be a final hurricane, as the last of the magic that made the land unfolds. After that, the land will no longer exist. And neither will your castle. Are you sure you want to go ahead?" Chernomor lifts his eyebrows, his gaze serious.

"I'm sure. To free everyone in this land, and fix my ancestor's mistake, we must do this." I turn to my friends. "Will I see you on the other side?" I ask.

"I'll be in Lake Mila." Cascadia smiles. "Look for me."

"And I'll be in the grove." Dub waves a branch-hand, and the *vily* inside him wave too.

The ground shakes again and Chernomor nudges me towards the door. "There's no more time for goodbyes. If the land falls apart everyone here will be lost. And to warn your family and friends in time, you must leave now."

I wave to Golov, Mora, Koshka, the Yaga house

and Deda Yaga, and turn to Feliks, thinking that he'll come through the doorway with me.

Feliks holds up the paper bag of *bulochki*. "There are two left," he says. "Share them with your Babusya when you get her to safety. And send her my love."

"You're not coming with me?"

Feliks shakes his head. "You make sure everyone near the castle gets to safety, and I'll make sure everyone in this land gets through during the unfolding." He lifts the paper bag higher and I take it from his hands and stuff it into my pocket. A whirl of emotions rushes through me: gratitude for Feliks's help, fear of what is about to happen and uncertainty about the future. I drop to my knees and pull Feliks into a hug.

"I'm sorry we couldn't save our home," Feliks whispers, hugging me back.

"Me too." A sob rises in my throat and I try to laugh it away. "But it's only a building. You all matter so much more." I wipe my tears away with the back of my hand.

"The spirits here will be free because of you, Olia. If you hadn't found and returned Chernomor's hat they would have remained trapped for ever, or all been lost if the land collapsed. So even though our journey didn't go as we planned, it's been more victorious than I thought possible. You saved something even better than Castle Mila. Be proud." Feliks pulls away from me and puts his hand over his heart.

"We are going to free everyone." I smile. "And you and Mora will be together again." My smile grows wider, but Feliks only nods sadly in reply.

I turn to the keyhole. It's like a tiny, distant star, so faint I can barely see it. I slide the key into it believing, with all my heart, that it will get me home. There is a loud, clear *click* and I pull the door open. A rush of wind blows from the land into the doorway so fast I stumble forwards, and have to put my hands on the edge of the doorway to stop from falling. I stare hard, trying to make sense of what I see through it, because nothing looks like it should. My castle is falling apart.

CHAPTER THIRTY-FIVE

THE STORM

Aurora Dome was unbroken when I entered The Land of Forbidden Magic, but now it's smashed apart. Beyond its torn roof I see the evening sky, heaving with dark, billowing storm clouds, and the endless curved domes of Castle Mila. But they don't look right. Many of them are twisted, broken and jagged, nothing like I remember them at all. Some are completely missing.

My heart plummets like a heavy rock thrown into Lake Mila as I stare at the devastation that I've not allowed myself to picture. My bedroom window – in fact, the whole of my bedroom wall – has been ripped away and my bed is teetering on broken floorboards. Roof shingles whirl through the air like angry birds, and the creak and squeal of the castle walls tilting and swaying is deafening.

Movement on the ground below catches my eye and I look down to see people gathered between the castle and the lake, surrounded by a random assortment of furniture and boxes. Babusya is in the centre of them, leaning heavily on her walking sticks, a worried frown creasing her brow.

Papa, Dinara, Luka and tens of other people are carrying more boxes away from the castle. My throat tightens as I realize they're risking themselves to empty the castle of our possessions.

"Go through the doorway." Feliks nudges me forwards, but I'm frozen. "Go to your family, Olia." He nudges me again. "I'll make sure you get down safely. The castle will bend to my will."

I swallow back my emotions and step through the doorway. "It's only a building," I whisper, trying to focus on what I must do now: climb down and get everyone to safety. But the sight of my family home so broken, and the knowledge that soon it will be flattened completely, makes my head spin, like a weather vane in a wild gale. I want to feel happy for the magical spirits who will be freed, but I'm filled with grief for the loss of all that I know.

Aurora Dome sways. It leans further and further, and panic surges through me as I skid across the floorboards – but then I glimpse Feliks and remember his power to control the castle, and how the dome tilted when we first walked this way. Trusting in Feliks, I let myself slide off the dome and land with a bump on another section of roof.

A warm tingle of magic flows beneath me and the roof bends and ripples, carrying me along; then the walls of the castle curve around me like a hammock and swing me down towards the ground in a smooth, swaying movement. Tears well in my eyes, because this feels like a last hug from the castle. The last time I'll feel its magic all around me.

I'm placed gently on the ground. I look up at the castle's walls, which are straight and still again, and whisper a thank you. Then I turn and run towards my family and friends.

"Papa!" I yell. He turns, sees me, drops the box

he's carrying, races over and pulls me into a massive hug.

"Oh, Olia, it's so good to see you." He squeezes me tight and speaks right into my ear, so I can hear him over the howling winds. "Babusya kept saying you were safe, but it hasn't stopped me worrying. Are you all right?"

"I'm fine. I'm sorry. I was… We have to leave!" I pull away from Papa and my voice rises as I remember how little time I have to get everyone away from the castle. "We have to go to the village, where it's safe. Where are Mama and Rosa?"

"They're already in the village, in Dinara and Luka's house. We didn't think Rosa should be out in the storm. Your Babusya shouldn't be either, but she wouldn't listen to me—"

"Olia!" Dinara and Luka shout in unison, interrupting Papa. They rush to me and I notice Dinara has a new, bigger bandage on her wrist.

"Your wrist." I look at it in concern. "Is it all right?"

"It's only sprained – the doctor says it'll be fine." Dinara crushes me in a huge hug before leaning back and staring at my clothes. "What are you wearing?"

I look down and realize over my torn and muddy pyjamas I'm still wearing the shining *rusalka* armour. "I found it in Aurora Dome, but there's no time to explain. Come on, we have to leave, now!" The wind screams as it wrenches a cluster of shingles from the roof above us and they clatter together as they're whipped away.

"You're right." Papa looks up at our collapsing home. "I'll gather all the villagers. You go ahead with Dinara and Luka. Their parents have invited us to stay with them tonight."

"You are coming straight away?" I ask in panic.

"Of course. But I need to make sure that no one is left here. This storm has made the castle unstable. Take Babusya with you and get her warm, please. She wouldn't leave without us so has been stood out in the cold for hours."

I nod and rush towards Babusya. She's leaning on her walking sticks near the lake shore, gravely staring up at the castle. But when she spots me, a huge smile grows on her face. "Magnolia," she whispers as I lean in to give her a hug. "Safe home at last."

"I'm sorry I couldn't save the castle, Babusya," I whisper back into her ear, my voice wavering. "This is the only way to free the spirits. The winds are going to get worse. They're going to flatten everything."

"Don't apologize." Babusya squeezes me tight, her bony hands and walking sticks digging into my back. "The winds of change are hard to fight. Perhaps they'll tear our castle down, but they won't tear *us* down. I'm just glad you returned safely and the spirits will be free."

"Me too." I squeeze Babusya back. "Papa says I should take you to Dinara and Luka's to warm up now." I release Babusya and offer her my arm.

She gives me one of her walking sticks, grips my elbow, looks up at the castle once more and whispers something that I think might be a goodbye. Then she pulls a sprinkle of salt from her pocket and throws it into the wind, turns, and we walk away from Castle Mila towards the spruce grove and the village beyond. I glance back one last time too, feeling like I'm leaving a piece of my heart behind.

CHAPTER THIRTY-SIX

THE NOTE

The evening sky over Lake Mila is leaden, cloaked by the burgeoning storm, and there's no sign of the harvest moon at all. If it has risen, it must be hidden behind clouds, but I can't help feeling like the winds might have blown the moon away, along with my castle and the missing piece of my heart.

A line of villagers, with their coats and hair flapping around them, light up the path through the spruce grove with torch beams so frail they barely cut through the darkness. Most of the villagers are carrying boxes or bundles of my family's possessions: pots and pans and jars of Babusya's herbs from the kitchen; blankets and cushions; clothes and towels; books and photograph albums. I notice some of the villagers carrying things they must have retrieved from the chaos in the Great Hall too: decorations and harvest foods that weren't smashed when Sun Dome collapsed.

I keep glancing back to look for Papa, and when I finally see him at the back of the line, carrying his big tool chest with the help of Dinara and Luka's papa, Mikhail, I breathe out a sigh of relief. Everyone must be out of the castle now and on the way to the safety of the village.

Babusya grips my arm tight as the wind gusts between the trees and tries to snatch the one walking stick she's using. Dinara moves the box she's carrying under one arm and offers her other arm to Babusya. Babusya thanks Dinara, gives Luka her walking stick, and holds on to both Dinara and me as she continues along the path.

I spot my favourite green jumper in the tilting box Dinara is holding, along with the rag rug I made with Mama, the jug and bowl from my washstand, and some of the treasures I've found in the roof domes over the years: rolled-up maps and gilt-edged books, art brushes and pots of inks and carved wooden boxes.

"You saved my things!" I smile at Dinara and she smiles back.

"Luka and I gathered up as many of them as we could before they were broken or lost."

"Is the family blanket safe?" I ask Babusya, my heart leaping into my throat as I remember it. The blanket is our most treasured possession, even more so now the castle is being destroyed.

"Yes," Babusya says breathlessly as she struggles against the wind. "Not only safe, but cleaned and mended. It's in the box Luka is carrying."

Luka hugs the box closer to his chest. "Are you going to tell us what you've been doing then, Olia? How did you get into Aurora Dome? I thought it was impossible to reach."

"Nothing is impossible for the princess of Castle Mila." I try to joke about being a princess, like I did with Dinara and Luka this morning, but I regret my words almost immediately. Since I learned about Ludmila, and how she created The Land of Forbidden Magic and banished all the spirits there, I'm ashamed of being descended from her and all my royal ancestors.

I don't even want to think about them any more.

"This armour you found…" Luka looks from the shimmering breastplate to the helmet I'm still wearing. "What's it made of?"

"I'll show you when we get to your house." I wonder if Luka and Dinara will believe the truth about the armour and what I've been doing. The Land of Forbidden Magic and all the spirits inside it are so fantastic, maybe they need to be seen to be believed. What if Dinara and Luka think I've made them up, or been confused by the storm or a bump to the head? I'm still pondering what exactly to tell them when we arrive at their home in the village.

The winds are calmer here, although they still whistle in my ears and whip up my hair. Papa and Mikhail and many of the other villagers go to store our possessions in the small hall in the school. But they tell me to go inside with Dinara and Luka and get Babusya warm.

It's a relief to enter Dinara and Luka's cosy kitchen, filled with the scents of fresh coffee and *plushki* cinnamon buns, and safe from the cold outside. Their stove is like ours, only smaller. Welcoming flames dance inside and heat radiates from it, enveloping the room in a massive hug.

I rush over to Mama, who is sat feeding Rosa in a quiet corner, and throw my arms around them both. I bury my face into Mama's neck, close my eyes and breathe in the sweet smell of her and my sister. "I've missed you both so much," I whisper, blinking away tears and smiling as I stroke Rosa's cheek with one finger. She's asleep, even though she's feeding, but a smile twitches on her lips when she hears me.

"Thank goodness you're okay." Mama hugs me back and kisses my cheek. "Is everyone safe out of the storm now?"

"Yes. Papa and Mikhail should be back any moment." I kiss Mama again, then I go to help Dinara and Luka's mama, Magda, who is getting Babusya comfortable in an armchair by the stove. I cover Babusya's legs with a blanket, and Magda pours her a coffee. Then I sit at Babusya's feet and, remembering the bag of *bulochki* Feliks returned to me, pull it from my cardigan pocket. The vial of the waters of life falls out too and I grab it before it rolls across the floor.

"I got the water you asked for," I whisper, slipping the vial into Babusya's hand. Then I reach into the paper bag and pass her a *bulochka* too. "Feliks said to share these last two with you."

"Where is Feliks?" Babusya whispers back, as I take the other *bulochka* from the bag. "Is he safe?"

There's a piece of paper stuck to my *bulochka* and as I peel it off I notice writing on it. I stare at the tiny, neat letters. Babusya leans closer so she can read the note over my shoulder.

Dear Olia,

I hope you are somewhere safe and warm with your family now. It was an honour and a pleasure to accompany you on this adventure. I'm proud of all we did together, and I hope you are too.

I'm sorry we couldn't save Castle Mila, but I'm forever grateful that we could free the spirits trapped in The Land of Forbidden Magic, especially Mora.

I know you will mourn the loss of your home. Castle Mila was a special place, but I truly believe it was special because of the people who lived and loved there. Your Babusya, parents, sister and you will find or build another home, and you'll make it just as special.

When Mora arrives back at the castle, she – like you – will have lost her home and, unlike the other spirits, she will be unsure where to go. So I have a favour to ask of you. Please would you find her, comfort her and make sure she's safe? And perhaps you'll help her to find a new home too?

Send her my love and tell her that being with her again after all these years, even if only for a short time, made me happier than I ever dreamed possible. I'm sorry that I won't be able to join her in her new home, but I will always be with her in her heart. Castle Mila was my life, but Mora is my eternal love.

Take care, Olia, and please remember to leave salt offerings in your next home. Your new

*domovoi will be young, and need plenty to grow
up strong,*
   With love,
   Feliks

"What does he mean?" The note trembles in my fingers and Babusya takes it from me.

"Oh, Feliks," she whispers sadly and a tear rolls down her cheek.

"What is it?" I ask again. "Feliks will come back, won't he? The wizard Chernomor is unfolding The Land of Forbidden Magic. Feliks should be freed with everyone else. I don't understand."

"Feliks is a castle *domovoi*." Babusya rests a hand on my shoulder gently. "If there is no castle, there is no *domovoi*."

"What?" I ask, all the warmth draining from my face.

"Feliks came to life when Castle Mila was created, and he will cease to exist if Castle Mila is destroyed. If this unfolding is going to raze the castle, then Feliks will disappear."

Anger flares through me, bringing the blood back into my face, hot and tingling. "He knew this! He knew this and he didn't tell me. Stupid, selfless *domovoi*, sacrificing himself for everyone else. Well, I won't allow it." I rise to my feet.

"Is everything all right?" Magda asks. She's bustling around the table with Dinara and Luka, pouring coffee and laying *plushki* on plates.

"Yes, I'm sorry. I just realized I forgot something at the castle." I frown, trying to work out how I can return to the castle and save Feliks without worrying anyone.

"It's not safe to go back there now." Magda glances out of the window. The storm is surging. "Perhaps you can get whatever it is tomorrow." Magda's words are no comfort at all, because I know that tomorrow there will be nothing left of Castle Mila, or Feliks.

I look at the door, filled with fear for Feliks and still wondering how I can escape and save him, when Papa and Mikhail burst through with a gust of wind. I rush to Papa, so overcome with emotions that tears pour down my face.

"Oh, Olia." Papa pulls me into a hug. "Are you all right?"

"No." I shake my head. "I'm not."

"I know seeing the castle like that is quite a shock." Papa glances over to Mama with a look of concern. "But everyone is safe and, once the storm has passed, we can think about repairs."

A sob tightens my throat, because Papa doesn't understand. He doesn't know that Feliks even exists, let alone that he's in danger. And he doesn't know that there will be nothing left of the castle to repair. Chernomor said it would be completely flattened.

"What's wrong, Olia?" Mama rises to her feet and carries Rosa, who is fast asleep, over to Babusya. "I've never seen you so upset."

I take a slow breath in, wondering if I have enough courage to tell my parents the truth; about magic, and the land beyond the dome, and the castle falling, and Feliks. It's all so fantastic. What if they don't believe me?

Mama lowers Rosa into Babusya's arms and walks over to me. "You can tell us, Olia. Whatever is on your mind, it's best to speak out. And I promise we'll do everything we can to help."

"Of course we will," Papa agrees.

Like Teffi opening her wings to fly, my bravery expands, and I feel stronger and surer than ever before. I need to tell my parents what I've discovered and convince them to help me save Feliks.

"Magic is real," I begin, thinking carefully about my words. Papa's brow furrows, as if he's trying to work out a complex riddle in one of his puzzle books, but Mama only nods calmly. "And the magical spirits Babusya sees are real too," I continue. "One of them is called Feliks, and although you might not remember him, he's always been a part of Castle Mila and our family. He's helped and protected and cared for us, and he's going to disappear, unless we go back to the castle and save him."

Papa ruffles his hand through his curly hair. I've never seen him look so unsure of himself. He glances over to Babusya, who gives him one of her steady, knowing looks. Then he turns to Mama, who smiles at him, her eyes twinkling. Finally he turns back to me and his face relaxes a little. "All right, Olia. Let's go to the castle and save Feliks the magical spirit." He smiles nervously and I beam.

"I'm coming with you." Mama puts on her hat and coat. "Rosa has just had a feed and she's fast asleep, so she'll be fine with Babusya for a while."

"I'll keep an eye on them both," Magda says.

"We're going with Olia," Dinara and Luka rush out at almost exactly the same time.

"And me," Mikhail says with a wide smile. He rises onto his toes, like Dinara does when she's excited, and his fair hair flops over his face, like Luka's always does.

My heart swells with so much hope I think it might burst. I whoop with excitement, and rush over to Babusya and Rosa. I stroke Rosa's silk-soft hair, whisper that I love her, then kiss Babusya. "We'll save Feliks," I say firmly, before turning back to my parents and friends.

"Feliks is a castle *domovoi*. But the storm is destroying Castle Mila, and if there is no castle, there is no *domovoi*. I know we can't save the whole castle from the storm, but if we can save a part of it, that will be enough."

"How do you know it will be enough?" Papa asks.

"If we believe it's enough, then it will be," I say confidently. "Because belief is more powerful than magic." Then I throw my head back and lead the way out into the cold, stormy night, determined to save my friend.

CHAPTER THIRTY-SEVEN

ETKA AND ZARYA

Inside the spruce grove, surrounded by dark, swaying trees, the wind whines and whistles through dense, tangled boughs. Beyond the spruce grove, the winds are louder, roaring, and I hear the creaks and groans of Castle Mila rumbling among them.

I run towards the castle as fast as I can, because I need to reach it before it's completely destroyed. My parents and friends run alongside me, their hair and coats whipping around them. I'm so angry at Feliks for not telling me that he would disappear with the castle, and angry at myself for not realizing it sooner.

When we first stepped out onto the castle roof together, Feliks told me that he and the castle were made of the same magic. And when the roof dome smashed near him, he clutched his chest as if in pain; then again, in the chasm, he did the same thing. I should have figured out this might happen, and I should have done something to protect him before now. "I *will* save Feliks!" I yell into the wind.

Mama grips my hand and squeezes it tight. "We will save Feliks!" she yells too, and immediately Papa joins in, then Dinara and Luka and Mikhail.

"We'll save Feliks!" everyone screams into the storm. My cheeks flush with warmth and bubbles of excitement explode. *I helped them all to believe!*

"Which part of the castle should we save?" Mama shouts over the wind.

"The kitchen," I shout back. I know in my heart that's the only choice. It's the strongest room in the castle and it's always been the heart of our home: where Rosa and I were born, where we've gathered for hot drinks and meals, where we've cosied up by the stove to read or talk or sew. It's where Babusya has slept, and where we've all slept during the coldest winter nights. "And if we can't save the whole kitchen, then we must save the stove," I add. Feliks lives behind it, and it's where we've always left him salt offerings.

I glimpse the waters of Lake Mila churning beyond the grove. I think of Cascadia's mother out there somewhere, hopefully about to be reunited with her daughter after five hundred years apart. And Dub's father, who is maybe in this very grove. An idea hits me like a wave and I gasp.

"What is it?" Mama asks.

"Dub's father!" I shout as loud as I can over the wind. "Dub's father, are you in here? I've seen Dub. He's on his way home."

"What are you doing?" Dinara jogs closer to me.

"Dub's father!" I shout again, looking at the tall, dark, swaying trees and trying to spot a rowan amongst all the spruce. "Please, I need your help."

Mama looks around curiously, while Papa, Dinara, Luka and Mikhail all stare at each other in confusion. I scan the grove, desperately hoping Dub's father is here and will reveal himself. Even if he can't help me save the kitchen for Feliks, if he would show himself it would help prepare my parents and friends for all the other spirits they might see at the castle. But there's no sign of a *leshy* at all.

"Who's Dub?" Dinara asks, bouncing on her toes.

"And who's his father?" Luka echoes.

Before I can think how to answer, a rowan tree steps out of the darkness and unfurls, revealing his limbs, his hands and feet. Berries, black in the night, dangle around his knotty face. "I am Dub's father, Etka. Have you really seen my son?" His eyes fill with sap and shine with hope.

Mama smiles and laughs like wind chimes in a breeze. Papa's and Mikhail's jaws drop open. Dinara and Luka each grab one of my elbows, their eyes widen, and for the first time ever I think they look alike.

"It's all right." I tap my friends' hands in what I hope is a comforting gesture. "This is a *leshy*, a tree spirit. His son is trapped in…" Thoughts whizz through my mind. I don't have time to explain everything about The Land of Forbidden Magic. "His son is trapped in Castle Mila." I decide to simplify things as best I can. "Other spirits are trapped in there too, but they're all going to be freed by the storm. Except Feliks – he's in danger and we must save him."

"Is my son in any danger?" Etka leans down to me, his face creaking as it twists with concern.

"No." I shake my head. "Dub is fine. But there's a *domovoi*, Feliks, who will disappear unless we can save a part of the castle. Will you help us?"

"I will try." Etka rises again.

"Thank you." I look from Etka to my parents and friends. "Do you still all want to come with me?" I glance at the bandage around Dinara's wrist. The thought of her, or anyone else, getting hurt because I brought them here makes my muscles tighten with fear. "The storm is going to turn into a hurricane."

"Of course we're coming with you!" Dinara bounces with excitement.

"I'm not missing out on this." Luka pushes his hair away from his face.

"Me neither." Mikhail puts his arms around Dinara and Luka and smiles.

Mama squeezes my hand again and Papa pats my back. "Come on," he says, "we're doing this together."

I glow with gratitude for my parents and friends as we run on towards the castle. "Do you know Cascadia's mother?" I shout up to Etka. Now he's straightened to his full height – over three times as tall as me – I'm not sure he'll be able to hear me. "Is Cascadia's mother in the lake? Can you call her?" I shout louder, thinking that the more help we can get, the better the chance of saving Feliks.

Etka steps out of the spruce grove and in two long strides, he's standing in the shallows of Lake Mila. "Zarya is Cascadia's mother. I will beckon her." Etka splashes the water with his branch-fingers and makes a noise over the wind, something like Cascadia's bubbling laugh but deeper.

There is a splash in the distance, followed by an echoing bubbling sound that grows louder and closer, until Cascadia's mother, Zarya, rushes out of the water in a wave. She looks like Cascadia, but is taller and has sadder, wider eyes. There is something familiar about her, from long ago, and I wonder if I met her before, when I was much younger.

"Cascadia is coming home," I say in a rush and

Zarya's eyes brighten. "All the banished spirits will be freed by the storm and everyone should be fine, except for the castle *domovoi*. He's called Feliks and he's my friend." My chest tightens and I inhale slowly to ease it. "I need to save a part of the castle, otherwise he'll disappear."

Zarya stares up at Castle Mila. "I will help...but there is very little left to save." Her voice is like waves over sand. I follow her gaze and the sight of the castle chills my bones so much they feel brittle, like they might shatter in the wind.

Both the north and west sides of the castle have fallen, and although most of the east side still stands, there's barely anything left of its beautiful roof. Nearly all of its domes are torn open. The shell of Aurora Dome sways violently in the wind. Inside it, the split into The Land of Forbidden Magic glows brighter with every moment.

"I don't think we have much time." I sprint towards the castle and the others follow. "We must save the kitchen, especially the stove." But I stop as we draw near because the walls are leaning and groaning ominously. "It's not safe to get any closer." My heart races as I try to think what to do.

"I can protect you all, if you stay in my branches." Etka kneels down and offers us his arms. Zarya splashes into a nook in his elbow while I turn to my parents and friends.

"Are you sure you want to come?" I ask again, still torn between wanting their help and not wanting to put them at risk.

Wordlessly, they all step closer to me. We link hands and arms and climb up into Etka's branches, ready to face the dangers together, to save Feliks.

CHAPTER THIRTY-EIGHT

GOLD ON THE WIND

The wind blasts through Etka's branches as he carries us towards the castle. Rust-coloured leaves and clusters of berries are torn from his head and whipped away. Etka nudges us up into the foliage on his shoulders, where he says we'll be safer from the gusts and he can hear our voices better.

I point to Aurora Dome swaying above us. "That's where Dub and Cascadia and the other spirits will escape from." Then I point down to where a section of the outer wall has tumbled, revealing the kitchen inside. "That's the room we need to protect, and the stove in particular. And we need to keep a lookout for Feliks, to make sure he comes here when he leaves the dome."

"I can pool on the roof near the dome and watch for the *domovoi*," Zarya shouts over the gale.

"Only if you're sure you'll be safe," I shout back.

"I'll be fine." Zarya wobbles in the wind as Etka's branch-arms stretch and grow so he can lift her up onto the roof, then she flows down into a puddle near what's left of Aurora Dome.

Etka kneels and peers through the broken outer wall into the kitchen. "I could climb inside," he offers. "And shield the stove with my body."

"Yes, please." I grip Etka's branches tightly, and so do my parents and friends, as he leans over and edges into the kitchen. Once inside, he curls his body around and over the stove, filling the room with his tangled branches and rustling leaves.

We all slide down from his shoulder onto the floor. It's like being inside a den in the woods, but with the kitchen stove in the centre of the den and a huge woody face above us.

The fire in the stove has gone out, but it still radiates warmth and – despite knowing that most of the castle is in ruins around us – it feels as much like home as ever. With a bloom of satisfaction, I realize I made the right choice about saving this room. If we can keep this small part of the castle from being blown away, I believe Feliks will survive.

Luka grabs my arm as the wind surges and screams and the ceiling is torn away in a sudden gust that makes my heartbeat bolt. Papa beckons everyone back into the shelter of Etka's branches and through them I see pieces of the castle tumbling and whirling through the night sky. Etka crouches lower as bangs sound all around us.

The walls shake, another section of logs collapses with a rumble, and Etka sways as he braces himself against the devastating winds. "Climb up to my shoulders again," he urges. "You'll all be safer there."

We clamber higher into Etka's branches and peer up through the spaces to see what's happening in Aurora Dome. Winds streaked with gold are flying from the split that leads to The Land of Forbidden Magic.

"What's going on?" Papa wraps an arm around me and follows my gaze. "What's that gold on the wind?"

"That's magic," I reply, my skin tingling. "There was a whole land beyond Aurora Dome, but a wizard named Chernomor is unfolding it. The magic being released is going to flatten Castle Mila."

Papa's eyebrows scrunch together with confusion. Mama puts her arms around us both and hugs us tight.

"Your castle." Dinara's face falls. "I'm so sorry."

Tears sting the back of my eyes. "It's only a building."

"We know it's more than that to you and your family." Luka looks up at me through his hair with such an expression of understanding that a tear escapes and rolls down my cheek.

"Castle Mila is special." I wipe the tear away. "When I first entered The Land of Forbidden Magic, all I wanted was to protect our home. But..." I pause and squeeze my parents' hands. "Now I know it's not the building that's important, it's the people. My home is wherever my family and friends are, and I'm not losing them. Also, there's a very good reason the castle must fall."

"What?" Mikhail asks in confusion. His arms are

wrapped protectively around Dinara and Luka and golden winds are reflected in his eyes. The winds are swirling down to the ground now, and the split above them is growing bigger and brighter.

"One of our ancestors, the Princess Ludmila, banished hundreds of spirits into the land beyond the dome against their will. Their lives are more important than any castle, and this is the only way to free them."

Mama nods in agreement, and although Papa still looks confused, he nods too.

"It doesn't seem fair that you have to lose your home because of something one of your ancestors did." Luka frowns.

Thoughts about my ancestors spin through my mind – not only about Ludmila and what she did, but about the things my other royal ancestors did in the real world. For hundreds of years they filled the castle with treasures, while people in the village went hungry. "You know, I think it's fair and right that we face up to what our ancestors did and try to make amends for it. And Castle Mila is a monument to the past. We don't need it to build a better future."

"They feel like words I've needed to hear for a long time, Olia." Papa pulls me into a warm hug. "You are brilliant and I love you," he whispers and I beam with pride. Mama, who still has her arms wrapped around us both, squeezes tighter.

"You're being very brave, *Princess* Olia." Dinara nudges me.

"It's a lot easier to be brave with all of you around me." I nudge her back.

The winds surge stronger. They howl into a gale and blast against Etka until he shakes with the effort it takes to stay in position. The split in the dome above us cracks wide open and an explosion of brightness bursts out. Then the thunder of hooves is thrown into the simmering sky and we all turn our faces towards the noise, like sunflowers turn to the light.

Chapter Thirty-nine

Unfolding

"It's the flying horses!" My hand whips up to point at the horses, who are galloping away from the dome on a stream of golden wind. They neigh triumphantly into the shining air rushing around them. "Look! There's Teffi. I rode on her back." My heart leaps at the memory and my sorrow about Castle Mila shrinks, like a fat bag of *bulochki* into a *domovoi's* pocket, as I watch Teffi fly to freedom.

My parents and friends track the colourful horses across the sky with wide, glittering eyes. "Where will they go?" Mama asks, as it becomes clear they're not going to land near the castle.

"I guess they'll return to where they lived before they were banished." I watch the horses disappear into the darkness over Lake Mila. "But I don't know where that is." I feel a pang of sadness that I might never see them again, and that Babusya and Rosa might never see them at all.

"Flying horses favour mountainous regions." Etka turns his face towards us and a gust of wind whips a branchful of leaves away from his head. I make myself a silent promise to find the horses again one day, with Babusya and Rosa. I've been so focused on showing Castle Mila to Rosa as she grows up but there is a whole world to share with her, bigger and more magical than I ever dreamed. Our adventures were never meant to be confined to one building.

"Look!" Mikhail shouts and points at the dome again. More spirits are escaping, all carried on glowing, golden winds.

The froglike *vodyanoy* is swept away over the lake and I wonder if he'll settle in the marshes on the other side. He's followed by hundreds of tiny, fluttering, winged fish spirits and other tentacled and scaled spirits from Water Dome.

Flaming hedgehog spirits, fire-breathing weasel

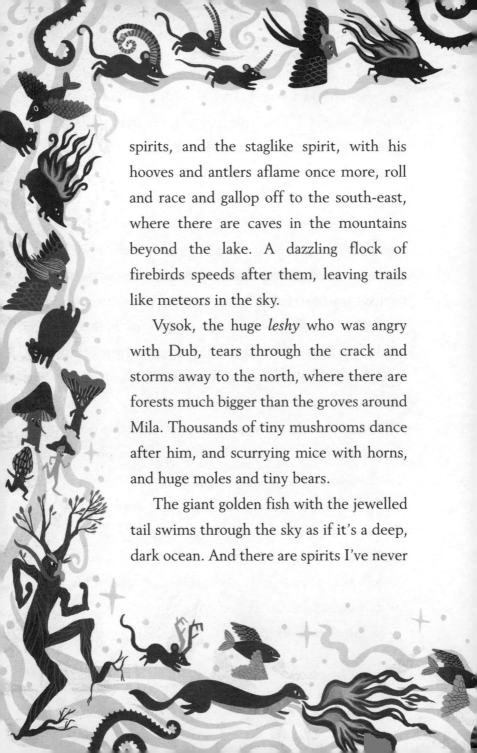

spirits, and the staglike spirit, with his hooves and antlers aflame once more, roll and race and gallop off to the south-east, where there are caves in the mountains beyond the lake. A dazzling flock of firebirds speeds after them, leaving trails like meteors in the sky.

Vysok, the huge *leshy* who was angry with Dub, tears through the crack and storms away to the north, where there are forests much bigger than the groves around Mila. Thousands of tiny mushrooms dance after him, and scurrying mice with horns, and huge moles and tiny bears.

The giant golden fish with the jewelled tail swims through the sky as if it's a deep, dark ocean. And there are spirits I've never

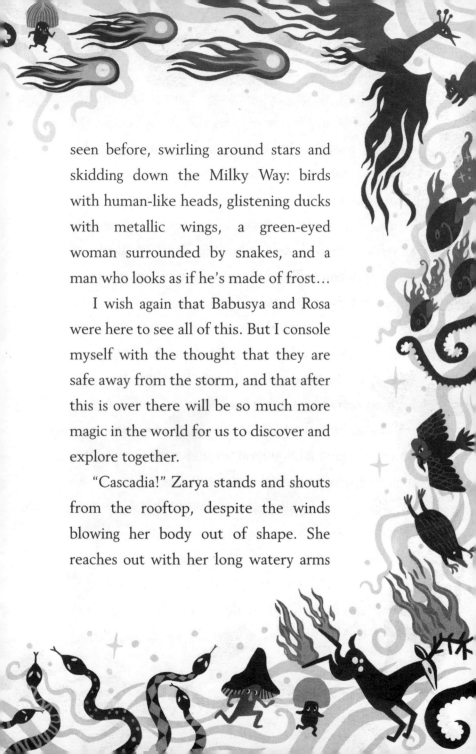

seen before, swirling around stars and skidding down the Milky Way: birds with human-like heads, glistening ducks with metallic wings, a green-eyed woman surrounded by snakes, and a man who looks as if he's made of frost...

I wish again that Babusya and Rosa were here to see all of this. But I console myself with the thought that they are safe away from the storm, and that after this is over there will be so much more magic in the world for us to discover and explore together.

"Cascadia!" Zarya stands and shouts from the rooftop, despite the winds blowing her body out of shape. She reaches out with her long watery arms and grabs Cascadia, who is an amorphous bubble carried on a flurry of golden sparks. Zarya pulls Cascadia close and they flow back into shape and hug each other so tightly that tiny fish dart between their bodies. My heart soars to see them together after so long apart.

More spirits fly free and I watch with my parents and friends, wide-eyed. The Immortal Cloak twirls and whirls with glee as it zooms off to the west. I hope it finds the spirit of life it belonged to. Feathered, furred, scaled and slimy spirits flee in every direction, along with grasses, flowers, bushes and shrubs... Every time a tree hurtles across the sky, Etka lifts his head, his eyes searching eagerly for Dub.

The split rends wider and wider, then the Yaga house stomps out, its enormous clawed feet struggling to get a grip on the magical wind. Bones dangling from its window sills and eaves rattle with delight, and Deda Yaga, riding on the veranda, cackles with elation, his one tooth glistening.

The house leaps off the wind and lands with a thump and a clatter right next to us, just the other side of the tumbling exterior wall. Deda Yaga's eyes gleam as they find mine and his smile widens. "Freedom!" he cheers, shaking his bone walking-frame in the air. I smile back at him, then beam when I spot Koshka curled around his leg. Mora is with them too, staring up at the split with her tail clutched between her hands. But there is no sign of Feliks.

Mama squeals with excitement at the sight of the house with chicken legs. But Papa, Mikhail, Dinara and Luka only gawp in shock. I try to give them a reassuring look, but Golov lands almost immediately, shaking the ground, and they all pale so much I think they might faint together in a heap. Then Dub rushes out of the split and launches himself at Etka, *vily* flying all around him. Dub and Etka entwine and embrace, creating an even bigger den-shield around the kitchen stove, and I whoop with delight to see Dub and his father reunited.

The storm winds tumble the exterior wall completely and long, thick logs are blown away as if they're tiny twigs. But it's so wonderful to see all the magical spirits happy and free, the loss of another wall doesn't seem to matter so much.

I glance at the stove to check that it's safe, then I scan the sky again, hoping to spot Feliks, who still hasn't emerged. Hundreds of spirits are flooding out of the land now, making it difficult to focus on any one of them. I strain my eyes, but they only leak tears into the wind.

"Feliks!" Zarya suddenly yells. "There!" She points to a swirling golden wind streaming towards us. With a rush of relief, I see Feliks struggling to balance as he descends rapidly through the air.

The wind ruffles his orange fur, whips up his beard and coat and spins him around. He leaps down as a fox, falls through Etka's branches, then lands with a clunk of his boots on the stove. He jumps off it immediately, then stares up at me in shock.

"Olia! What are you doing here? You must leave immediately. The last winds will be the most powerful."

"I know. They'll be strong enough to destroy the castle and *you*." I glare at Feliks accusingly.

"You read my note too soon." Feliks winces.

"I read it just in time. We're here to save you."

I look at my parents and friends, old and new. "If we can keep the stove standing, I believe you'll survive."

"It's no use." Feliks shakes his head rapidly. "*Everything* will be flattened, and if you don't all leave now, you'll be hurt. Please, go."

"We aren't going anywhere." I beckon everyone to draw close around the stove. Mora rushes to Feliks and pulls him into a hug. "If there is anything useful in your pockets that might help shield the stove, now is the time to get it out," I suggest to Feliks.

"I do have that banqueting table." Feliks rummages in his pocket and expands out an enormous mahogany table followed by tens of velvet-upholstered chairs, and we stack them around the stove, tangling their legs together to make a barricade.

"May I have the sword too, please?" I ask, an idea sparking in my mind.

"Sword?" Mama's and Papa's eyes widen in horror as Feliks expands the sword from his pocket.

"It can cut through magic, which is what these winds are made of." I slide the blade from its sheath, stand in front of the barricade, lift the sword with both hands and brace myself for the final, most powerful winds. Mama and Papa glance at each other in concern, but step beside me.

The last few spirits are emerging through the split and either flying or running away. More *vily* appear and gather with the others in Dub and Etka's branches.

Chernomor appears last, flying down on his swan. They land near us and, after the swan trumpets loudly, everything goes eerily quiet. I hold my breath, knowing in my heart this is the calm before the final hurricane strikes.

Chernomor looks over to us, his silver eyes as bright as stars. He nods a warning and I turn to check the others. Feliks, Mora, Cascadia and Zarya are behind the barricade and have their arms linked together around the stove. Dinara, Luka and Mikhail are sheltering in Etka's branches. Etka is entwined with Dub, making a den-shield over the stove. The house with chicken legs is close by, crouching low, with Deda Yaga and Koshka on its porch. Golov is kneeling beside it, his arms out as if he's going to protect us all.

I take a deep breath, look at my parents beside me, then root my feet firmly to the ground and grip the sword tighter. Chernomor holds up his hat in one hand and with his other hand he reaches towards the split. He takes hold of something heavy and invisible and *pulls*, and there is an eruption of blinding golden light.

Wind hits me with a powerful punch. In a split second I'm lifted off my feet and tumble through the air, desperately trying to control my body. Cracks and crashes sound all around. The banqueting table and all the chairs zoom away, still tangled together. My parents and friends are shouting and screaming. I force my head to turn to look for them, and see everyone being tossed around by glowing winds. I try to focus, to orientate myself and find the stove. Finally, I spot it below me, exposed and alone. All of us have been ripped away from it by the force of the wind, and it's wobbling, teetering, about to be blown away too.

"No!" I yell and swing the sword. Golden sparks fly from its glowing blade as it slices through the wind.

I fall to the floor, hard, in front of the stove, curling into a ball as my breath is knocked out of me. But I rise to my feet as quickly as I can, knowing that I must fight back these winds to save *everyone*.

CHAPTER FORTY

CUTTING MAGIC

I grip the heavy sword with both hands and swing it through the air. The winds stop at the blade and calm, still air pools around me. The stove stops wobbling and, with a rush of relief, I see Feliks's orange fluffy tail entwined with Mora's smooth black one curling out from beneath it.

"Feliks!" I shout, nudging his tail. "I can use the sword to cut through the winds!" I move in a circle around the stove, waving the sword up and down, back and forth, and the patch of calm air swells wider, enclosing us all in a safe space.

Feliks creeps out from beneath the stove. One of his hands is holding Mora's and the other is clutching his chest. He looks pained and scared and my own fear rises as I see how much the castle disintegrating is physically hurting him. A gust of wind breaks through and ruffles his fur. I swivel round and swing the sword again to protect him and our little dome of calm.

Still rotating the sword, I stare into the storm, searching desperately for my parents and friends. "I can't see any of the others!" I shout, my voice cracking as worries tighten in my throat. "We need to find them and bring them here."

"There's Golov." Mora points behind us, and I turn to see him lying on the floor, his giant fingers digging into the earth to stop himself from sliding away.

"Golov!" I shout, but he doesn't hear me over the winds.

"I'll go to him." Mora shrinks to the size of a sparrow.

"You'll be blown away," Feliks protests, trying to scoop her into his hands.

"I'll land on his chest – nightmare feeders always do. Then I'll help him find the others and we'll bring them all here." Mora scurries up to Feliks's fluffy nose, kisses it, then jumps into the wind and zooms away.

I want to watch to see if Mora does land on Golov's chest, but I must focus on the winds that keep breaking through with whistles and screams. I slice through them when they come, and they fall away like great sighs.

"There's the Yaga house." Feliks points towards Lake Mila, where the house is stumbling out of the shallows, leaning into the wind, with its bones trailing behind it. It's struggling, but slowly managing to draw closer to us. It stops and nudges something large onto its veranda with one of its great clawed feet, and I realize it's Etka and Dub, still entwined, who must have fallen and skidded over to the lake shore.

"Can you see my parents and friends?" I shout to Feliks in panic as I wonder how far they've been flung by the wind. They don't have a magic sword to protect them, and the thought of them getting hurt terrifies me.

"Not yet." Feliks frowns. "But Golov is on his feet now, and I'm sure he's searching for them."

The Yaga house staggers up to us and crouches down beside the stove. It's being blasted by winds. Bones are being ripped from its window sills and pieces of its black roof are lifting, about to be torn away. I race around it, swinging the sword frantically to deflect the gusts.

Making a bigger circle of calm is difficult, and by the time I complete a full loop, winds are breaking through again, but I manage to fight back enough of the gales to stop the house and the stove from being blown away.

Deda Yaga, who is stood on the house's veranda, clinging onto his bone walking-frame with one hand and clutching Koshka with the other, says something to Dub and Etka. They nod and clamber off the veranda, then circle their branches around the stove to shield it again.

Scores of *vily* are sheltering amongst Dub's and Etka's leaves, looking out at the storm with wide eyes. The wind howls and I glimpse Feliks through the leaves too, huddling against the stove with his tail wrapped around himself and his eyes shut tight. He looks so scared and fragile, I want to rush to him and tell him that it's going to be all right. But all I can do is keep slicing through the winds to protect him and the stove.

My eyes are frantic as I keep searching for my parents and friends in the chaos of the storm. I need them here, safe with me. Finally, just as I'm wondering how I can protect the stove *and* go to find the others, Golov appears. He crashes to the ground next to the house, and my heart balloons with relief as Mama, Dinara, Luka and Mikhail jump from his hands and come rushing over. Cascadia and Zarya splash down too, followed by Chernomor and his swan, and then Mora, who steers everyone to the stove and beckons them to crouch down beside Feliks.

"Where's Papa?" I ask in panic when he doesn't appear.

"I haven't found him yet, but I will." Golov lumbers off again, leaning into the winds, his owls sheltering deep inside his hair and beard.

My stomach churns with worry, but I carry on circling the stove and the Yaga house, slicing back the winds. Knowing that Mama and my friends are safe inside the dome of still air gives me a surge of energy and I move faster, fighting back the winds to protect them all.

"Golov has Papa!" Mama shouts from behind me and I almost drop the sword with relief. "I can see them sheltering behind the spruce grove. I'm not sure Golov can get back through the winds now."

The storm is roaring, forcing me to swing the blade higher and faster. Calm blooms around us, but beyond it the winds rise and raze everything in sight. Castle Mila tumbles down and is blown away, piece by piece, chunk by chunk, room by room. I watch what is left of the roof domes and the walls and the floors tear apart and fly away.

My heart tumbles like the castle, feeling bruised and broken, but I cling on tight to the memories the wind can't take. Babusya snoring by the fire, her mouth wide open. Papa and I watching hawks hunting and cranes dancing from the roof. Mama showing me the stars from Astronomer's Dome, telling me that's where we all came from and where we'll all return. Rosa, moments after she was born, as new and sweet as a rosebud, nestled in my arms.

I keep moving in an endless circle to protect this small dome of home, which contains Mama and my friends, old and new. The storm seems to go on for ever, and my arms ache until they burn. But I believe with all my heart that Golov will protect Papa and that I will stop the winds and protect everyone else.

Mama offers to take over, but when her hands touch the sword it stops glowing and winds rip through the calm with a screech. I remember Koshka saying that only someone with royal blood can wield the Giant's Sword, and I think maybe because Mama wasn't born into our family, it won't work for her.

"Thanks for trying, Mama." I take the sword back. "But I think I have to be the one to make up for the mistakes of my royal ancestors." A bitter taste fills my mouth, because I know I'll never be able to make up for everything Ludmila did, and although the spirits are free now, it doesn't erase the five hundred years of banishment. But it does make it easier to watch Castle Mila fall, because I know now that it divided people and spirits.

The best bits of the castle – the things that made it our home – are my family, my friends and my memories, and I won't let the winds take them away. Sweat runs off my skin. I feel like I'm in a trance, moving around and around in a great circle, swinging the sword in sweeping patterns.

One. I slide the blade up through a golden wind, to protect Mama and my friends huddled against the stove, and I think of Rosa, born right here in the kitchen. *Two.* I leap over Feliks, swing the blade down, and say goodbye to the castle's long and winding corridors, but hold on to the memory of sliding along them. *Three, four, five.* I take three running strides around the Yaga house, cut back a shining gale, and wave goodbye to the faded and torn tapestry of the royal crest. *Six.* I race round to the stove again and slice through a squall. One of the portraits of my royal ancestors frowns as it zooms past. *Seven, eight, nine.* The Giant's Sword glows as I fight back the storm and say goodbye to Musician's Dome and Astronomer's Dome and all the secret doors and passageways behind walls, and my third-floor bedroom where Mama sang me to sleep. *Ten.* I watch the ruins of Castle Mila disappearing into the distance, while holding tight to the memories I've made there, and start all over again. *One.* I slide the blade up…

When there is nothing left outside the dome of calm but flattened grass and the cracked remains of a shallow stone foundation, the winds stop howling and the blur of moving air stills. Finally I see the surface of Lake Mila, its white-tipped waves diminishing into dark, rolling ripples.

Feliks and Mora appear at my side. "I think you can lower the sword now, Olia," Feliks whispers, holding up his furry hands.

I let the sword fall to my side. Every muscle in my body is trembling, and I shiver as a gentle breeze strikes the sweat on my brow. "Papa…" I whisper, my heart pounding as I scan the grove for him and Golov.

"Over there!" Mama points and I make out the huge mound of Golov crouching behind the tallest spruce trees for shelter. He rises to his feet and places something gently onto his shoulder.

"Papa!" I shout and wave in excitement as Golov

walks over to us and lowers Papa to the ground. Mama and I pull him into a hug and we squeeze each other tight with relief.

Then we look around to check everyone else. Dinara, Luka and Mikhail are huddled together by the stove. Chernomor is resting on his swan near it too. Deda Yaga and Koshka are on the Yaga house's porch, along with Cascadia and Zarya. And Dub and Etka are entwined nearby. My castle might be gone, but everyone is safe, and I smile.

The storm has passed and the sky is lightening to a pale blue-grey. With a snap of surprise, I realize it's almost morning. My heart leaps as I spot the harvest moon, fat and red, sinking in the west.

Papa follows my gaze. "Who needs a harvest moon feast with music and dancing when you can have magical winds and flying spirits?"

I hug my parents tighter. Then I crouch down and take Feliks's hand in my own and squeeze gently. "I'm glad you're still here," I whisper with a smile.

"So am I." Feliks squeezes my hand back, entwines his tail with Mora's, and smiles too.

CHAPTER FORTY-ONE

DAWN

Mama and Papa return to the village to get Rosa, Babusya and Magda. But they tell me to wait with my friends, so I sit on the floor, catching my breath after the long night fighting the wind. Everyone is gathered around the stove, except Golov, who is using the dome of the Yaga house like a pillow, and Deda Yaga and Koshka, who are both sitting on the house's veranda, staring out across Lake Mila.

The water is smooth and flat as a mirror and perfectly reflects the sky, which is burnished orange with the approaching dawn. The sun peeps above the horizon and throws beams of light into the world, filling me with wonder.

All that is left of Castle Mila is the kitchen stove and a small circle of uneven wood-block floor. But my family and friends are safe, all the spirits are free, and Feliks is alive. A huge smile aches my cheeks.

"What a beautiful sunrise," Deda Yaga says from the house's veranda and the house blinks all its windows in agreement. Koshka leans against Deda Yaga and a purr rumbles in her chest.

"Are you pleased to be back in this world?" I ask Koshka.

"It's not a bad place to be, I suppose." She flicks her tail as if in irritation, but there's a smile twitching at the corners of her mouth too.

Cascadia rises to her feet, her watery body twinkling golden in the light. Her eyes swirl larger at the sight of the dawn, and her mouth drops open so wide that a tiny shrimp falls out and scuttles back into her foot. "I haven't seen a sunrise for five hundred years." Cascadia wavers so much I think she's going to splash into a puddle, but her mother, Zarya, grabs her hand and she regains her shape.

Zarya flashes a row of pearly teeth like Cascadia's,

with a few strands of lake weed flowing between them. "Thank you for bringing my daughter home," she bubbles.

"Home." Cascadia edges towards the lake. "I can't believe I'm back after all these years. Thank you, Olia. I will see you again, won't I?" She glances up to where Castle Mila stood and her eyes darken to a deep-water blue. "Where will you live now?"

"I'm not sure." I bite my lip, wondering what will happen next. I haven't had a chance to talk to my parents about the future yet, and Babusya hasn't even seen that the castle is completely gone. I wonder how she'll feel about it, and about moving somewhere new, after living in the castle her whole life.

"You can all live with us in the village." Dinara stretches and rises to her feet.

"It would be a squeeze, but you'd certainly be welcome to stay for as long as you needed," Mikhail says.

"Thank you," I say, although the thought of leaving this place, even with the castle gone, makes my heart ache. I can't imagine waking without this view, and not chasing Babusya to the grove every morning. I step next to Cascadia, who is so eager to splash into the lake that she has tiny white-tipped waves all over her. "Wherever I end up living, I'll come here often to look for you."

Cascadia throws her watery arms around me, coating me in cold droplets that make me shiver. "Then I'll see you soon. I have to go. I've been waiting to swim in those waters for five hundred years."

"Thank you for everything." I smile as Cascadia lifts her arms and the water droplets she left on me rise and flow back into her hands.

Cascadia surges away and Zarya chases after her. Their voices are like a stream rushing, filled with freedom and joy, and it's impossible not to beam as they dive into the shining waters of the lake and disappear. Ripples expand from their splash, distorting the reflected sunrise.

"We're going home too." Dub holds a branch-finger out to me. "Will you visit us in the grove?"

"Of course." I hug Dub's whole arm. *Vily* flutter amongst his leaves. "Oh, will the *vily* be all right?"

I ask with concern. "How will they get the blood flowers they need?"

"The pool of the waters of death, along with the blood flowers, will have returned to the cave it was in before Ludmila folded it into The Land of Forbidden Magic," Etka says. He offers me a branch-finger, which I hug too.

"Thank you, both." I wave as Etka and Dub walk slowly to the grove, where they seem to melt into the other trees.

"Now it's my turn to leave, little one," Golov booms, leaning down to look at me. His cheeks plump into huge pink mounds.

"Where will you go?" I ask, wondering where a giant could live in this world.

"The caves in the mountains. They're an old family home, on the giant side. Will you join me, brother?" Golov glances at Chernomor, who is encased in his golden robe and snuggled up against his swan by the stove.

Chernomor looks up at Golov in shock. "You would let me join you after what I did?"

"I think it's time to move on from that," Golov says. "Let's make a fresh start in the mountains. Our mother may still be there."

"Do you think so?" Chernomor's silver eyes shine. He rises to his feet and holds his hand out to me. "Thank you, Olia. You've brought us all home."

My cheeks flush with warmth as I shake Chernomor's hand. "I couldn't have done any of it without you and the others."

Chernomor lifts the floppy green hat and offers it to me. "I'd like you to have this, as thanks for what you did. Not many humans can see and feel magic. Perhaps you could use the hat to become a wizard yourself?"

My mouth drops open and my fingers twitch towards the hat. But then I let my hands fall back to my sides and shake my head. "Thank you, but no. I can see and feel magic without your hat. I've always been able to, although for the last few years I've struggled because I let doubts grow in me – doubts about magic and my ability to see it. But now I know to trust in what my heart sees and feels."

"That's a fine choice, Olia. And I'm sure you'll find plenty of magic in this world." Chernomor climbs up onto his swan, who bugles so loudly that I take a step back.

Golov smiles down at me again. "Goodbye, Olia. Thank you for everything." I wave as he paces away. The ground shakes with his every step and his owls swoop and hoot around him. Chernomor flies near Golov's ear, on the neck of his swan.

I scan the lake, suddenly wondering if anyone from the village is out fishing and might spot the giant, but there are no boats on the water and, within a few paces, Golov disappears into mist, as if the world is cloaking him. I remember what Babusya said about seeing with your eyes and your heart, and I wonder if everyone would be able to see Golov anyway, or only those who were looking for magic.

I turn to Deda Yaga and the Yaga house. "Where will you go?"

"We like it here." Deda Yaga smiles. "There's a lovely view of the lake, especially now, at sunrise, and the grove too. It's the perfect spot for a house."

"It is," I agree. "Or it was..." I look around at the empty space where Castle Mila stood and I sigh. "But how could we explain to the villagers about a house springing up overnight? Especially one with..." I glance at the few bones left dangling from the window sills and eaves.

"We could take the bones down, if you think it's necessary." Deda Yaga smacks his lips together. "And as far as explanations go, you'd be amazed what people will believe. We could say this house was inside your castle, hidden in a wing somewhere. As unlikely as that sounds, people would believe it over what they consider to be even more unlikely explanations."

"I suppose so. But don't you want to go off... guiding the dead?"

"The dead will find me when they need me. And the house and I will wander again. But for now, we'd like to stay and watch a few of these lovely sunrises. And I hear you need a new home," Deda Yaga adds with a wink.

Emotions tumble through me: a jolt of shock, a shiver of nervousness, a sparkle of hope.

"This house is far too big for me," Deda Yaga continues. "I would happily welcome you and your family here, for as long as you need."

"I don't know what my parents will think of that…"

"I think you're about to find out." Dinara nudges me and points to the spruce grove. My parents have emerged from the path between the trees, walking hand in hand. Papa is carrying Rosa close to his heart in her bright green wrap. Behind them, just visible through the trees, is the silhouette of Babusya walking alongside Magda. Although Babusya is using her sticks, she's not wobbling as much as usual. I smile as I wonder if the waters of life I gave her have already helped with her rheumatism.

Mora grabs Feliks's hand and they both shrink and disappear behind the stove. Deda Yaga rises to his feet, leans on his bone walking-frame and straightens his hat and coat proudly, while Koshka slinks nervously behind him.

A huge smile widens on my face as I race towards my family. Because even though Castle Mila is gone,

I now understand it wasn't really my home. My family are my home, safe and strong, and they're still here, right in front of me.

CHAPTER FORTY-TWO

TANGLED MAGIC

Mama breaks away from the others and sprints towards me. She's faster than Papa, because he's wearing the baby wrap with Rosa tucked inside. I rush to Mama and she pulls me into a massive hug and kisses the top of my head. Then she gazes up at the Yaga house, her eyes sparkling. "I'm so pleased the Yaga house stayed. Until last night, it had been years since I'd seen one."

"How do you know about Yaga houses, Mama?" I look at her in wonder.

"I grew up in one." Mama keeps a tight hold of my hand as she walks towards the house's veranda. Deda Yaga smiles a gummy, one-toothed welcome. "Star-filled greetings," Mama says with a smile. She walks straight to Deda Yaga, leans over his bone walking-frame and kisses his cheek. Deda Yaga blushes in response. "I'm sorry, I don't recognize you." Mama tilts her head. "I thought I knew all the Yaga."

"I'm Yaga Sergey, I've been—"

"Missing for five hundred years!" Mama exclaims. "You're a legend. You must tell me everything. I'd offer to make coffee but my home has blown away…" Mama looks around at all the empty space. "But we saved the stove of course. If you wouldn't mind lending us a few kitchen things, we could make coffee out here and watch the sunrise."

"That would be lovely. I'll get some firewood and a coffee pot and mugs…" Deda Yaga's voice is drowned out by the rattle of his walking-frame as he clumps and clatters towards the front door.

Papa arrives on the veranda and wraps his arms around me, enveloping me in his warmth. Rosa, tucked up in her baby wrap, murmurs. She opens her eyes and looks up at me and my heart swells with love.

Noise and bustle rise around Papa, Rosa and me. I'm vaguely aware of Mikhail trying to explain the

Yaga house's appearance to Magda, but it all seems far away from our little dome of calm. I offer Rosa one of my fingers and when she wraps her own tiny fingers around it, I beam with happiness.

Mama calls Dinara and Luka over to help Deda Yaga, and they disappear into the Yaga house and emerge loaded up with firewood. Mikhail and Magda get the stove lit and it chuffs smoke into the orange sky as flames dance inside it.

Babusya grabs my arms and pulls me into one of her bony, awkward, walking-stick-filled hugs. I try to tell her that I'm sorry about the castle, but she shushes me.

"I already said my goodbye to Castle Mila. But where is Feliks?" she asks.

"He's with his wife, Mora, safely behind the stove."

Babusya blinks away happy tears and hugs me even tighter. Papa brings her a chair from the Yaga house and gets her comfortable beside the stove, while Mama chats to Deda Yaga. They disappear into the house, and when they re-emerge, Mama is carrying a dark loaf of *borodinsky* bread topped with coriander seeds. She sets it to warm in the stove, and puts coffee on to brew.

Dinara and Luka carry more chairs out of the Yaga house and everyone sits around the stove, talking fast about the storm and the sunrise, the departed castle and the arrival of the ebony house, and possibilities and plans for the future. Mikhail asks Papa if we'll rebuild the castle, but before he can answer Magda suggests we move to the village, and starts listing all the empty houses.

"I have an idea," I say, glancing over to the stove, and thinking about Feliks and Mora snuggled safely behind it.

"What is it, Olia?" Mama asks, and everyone turns to me.

"Well, instead of rebuilding Castle Mila, we could build something new here, around the old stove. Instead of being huge, with thirty-three domes, it could be a small home, just big enough for us. But maybe we could build a hall right next to it, with one or two domes, for everyone in the village to use for celebrations." I look up at my parents and Babusya hopefully.

"I think that's a wonderful idea, Olia," Babusya says, her eyes gleaming.

"I agree." Papa rests a hand on my shoulder. "But there's nothing of the castle left. And it's a huge job to build a house from scratch, let alone a hall too."

"Everyone in the village would help." Mikhail leans forwards and Magda, Dinara and Luka nod in agreement. "It would be a wonderful thing for everyone to do together. Talking of which, Magda and I are going to pop back to the village, but we'll return soon." Mikhail and Magda rise to their feet, wave a farewell and wander towards the spruce grove.

Dinara and Luka stay sitting around the stove with us. "If everyone helped, we could build a house and a hall in no time," Dinara says.

"And you're welcome to stay in my house while you build something new." Deda Yaga looks up at the Yaga house proudly and it winks its windows. I glance at Papa to see his reaction, and catch him winking back.

Mama nudges Papa. "It would be fun."

Papa looks out across the lake. "This is a beautiful

spot, and it would be nice to create a new home here. I've always had mixed feelings about Castle Mila."

"Really?" I look at Papa in surprise. "I thought you loved the castle. You and Mama have always worked so hard to look after it."

"I was just doing what I've always done, without really thinking about it." Papa runs his hand through his hair. "For generations our family has maintained and repaired the castle. It was our family home, so I loved it for that, but it had a blemished past."

"Now the castle is gone, we can forget all the bad things our ancestors did," I say, trying to comfort him.

"No." Papa shakes his head. "We should never forget our history. Even if our ancestors make us feel guilty or ashamed or angry, we need to remember what they did and turn those emotions into something good."

"How?" I ask, unsure what Papa means.

"By doing what you said, Olia, when we were all in Etka's branches before the final storm. You said we should 'face up to what our ancestors did and try to make amends for it' and you were right. We have to accept our mistakes, even if it's difficult, and think about what we can do to help make things right. And we have to put our efforts into moving forwards and building a better future for everyone."

"Like you did in The Land of Forbidden Magic." Babusya passes me a mug of steaming, spiced milk and a slice of *borodinsky* bread.

"Sounds like you have a story to tell us, Olia." Mama raises her eyebrows.

"I'd rather hear your story first." I sip my milk and smile. "Why didn't you ever tell me that you grew up in a Yaga house?"

"I thought Yaga houses might be the kind of thing you have to see to believe." Mama glances back at Deda Yaga's house. The bones dangling from its sills sway and rattle with pride. "But now you've seen one, I'll tell you about my childhood, if you like."

"Yes, please." I take a bite of the soft, warm bread, and snuggle deeper into Papa's arms, right next to Rosa.

"When I was your age, I was a Yaga," Mama begins. "Yaga Marinka, living with my grandmother in a house with chicken legs..."

The sun rises higher as Mama tells her story. Lake Mila reflects its golden light and the spruce grove shines as if it's been gilded. Mama talks about how she grew up and carved a future for herself, different from the one she had expected, and I think about the future of our family, friends and the villagers too.

I nestle closer to Rosa and breathe in her sweet baby smell. To think I'd been worried about how to be the best big sister! I thought I needed to be strong and brave and good, and show her all the magic in the world, and save the castle so we could explore it together. But as I look into Rosa's tiny, peaceful face, I realize all I need to do is be here for her.

We won't get to explore Castle Mila, but we'll explore plenty of other places. The world will be even more wondrous with my spirit friends to visit, and more magic to discover. But it really doesn't matter where we go or what we find. What matters is that we do it together.

As Mama finishes her story, a long line of villagers emerge from the spruce grove, led by Mikhail and Magda. They're carrying baskets of fruits and breads, and pies on plates, and jams of every colour and flavour imaginable. Picnic blankets are spread out where the Great Hall used to be, loaded with foods and decorated with flowers and berries.

Luka plays music with the band while Dinara and I dance with more of our friends, and the sun rises high into the sky, looking like it's cut from orange velvet and threaded through with gold. The celebrations are bigger and merrier than ever before, because this year we say goodbye to Castle Mila.

I gaze around at the empty space where the castle once stood, and I see people glittering and whirling through the air like magic. Everything has a shining hue and, with a twist of confusion, I notice shimmering threads, almost invisible in the light, tangled over everyone. The threads connect us all to each other, and to the land, and to the newly revealed horizon, which stretches and sparkles far into the distance. The threads even rise up into the sky, where a clattering of jackdaws wheel through sunbeams.

It's like there's a castle of tangled magic all around us, linking us together and keeping us safe and strong.

Home, I think, is even more than my family and my friends. It's all the people and all the spirits who share this whole world with us too.

Babusya's words echo in my mind: *"Do you know what the winds of change are, Olia? They tear things down, to make you see."* A ray of understanding glows through me. Babusya wasn't talking about the storm and the castle. And the winds didn't have the power to change anything. But I did. I tore down the doubts inside myself, and now I can see magic in me and in everyone, everywhere. And in my heart I found bravery, and it grew, like a banqueting table expanding from a *domovoi*'s pocket, until it was big enough for me to believe in myself.

I go to Babusya, who is still sat in a chair beside the stove, and I drop a kiss onto her cheek. Curled in her lap is Koshka, purring, and I stroke her soft fur and smile at them both.

Babusya glances to a box near her chair. The family blanket is folded neatly inside it, along with Babusya's sewing kit. "Would you like to sew your patch on?" she asks.

I take the patch I made from my pocket, and look at the picture of me holding Rosa, with our family and friends all around us, surrounded by magic. Although I sewed everyone in the shape of the castle, I didn't sew the actual castle, and I think about how I must have known all along in my heart that home wasn't the building, but the people.

I place the patch carefully on top of the blanket. "Maybe I'll sew it on later." I smile as an idea sparks into my mind. "Or perhaps it could be the first patch of a new blanket."

"That's a fine idea." Papa appears beside me and lifts Rosa out of her wrap. "Would you like to cuddle your sister, while I dance with your mama?"

"Yes, please!" I sit in a chair beside Babusya, and fold my arms around little Rosa. She's awake, her limbs unfurling and waving about. She spots something flying over my head. Her eyes shine and she makes a soft cooing sound. I turn in time to see a tiny, winged fish spirit flutter away.

"Did you see magic?" Babusya whispers, her eyes twinkling.

"Rosa did." I smile. "And I see it too. Everywhere. In the people here, and on the horizon, and…" I glance at my dark-haired papa and my red-haired mama, who are dancing nearby, surrounded by glittering light. Not far away from them, curling out from behind the stove, are two entwined tails. One of them is fluffy, like a fox's, and the other is smooth, like a shrew's. Warmth floods through me, making my skin tingle. I look back at Rosa, snug and safe in my arms. "And I see magic right here, in the heart of our home."

OLIA'S GLOSSARY

balalaika: a musical instrument with
a triangular body and three strings
borodinsky: dark brown rye bread, sweetened
with molasses and flavoured with coriander
and caraway seeds
bulochka (plural *bulochki*): a soft bun swirled
with a creamy poppy-seed filling
Deda: a Russian word for a grandfather or
old man (shortened from *Dedushka*)
domovoi: a protective house spirit from
Slavic mythology
firebird: a magical, glowing bird from
Slavic mythology
grenka (plural *grenki*): bread that is soaked
in milk and egg, then fried

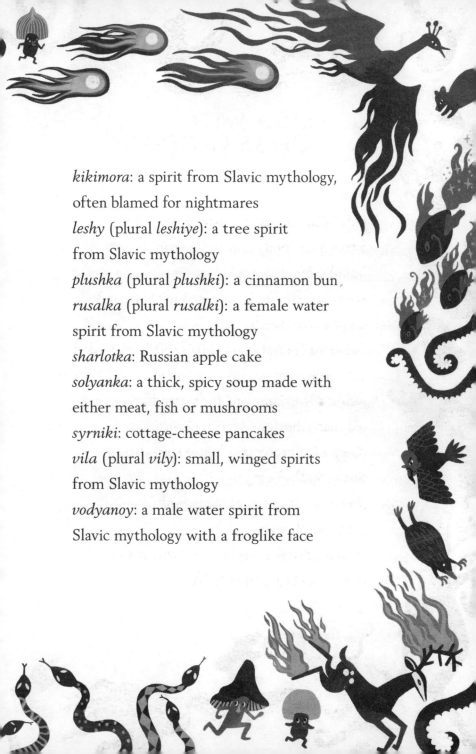

kikimora: a spirit from Slavic mythology, often blamed for nightmares

leshy (plural *leshiye*): a tree spirit from Slavic mythology

plushka (plural *plushki*): a cinnamon bun

rusalka (plural *rusalki*): a female water spirit from Slavic mythology

sharlotka: Russian apple cake

solyanka: a thick, spicy soup made with either meat, fish or mushrooms

syrniki: cottage-cheese pancakes

vila (plural *vily*): small, winged spirits from Slavic mythology

vodyanoy: a male water spirit from Slavic mythology with a froglike face

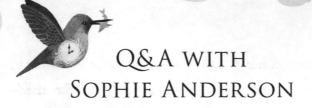

Q&A WITH
SOPHIE ANDERSON

What's your favourite place to read?
Nestled into a comfy chair at home with the blanket
my grandmother knitted me, or in a hammock in my
garden surrounded by birdsong. But I also love how
reading whisks you away to wondrous places, making
it the perfect way to escape wherever you might be!

*You're setting off on adventure... Where are you going
and what are you doing?*
I'm opening a book! Or I'm going for a walk with my
family to explore a woodland, mountain, lake or
beach. We're prepared to get wet and muddy, and
have a picnic with us. If we're feeling particularly
adventurous, we might be taking our canoe, too.

What is the perfect fairy-tale food to take on a quest?
Something freshly-baked, pocket-sized and sturdy

enough not to fall apart. Cheese or herb scones smell and taste delicious, and can be made quickly from only a few ingredients. A handful of dried fruit is also a good idea, for emergency energy and to leave as offerings for any spirits.

Do you have a favourite clock?
I remember standing with my mother beneath a clock in the centre of my hometown, waiting for it to strike the hour because figures would then dance out of doors in the clockface. My husband has fond memories of watching a clock in his hometown too. I love the idea that we carry childhood clocks in our hearts.

If you could travel to any moment in history, which moment would you choose?
I'd love to see my grandmother as a young girl, in her homeland of Prussia. Her eyes sparkled when she

spoke of her childhood spent swimming in lakes, exploring enchanted woods, and collecting pieces of amber washed up on beaches. It would be wonderful to live those stories with her!

Where do your characters' names come from?
Most are inspired by Russian folklore or Russian words – for example Koshka means cat, and Golov is from *golova* which means head! Olia is a form of Olga, which means blessed, and magnolias are one of my favourite trees. They bloom early in spring so make me think of new beginnings – something Olia experiences.

How and where do you look for magic?
I open my mind to possibilities and try to see with my heart. I listen to the whispers of the wind, smell the rain, and stare into dewdrops on spiderwebs. I splash in waves and gaze at stars, search my dreams, and wander through art, music, and books. I sip hot chocolate, and look for kindness, laughter, and love. And I've found Babusya is right: magic is everywhere you believe it to be.

Unravel the Magic:

A timeline of writing with Sophie Anderson

Five steps to plotting an adventure: how to unravel your own ideas and turn them into something magical!

1. Gather your inspirations...

Look around curiously and you'll find anything can spark an idea. Write notes or lists, collect or sketch pictures of things you might like in your story. This could include characters (somebody like you? A talking lizard with a slight resemblance to someone you know?), settings (a community like your own? An igloo on a cloud?), objects (a music box like one you saw in a shop? A velvet waistcoat?), and even words you like (serendipity? Kerfuffle?).

2. GET TO KNOW YOUR CHARACTERS...

Think about what they look like; how they talk, laugh, and move; how they spend their days, and what their hopes and dreams are. Try writing an interview for them with interesting questions like, what is your most treasured memory? How would you change the world? Or, what is the most embarrassing thing that ever happened to you? Then imagine you are the character and answer the questions!

3. THROW SOMETHING AT YOUR MAIN CHARACTER...

Stories often start with an inciting incident – an event that propels the main character into an adventure. In *The Castle of Tangled Magic* it was a fierce storm. But it can be a less dramatic event too – in *The House with Chicken Legs* it simply involved the main character, Marinka, meeting someone she wanted to be friends with. Think about what you could introduce into your main character's world that might set them off on a new and exciting path.

4. RAISE THE STAKES...

The inciting incident should make your character want to do something. The storm made Olia want to save her castle. Meeting a potential friend made Marinka want to change her destiny. What does your character want to do now? And what will happen if they can't do it? Will they lose something they love? Or will the world end? The higher the stakes, the tenser your story will be!

5. BELIEVE IN YOURSELF.

Humans are born storytellers. When you draw a picture, hum a tune, play an imaginative game, daydream, or tell someone about your trip to the shops, you are weaving a tale. We spend our lives surrounded by stories. They are in the news, in books and magazines, in movies and TV shows, and in our conversations with others. You know in your heart what makes a good tale, so trust yourself. Stories are part of the magic inside us all, and to unravel it you only need a little faith and courage!

ACKNOWLEDGEMENTS

The Castle of Tangled Magic was woven with the help of many people and is threaded through with all their wizardry. Golden ribbons of gratitude fly out to:

My husband Nick for his love and support, the banqueting table, the dancing mushrooms, and other wonders too numerous to list. You are the magic in my world.

Our children for their love, encouragement and understanding: Nicky for the star-shaped rainbow and perceptive editorial thoughts; Alec for the *Almasty* (we know he's roaming the mountains of Earth Dome) and for drawing the first map of the land; Sammy for the fire-breathing rabbit who became a weasel and many more imaginative suggestions (I hope the cupboard with the flying eye has its own book one day); and Eartha for the hummingbirds who fly straight and the warm cuddles while I worked. I adore you all, my four spirited whirlwinds.

My agent Gemma Cooper for creating magical doorways, holding them open, helping me through them, and making sure I don't fall back out.

My editors Rebecca Hill and Becky Walker for giving me the needle and thread to create this tale, and helping me unpick and re-stitch until the story held itself together. And a huge thank you to Rose for lending me her enchanting name.

Illustrator Saara Katariina Söderlund and designers Katharine Millichope and Sarah Cronin for bringing Olia, the spirits, and two worlds to life so beautifully. I am in awe of your creative brilliance.

Every one of the kind, talented, and dedicated professionals who make up the gorgeous patchwork of Usborne; Sarah Stewart for the incredible more-than-a-copyedit, Anne Finnis and

Gareth Collinson for the proofread, Katarina Jovanovic and Stevie Hopwood for outstanding publicity and marketing yet again, Penelope Mazza for the amazing animated cover, Christian Herisson and Arfana Islam for tirelessly championing my characters and stories, and the whole publishing and sales team. I am truly blessed to be part of the family.

The poet Alexander Pushkin and the translators who have enabled me to read and be moved by his glorious work, especially Walter Arndt and D.M. Thomas for their translations of the epic fairy tale *Ruslan & Ludmila* which I have reimagined many elements of in this novel.

My parents Karen and John, my brothers Ralph and Ross, my grandparents Gerda and Glyn, my parents-in-law Sheila and Frank, and my soul-sisters Lorraine and Gillian, for being ever-present shining stars.

The many writers and illustrators who have inspired me and shown me kindness, with an extra hug to James Mayhew for his friendship, for Koshka, and for introducing me to Kitzhi; to Sarah McIntyre for *bulochki* and other treasures; and to Kiran Millwood Hargrave, Michelle Harrison, Yaba Badoe, Gabrielle Kent, and Cerrie Burnell for being a coven of wise witches and marvellous mermaids.

All the heroes who put books into readers' hands: the booksellers, librarians, teachers, book reviewers and book bloggers, with a special gust of appreciation to Fiona Noble, Alison Brumwell, Jo Clarke, Galina Varese, Ashley Booth, Steph Elliott, Scott Evans, Gavin Hetherington, Liam Owens, Liam James, and Karen Wall. And to Fiona Sharp and Durham Waterstones children's book group for sharing their fantastic ideas with me.

Above all, thanks to my readers who turn ink on a page into real magic, glowing in hearts and minds, and connecting us together with shimmering threads that keep us safe and strong.

All we have to do is believe…